People talked about the ads that Jim Bower wrote—
and that was why Bower was in trouble.

THE ADVERTISING MAN . . .

"What's most impressive about *THE ADVERTISING
MAN*—what makes it the sort of book that is the best
thing about whatever day you happen to have read it;
one of those books you can hardly wait to get back to,
even if the weather is golden or your favorite movie is
on T.V.—is that Jack Dillon gets you concerned about
his man with the gray-flannel Pentel pen."

—Christopher Lehmann-Haupt,

"Unusually good—a winner."

"Beautifully written . . . simple, direct, powerful . . .
No frills. Only the transparent prose of a writer who
knows what language can do and can do what he
wants with language. . . . In the ad business that kind
of writing can sell a lot of soap. Mr. Dillon proves that
in fiction it can do a great deal more."

the advertising man

A NOVEL BY

Jack Dillon

A FAWCETT CREST BOOK

Fawcett Publications, Inc., Greenwich, Connecticut

THE ADVERTISING MAN

the
advertising
man

tuesday

It began on our twentieth anniversary and it began before I woke up.

I was back in the fifth grade. I didn't know the answer to something and George Brice did. There he was, plain as day, two rows over from me with his hand up. It did not seem strange to find George Brice in the fifth grade. It was perfectly natural. He got nothing but 100s and his mother loved him.

I woke up and got up. George Brice. Christ.

I went into the bathroom and washed my face and then I

7

remembered and went back to the bedroom and kissed Melinda. "Happy anniversary."

"What time is it?"

"Six."

"Six?"

"I have to make the seven-thirty. We have a mix at nine."

"Do you know how to boil an egg?"

"I guess so. It's like giving it a bath, isn't it?"

"God."

When I went downstairs, there she was, half asleep, put-out-looking and pretty. I sat down at the table. One soft-boiled egg. One piece of toast. "We'll go out for dinner tonight, okay?"

"And celebrate?" Melinda gave me the little smile she saved for parking lot attendants. We had been nipping at each other's heels for some time now. Maybe that was the way people got after twenty years.

I said, "Nobody else is going to celebrate it."

"Well, if you want to. There's a new place I suppose we could try. I forgot the name of it but it's French and it's supposed to be good."

"It doesn't have to be good. It just has to have air conditioning and a liquor license." It was the middle of August.

"Where did you say you were going?"

"Mix. That commercial we did for the bank—the one about loans? We have to change it."

This brought her first look of interest of the morning. "That one's cute. What are you changing it for?"

"FTC. They aren't allowing any propositions these days without the fine print that goes with them."

"Couldn't you talk to George Brice about it?"

I said, "It doesn't have anything to do with George Brice. The FTC is the Federal Trade Commission." I lit a cigarette to finish my coffee with. It was six thirty-five and I still had to put my tie on. "And no, I don't want to talk to George. I think I'll just wait for George to talk to me."

"Well, that sounds fraught with meaning. Why don't I understand it?"

"Just put it under the heading of new president and old guard. If George wants to start changing things, he'll have to tell me about it. I'm not going around to ask him."

I went up to the bedroom and found a tie and then transferred all the usual stuff from yesterday's jacket to today's. Melinda got back into bed. "What on earth would he want to change? Everybody knows Gibbs & Wilson. My God, they even know your commercials at the liquor store."

I took my keys from the top of the bureau and separated the ignition key from all those other keys. "Ask the board of directors. They hired him."

"You don't mind my not getting you a card? I mean, you're not going to spend the day brooding about it?"

"What card?"

"Our anniversary. It's so trite, giving each other cards."

"Oh. Yeah. We don't want to be trite, right?"

The mix was at Walker Sound at Fifth Avenue and Fifty-fourth Street. We had booked the studio from nine to ten. It was not a complicated job. We were just going to record a new announcer track and mix it with last year's music and effects tracks.

I walked uptown from Grand Central. The Newsweek tower said that it was already eighty-nine degrees. I could hear myself breathing. This was no weather for running.

It was nice to know they knew your commercials at the liquor store. I wondered if there was any way of putting the liquor store in touch with George.

George Brice had been the executive vice-president of General Drug. He was going to tell us just how to bring in packaged-goods accounts.

Packaged goods were brands you bought in drugstores and supermarkets—aspirin, toothpaste, soap and so on. The advertising budgets on some of these ran over twenty million dollars a year. This was the kind of money George was there to get for us.

We were now all going to learn from George.

Walker Sound had three studios—A, B and C. In A and B they had projectors. C was for radio spots or TV audio where synchronization with the picture was not particularly critical. We were in B.

I stopped in the hall and poured a cup of coffee from the Silex and took it into the studio.

Our announcer was an actor named Morgan Flemming. I had chosen him from an audition that casting had put on our Sony videotape machine. He was in the announcer's booth rehearsing.

"A little more up, Morgan. We're selling the bank, let's don't give it away." This was our producer, Fran Siltz. She was a busy little girl and she made me nervous.

Bob, the engineer, was still setting up the tape. "Hi, Jim. You walk up in this weather?"

I took off my jacket and loosened my tie. "I walked part of the way and swam the rest. Hank, you bring everything?"

Hank owned the editing house. "Even last year's voice track, Jim. Sorry you had to change this. I liked it the first way."

"Write your congressman."

In this commercial, all you saw was face after face—embarrassed, annoyed, uncertain, frozen, shocked and like that. We did not even show you a smiling banker when we got to our message. We just went right on showing you friends who did not want to see you.

The original script had been nice and simple:

There's just one difference between borrowing money from a friend and borrowing from a bank. Friends don't like it and banks do. At Manhattan, we don't even know why they're called "personal" loans. We figure you've brought us your business and heaven knows banks want business. So don't try your brother-in-law or your best friend. Drop in on Manhattan. Wouldn't you rather be treated like a customer than a pain in the neck?

The lawyers had said that there was more than "just one difference." You paid interest to the bank. I had said that that went without saying. The lawyers had said that nothing went without saying.

Th bank had also used the occasion to decide that the phrase "pain in the neck" was offensive.

First I had done the normal amount of screaming. And then, of course, I had changed it:

There are a number of differences between borrowing money from a friend and borrowing from a bank—and the first one is that friends don't like it and banks do. At Manhattan, we don't even know why they're called "personal" loans. We figure you've brought us your business—and interest always interests banks. So don't try your brother-in-law or your best friend. Drop in on Manhattan. We won't pretend we aren't home.

I said, "Fran, how are we doing?"

"He's just about got it, Jim. Morgan, would you run

through it once, please?" She even had a busy little voice, I thought.

Morgan started right in. *"There are a number of differences between borrowing money from a friend and borrowing from a bank—"*

I just sat there. Morgan Flemming's voice was not the voice that I had heard on the Sony.

I closed my eyes. Who did he sound like?

Jesus Christ, he was Walter Cronkite.

Busy little Fran. She couldn't leave the talent alone.

When Morgan finished, Fran said, "He's almost got it. Just a little more up, Morgan. Jim, I think we could put one down."

I said, "Bob, put up last year's track, will you?"

Fran came over. "Do you have a problem, Jim?" She was a cute little girl with cute little breasts that wandered around inside her sweater with nothing to fence them in. She had learned the business in a little TV station in Ohio. Commercials were supposed to be enthusiastic, weren't they?

I said, "He sounds like he's covering the Rose Bowl." I hated mixes. They put a hole in your day. "Morgan, we're putting up last year's track. Come on out and listen."

Fran sat down and lit a cigarette. Puff, puff, puff. After all her work, I had to come along and ruin it.

Bob played the old track. Morgan Flemming, a tall, red-headed man in his thirties, stood there outside the announcer's booth, listening. Then he said, "Conversational—that what you mean?"

"Yeah. You're just talking to a friend over a drink, okay?"

Fran said, "Just a little more up and I think we'll have it."

I said, "Not a little more anything. Let's try a dry run, then put one down and see."

After the dry run, Fran said, "A little brighter on the last line, Morgan."

Will you shut up, I thought. But I did not say anything. You can only give an actor so many changes to absorb at once.

On the third take, Fran said, "That was perfect."

I said, "I know it was. Now let's do it again. Morgan, on the last line, just throw it away."

"You don't want me to hit it? I can make it a little brighter, if you like."

"Just throw it away. Hit it and you'll kill it."

Fran said, "Give us some different readings on it, Morgan. Some up, some down—have fun with it."

I left after the recording and the mix. Fran had to wait to have the tape transferred to mag.

I walked down Fifth and over Forty-fifth and down Lexington. Max Gibbs had had to go over to the bank himself to sell this spot. The bank had not really liked it.

"It's the tone of voice, Max. It just doesn't sound like us."

"Don't you know what you have in this spot? This is a gut truth. Banks scare people."

"But saying the bank wants business—Max, it makes us sound like a store."

"Let me tell you something. People like stores and they don't like banks. Going to a bank for a loan is like going to a hospital."

It had gone on for almost an hour. "Max, can we at least change 'pain in the neck'?"

"Why? Because it isn't bankers' talk? You aren't advertising to bankers."

That had been the nice thing about working for Max. He had even had a set speech when he hired you. "I don't ever want to see an ad from you until you know in your gut it's right. Not in your head. Your gut."

And now Max was dead and we had George, who was going to tell us all about packaged goods.

George had been with us four months and had not been around to see me once and I already knew more about him than I wanted to.

He had sent me two talks he had given before the American Management Association, along with a book on copy testing. One of these talks was on research "to make your advertising dollars work harder." The other was on the marketing of General Drug's headache tablet, Relief.

General had run the same commercial for a year. There was a diagram showing where the headache hit, if you had a nice simple head like the diagram. Then little cowboys came in on horses and killed the headache. These cowboys were Sooth-X. This was Relief's miracle ingredient.

The commercial ran thirty seconds. Then you were ready for General Drug's little message about stomach acid. General bought one-minute time spots and piggybacked thirties in them.

According to the talk George sent me, he had tested his Relief commercial against thirty-five other commercials and

Relief had broken every sales record there was. He had practically tested every word of it.

This was not exactly doing it by your gut. This was painting by the numbers.

It was ten-thirty when I got to the office. In my mail was a notice that I owed the company $3.97 for personal phone calls, a memo offering a discount on Mountainaire air conditioners, now that it was the end of August; and a three-page memo on "disclosures and disclaimers" in TV commercials.

I gave this memo a try but I did not understand it. As nearly as I could tell, if you wanted to say your whoozis was 25 percent cheaper than their whoozis, you had to stop the commercial and explain that this was based on suggested list prices compared to their Model X or something. There was an example, but I did not understand that, either.

Edna, my secretary, came in. Edna was a tall, cool blonde. She was twenty-three years old and had that little sneer girls bring home from Vassar. "Accounting is dunning me for your phone bill."

"Tell them I'm out of the country."

"Is it that you don't have three dollars and ninety-seven cents or is it the principle of the thing?"

"It's the principle. I could raise that kind of money if I had to."

"The traffic boy was around. Something about a Federal ad for Buffalo."

"Barney Marker's doing it."

"I gather it's late."

"Get Barney on the phone."

She went out to her desk and presently my intercom buzzed. It was Barney Marker. "Jim? You wanted to talk to me?"

I said, "What's the story on the Federal ad for Buffalo?" Federal was Federal Airlines.

"We're still working on it, Jim. We just got the requisition a couple of days ago."

"How did you make out with the California ad?"

"The client wouldn't buy it. That's five they've shot down, Jim. I told Sermon maybe you ought to do it."

Barney was in his early twenties. This was his first year in the business. I said, "Your assignment, Barney. Give it another try."

"All right, but Sermon's getting a little nasty. He says he's tired of going over with ads Federal won't buy."

I said, "I feel awful about that."

Jeff Sermon was the account executive on Federal and I knew why he was nasty. Life would be easier if he could tell Federal all the writers on their account were big shots.

Brook Parker came in. "What kind of plane tickets are they supposed to send you when they want you to give a talk somewhere?"

"I don't know. What kind did you get?"

"Coach. They want me to give a talk in London and they sent me tickets on coach."

People always wanted Brook to make speeches. There had even been a book of his ads published. Brook was creative director. He made seventy thousand dollars a year, drove a 1930 Cadillac, dressed like a British banker and had chili for breakfast. On business trips, Brook flew first class.

I said, "Why don't you ask Marion if we'll make up the difference?" Marion Simons was our treasurer.

"He said there's nothing in it for us. We don't have an office in England." Brook sat down on my sofa and lit a cigarette. "I don't know if I want to do it, anyway. They never know what you're talking about. Do you know what they want? They want you to tell them how to do it, in forty minutes with questions from the audience."

"Well, if you don't want to go, what's your problem?"

Brook had, every now and then, a little boy's grin. "It's still a trip to Europe."

"What the hell—pay the difference yourself, then."

"That's in bad taste."

I just looked at him. "You just lost me. What's in bad taste?"

"Paying the difference yourself. It's business, isn't it? I don't fly coach on business."

"Brook, I don't know what to say." Brook was a genius. He could take absolutely nothing and make a problem out of it.

"Would Bernbach or Ogilvy do it?"

"What, pay the difference? I don't know. Probably."

"Wouldn't they think it was in bad taste?"

Barry Gorner walked in with a container of coffee. "Gentlemen? Any gentlemen in here?"

Barry was thirty-six, curly black hair, slim and dapper. Brook said he looked like a classy crook. Max Gibbs had hired him to set up our research department, because when clients wanted to see your research department, you had to

have one. Max himself had had no use for it. Right up to the
day he died, Max kept asking us what Barry's name was.

Brook said, "Jim used to be a gentleman."

I said, "I'm still a gentleman. That isn't a thing you lose."

Barry said, "I wanted you guys to be the first to know. No
more pulling rank on the honest people in research."

Brook said, "There are no honest people in research."

I looked at Barry and funny little thoughts crossed my mind.
"Barry? Don't tell me you're a vice-president?"

"I am. Fellows, after all these years, I finally got somebody
to listen to me."

Brook said, "Listen to you what?"

"I've had a report in my desk for four years now on just
how a research department should be run, and guess who's
interested in it?"

I said, "George Brice."

"You win the Argyle socks."

Brook put out his cigarette. "Brice is spending a lot of
time with you, eh?"

"Well, sure."

I said, "That's nice. He hasn't been spending any around
here. Just what have you guys been talking about?"

"Fellows, the key word is *norm*. Find a way to relate the
norms and all doors will open to you."

Norm. It was one of the magic words in research, right up
there with abracadabra.

Brook said, "That what you and George have been doing?
Relating all those little norms? You must have a lot of them
by now."

Barry said, "You can't relate them. That's what we've been
talking about—finding some way to do it. Look, you know
what a trailer is, right?"

I said, "It's the preview of next week's show. Just before
'Gunsmoke' goes off, you get the trailer for next week's
show."

"Wrong. A trailer is a trailer. You park it outside supermarkets and ask all the ladies to come in and watch a fifteen-
minute show. They get the show but you slip a few
commercials in, too. Now, when they come in you ask them
how they feel about Brand X, okay? And then you ask them
how they feel about Brand X on their way out. And if Brand
X is just all right on their way in and just wonderful on their
way out, you have an indication your commercial is not an
out-and-out stinker."

I said, "Barry, you didn't happen to mention, during all these little talks with George, that we kind of don't go around asking little old ladies whether our commercials are any good?"

"Come on, Jim. This is just making sure. You test something and the clients have to listen to you, that's all. Now, the problem is you get one kind of norm from trailer tests and another from twenty-four-hour recall and nobody knows how to relate them."

Brook said, "All this is what George Brice made you a vice-president for, eh?"

"He likes an idea I have for cross-indexing the norms. I figure if you could set up a formula you could relate the norms for trailers, Schwerin, twenty-four-hour recall and any other tests where a norm can be fixed."

Barry was pretty excited by all this.

Brook said, "You know what, Barry? I hope you and George will be very happy."

I did not say anything. It had started, I thought.

It was not just that I was the copy chief and a vice-president of the place, or even the fifty thousand dollars they paid me.

It was that Gibbs & Wilson was Gibbs & Wilson. All this seemed to be coming to an end.

I was forty-eight years old. I had worked for Max for ten years.

But before that, I had spent ten years with the Mercer Agency, and ten years with Mercer was—well, it was ten years with Mercer.

You talked to this sales manager about nylon fibers and that sales manager about fluorescent lamps and some other sales manager about roofing shingles and you came back and wrote the ads.

You were a processor of words. They gave you the story and you gave it back to them in an ad. Sound ads. Even clever ads. The account men decided whether they were any good. The account men decided everything.

I could still remember my last year there, writing American Credit ads for *Business Week*. "Who's putting the capital in your capital equipment?" Ads like that.

Of course, you were always free to try something new. If you could sell it to the account man, fine. If you couldn't, you couldn't. I could still remember that, too.

"I will loan up to 10 million dollars
to the company that can show me
they will make a profit with it."
                John H. Raymond
                President, American Credit

The account executive on American had been an ex-basketball player named Ernie Clifford. Ernie was reasonable and had dandruff and knew just where he was working. "Come on, Jim. Are you serious?"

"What do you mean, am I serious?"

"I can't show them anything like this."

"Why not? That's the proposition, isn't it?"

"It just doesn't sound responsible, Jim."

"Ernie, for Christ's sake, if you need money and you see that ad, do you mean you'd just turn the page?"

"Come on, Jim. It doesn't even sound like an ad. What do you want, the lecture on American and corporate image?"

"Ernie, let's really protect their image. Let's don't run any ads."

It was, of course, not just this one ad that had got to me. I had begun to wonder what I was doing there at all.

Most copywriters who got anywhere in this business did it in their thirties. There I was at Mercer, thirty-eight years old and still making $11,500 doing what I was told.

That was the week that Gibbs & Wilson had run an ad in *The New York Times* for a copywriter. I had been a little put off by Gibbs & Wilson. They were small and hot and I had heard that nobody worked there but young geniuses. I did not know if they would even look at a résumé from Mercer.

But I took the American ad and some others that Mercer had known better than to show clients and put them in the mail anyway. A week later a man named Alvin Baker called me. He was the copy chief at Gibbs & Wilson. Max Gibbs wanted to see me.

I did not know what I expected at Gibbs & Wilson but I did not expect Alvin Baker and Max Gibbs.

I went to Alvin Baker's office first. It was ten years since I had applied for a job, but I still remembered the polite little fencing.

That's a little higher than we had in mind.

You understand we're talking to several people.

The first thing Alvin Baker said was, "Jim, would you like to see an ad I just wrote?"

I did not know what to say. You would think I was already working there. "Sure."

He handed me a sheet of canary yellow typing paper. "Do you know Brothers beer, Jim?"

"I've heard of it, but I never tried it." It was an upstate brand.

> "I will close the brewery before
> I will make a light beer."

It was a long ad, all small plain words. Brothers beer was still made the way they made it in 1905. You believed every word. You would think your uncle Hank wrote it.

What kind of interview was this? They were showing me their ads. I said, "That's a nice piece of copy. Is the beer that good?"

"Oh, Jim, that's one of the great beers in the country. You should try Brothers beer."

"Well, I hope they know what an ad they have there."

"Oh, they're wonderful people. Do you know what they do when they like an ad? They write me a letter, Jim."

The beer was wonderful and the people were wonderful. It made me a little uneasy. "That's a nice client to have."

"But that's what they come to us for, Jim. Jim, this isn't Mercer. There isn't another place like this in the world." Alvin Baker was smiling and staring at me, as if there were something that I was supposed to understand. "Jim, the only thing that counts here is great work. Do you want to know something? If you do come up with an ad the client won't buy, he won't change it. The account man won't even change it. Nobody changes your copy around here but you, Jim."

"That's going to take some getting used to," I said with a little laugh.

Alvin Baker said, "Jim, do you know that Max read every ad you sent us? He said he could even tell where the client changed your copy."

"He read all those proofs?"

"In the shingle ads, you used the words *we* and *us*. They aren't in the American Credit ads once."

"That was the account executive. No first person pronouns. I think there's some kind of policy at American against sounding as if any real people work there. How did you ever pick that up?"

"We couldn't figure out why your shingle ads were warmer

than American's. It was Max who spotted it. Jim, how much
are you making at Mercer?"

"Eleven five."

"We're starting you at fourteen. That's just to give you a
little raise to celebrate. Jim, do you know something else
Max said? He said you had much better headlines in some
of your body copy than the headlines you used."

"I did? I didn't know that."

"Max figured it was because you couldn't get away with
them as headlines."

"No. I wish I could say it was on purpose, but I just didn't
know it."

"You should see some of the ads Max made out of your
ads, just by taking some of your other lines and making
headlines out of them. Jim, is your seat belt fastened?"

"What?"

"For the trip upstairs."

Max Gibbs' office looked like the kitchen in an old farm-
house. He did not have a desk. Just a big round oak table,
the kind you had dinner at if you had six kids. The man who
stood up to shake hands with me was about fifty, light blue
eyes, silver hair, nice smile, the build of a middle-aged middle-
weight. "Come in, Jim. Come in. Did Alvin tell you we think
that American Credit ad is one of the world's great ads?"

"Well, I can't say Mercer liked it much."

Alvin Baker said, "Do you know what they said, Max?
They said it didn't sound like an ad."

Max Gibbs laughed out loud. "What did you expect? Who
wants ads the client won't like? Jim, if we had American
Credit, I'd have been over there with that ad myself. Jim, if
you smoke, go ahead. If the cleaning woman doesn't find
something in the ashtray, she'll think we goofed all day. Alvin,
did you ask Jim what I asked you about?"

"I didn't get to it, Max."

Max Gibbs said, "Well, kid, I guess what we're wondering
is why you stayed at Mercer for ten years."

I said, "I don't know. One year just followed another, I
guess. I guess I just thought it would be the same anyplace
else."

"You did ads like this and they didn't think they were any
good, so you didn't think they were any good?"

"Well, no. I thought they were pretty good. If the account
men don't buy it, what can you do?"

Max Gibbs said, "Alvin, why is it that every good writer we find needs somebody to take care of him?"

Alvin said, "Maybe it's because good writers give too much of themselves away, Max."

Max Gibbs said, "Jim, we noticed something unusual in your work. Not just the roughs, but the ads that actually ran. One thing we saw was that you could go from account to account and come up with just the copy you needed. This guy writes like talking, Alvin, do you know that?"

Alvin said, with a little laugh, "Yes, Max, but he had clients who knew just how to fix it."

Max Gibbs said, "But we did notice something else. Jim, you don't always seem to know a good headline when you have one. Did Alvin tell you I found better headlines in your body copy than some of the headlines you used?"

Alvin said, "I mentioned it, Max. I think that might be because he didn't have the time to look his copy over after he did it."

Max Gibbs said, "Jim, let me tell you something. We don't get our clients on the golf course. They only come to us for the work we do. We can't use any secret ads around here. If our ads aren't the best in town, we're out of business."

Alvin said, "You understand you're one of us now, Jim. We have to bring this up because we've got to get the best you can give us."

Max Gibbs said, "Kid, do you know what we want? We want the lines you've been afraid to use as headlines."

Alvin said, "Tell Jim about Non-Temp, Max."

"Non-Temp. Okay." Max Gibbs took a deep breath. "Jim, Non-Temp was an account we fired. Every time we sent an ad over, they changed it. I'd call them up, I'd go over to see them, I'd tell them they were ruining a great ad—and, Jim, they didn't even know what I was mad about."

Alvin said, "Jim, they kept changing our ads and telling us how much they liked us."

Max Gibbs said, "And if it tells you anything, Jim, they were billing over a million when we threw them out."

I did not get all this. A fourteen-thousand-dollar copy job and here was the president, taking all this time to talk to me.

I said, "Well, I know Mercer dropped one account because it was crooked and I think they dropped one because the client wanted us to pick up girls for him, but they didn't stop any accounts because they changed any ads."

Max Gibbs said, "Kid, let me tell you something. Mercer's

in the account-keeping business. That's all right. Most agencies are. But this isn't one of them. Do you know what we
do here?"

"I know you're doing just about all the ads anybody's
talking about these days."

"Jim, that's only the result of what we do. Alvin, what do
we do here?"

Alvin said, "Jim, we don't let anybody keep those ads from
being done. I saw Max take a pencil out of an account man's
hand once and break it."

Max Gibbs said, "Isn't it ridiculous? Agencies pay a good
writer to come up with something and then they all sit around
and improve it. Well, talent's the only thing I can afford
around here. I can't afford all those other guys."

Alvin said, "Do you know what it's like here, Jim? It's like
getting out of the army."

Max Gibbs said, "We just have one ground rule, Jim. I
don't ever want to see an ad from you until you know in
your gut it's the best ad you ever did. In your gut. Not in
your head. I don't care if it's late. I don't care if we miss an
insertion."

I said, "Okay."

Max Gibbs said, "I don't want you staying at fourteen
thousand, either. That's a lousy salary."

The day that I started, Alvin Baker called me into his
office. "Jim, we're going to put you in with Brook Parker on
Paragon for a while. Do you know who Brook is?"

"No, but I know the Paragon ads." The Paragon was a
twelve-thousand-dollar sports car. It was one of the campaigns
that everybody was talking about.

> The speedometer cannot be seen
> from the passenger seat.

Alvin said, "You don't know Brook Parker? What did they
do at Mercer, lock you in a closet? Jim, Brook's the greatest
art director in the world. Jim, Willow cough drops?"

Willow cough drops, too? Who was this Brook Parker?
Willow was one of the stories they were even telling in the
halls at Mercer. The cough drops were bitter and Gibbs &
Wilson had figured, okay, they're bitter.

> If they taste good, see your doctor.

According to the story, Willow had said this was negative, and Max Gibbs had said it was not as negative as their cough drops. Willow wanted to test it. Max Gibbs had said tests were for classrooms. Willow tested it anyway, and the research people said it was a disaster. Max Gibbs had told Willow to run it or get another agency. They ran it and sales went out of sight.

I said, "Brook Parker did that?"

"Don't be surprised if Brook writes better headlines than you do," Alvin said. "Did the writers work with the art directors at Mercer?"

"Work with them how?"

"Sit down and get the idea together."

"No." I had never worked like that and I did not want to. How could you think of anything with somebody watching you?

"That's the only way we do it, Jim. Come on. I'll take you around to Brook's office. Brook's a genius, Jim. He's really a genius."

Brook Parker's office looked like an operating room. Big, white and stark. Sitting on a high steel chair at a drawing table was a man who looked like an eagle. The Roman nose. Pale eyes. He looked at me as if I were a piece of liver.

Alvin said, "Brook, this is Jim Bower."

I said, "Hi. I guess we're going to be working together." I held out my hand. At first, he just stared at it. He finally shook it and said, "We are?"

Alvin said, "Jim did some great ads for Mercer. Ask him to show you his book, Brook."

"Nobody ever did great ads for Mercer."

I said, "If it helps any, they didn't run."

Alvin said, "Well, time to lock the cage now. May the best man win."

He left and for some time Brook Parker did not say anything. Then he said, "Funny guy, Alvin Baker." He inhaled and exhaled cigarette smoke. "He's too good to be true but he's true."

I said, "Well, I guess what I'm supposed to do is think up some ads, eh?"

Brook Parker did not say anything at all. He smoked his cigarette and looked out the window.

I said, "Is there anything I ought to know about the Paragon that I haven't read in the ads?"

"If there was, you'd have read it in the ads."

I said, "So what we have is a twelve-thousand-dollar coupe, two seats and twelve cylinders. Seems like a waste."

"What does?"

"Twelve cylinders for a car that size."

"Oh." He sounded disappointed. I think that he had expected some new insight about the car from me. Now he went back to looking out the window. That left me the wall to look at.

I had never worked this way with an art director before.

At Mercer, you got the idea yourself and sold it to the account executive and then brought it around to the art department to get a decent layout for it. Having to think of an ad while an art director was sitting there like a teacher was not my idea of fun. I wanted to ask how much time we had, but I was afraid it would be a sign of weakness.

I sat with a pad in my lap and thought of silly things.

The Paragon of virtue.

Finally, I said, "Here's something: *$12,000 will buy 3 good cars or one great one.*"

Brook Parker shifted his weight a little on his high steel chair. He seemed to have the same expression that snakes get when they contemplate a sparrow.

He said, "We don't do ads like that here."

Just like that.

He did not have anything else to say.

I began to wish it were time for lunch. I wanted to get out of that room. I began to get a little sore. This guy did not even talk to you.

The hell with him. If he was not going to talk to me, fine.

Then Brook Parker took a felt-tipped Pentel pen and drew two car seats on his layout pad. He tore the page off and stuck it on his wall with two pieces of tan masking tape. Then he went back to his chair and sat down and looked at it.

There was nothing on the page but two car seats, facing you.

I said, "*12 cylinders. 6 for each of you.*"

He turned on his chair and looked at me for some time. Then he got up and wrote this on his layout:

12 cylinders. 6 for each of you.

Then he went back and sat down and looked at it for a while.

Then he said, "You going to be on Paragon steady?"

I said, "I don't know."

"I'll talk to Max about it. Come on."

"Where are we going?"

"Up to Coleman's office. Bob Coleman's the account supervisor on Paragon."

I said, "What do we do if he doesn't like it?"

"He'll like it. He'll just say he doesn't."

We went upstairs to an office the same size as Brook Parker's, but more comfortable-looking. In a huge leather chair behind a long black desk was a big, athletic-looking man in his early thirties. He had pure white hair and looked like the colonel in a war movie.

He said, "Hello, Brook."

Brook Parker put the layout on his desk. He did not say anything.

Bob Coleman looked at it. Then said, "I don't get it."

Brook Parker said, "Fine. We'll stay here until you do."

"Brook, I can't take an ad over to the client if I don't understand it myself."

Brook Parker said, "Don't go anywhere, okay?" He left the room.

Presently he came back with Max Gibbs. Max Gibbs said, "Okay, boys, what down is it?"

Brook Parker said, "Bob doesn't get this."

The colonel from the war movie said, "Brook, we already have a headline for this ad. *$6,000 each.*"

I just stood there. I thought *$6,000 each* was a swell headline. I wondered why Brook Parker had not told me about it.

Brook Parker said, "We've done enough ads about price."

Max Gibbs said, "Brook, I agree. I think this is a very good way to go. Bob, this is a very good ad."

Brook Parker said, "Jim did it. Jim or Jack?"

I said, "Jim."

Max Gibbs said, "I thought you just started this morning."

Brook Parker said, "Yeah. It took him almost an hour."

Max Gibbs turned to me and said, "If you don't follow all this, Jim, we've already sold this ad to Paragon with Brook's headline. That's what we have here, Jim. Fellows who can throw out their own ideas when they see a better one."

Bob Coleman said, "Okay, where does it go from here? What do I tell Paragon when they want to know why we changed an ad they've already bought?"

Max Gibbs said, "Bob, let me take care of it. I have to see them, anyway. Let me take this over."

On the way out of Coleman's office, Max Gibbs put his arm around my shoulder and said, "Well, kid, you're off to a good start. Just don't brood about living up to it. Take it as it comes."

I said to Brook Parker afterward, "That was a nice thing for him to say. What made him think of it?"

Brook Parker said, "Me. He wasn't even talking to you."

I worked for Max Gibbs for ten years. I went from the new copywriter in the place to copy chief. It was nice, having people ask if I wrote the 19th Century vodka ad: *Tell your mother-in-law it's potato soup. She'll love it.* It was nice to be asked if I did the cancer commercial: *You die a little every day. Would you like to try for a lot?*

Old friends from the Mercer Agency looked me up sometimes for lunch and told me that Ernie Clifford was still there, working on American Credit. And then that Ernie Clifford was not there any more, that Ernie had been let go.

Then one day Max Gibbs took a cab uptown to a client meeting and a bus ran into the cab. That was the end of the best ad man I knew.

This had happened six months ago. I could not say I was glad to hear that our new president had been spending all his time with Barry Gorner in research.

All this was on my mind that morning as I started work on a Federal Airlines ad.

I had been working on this ad for two days but I had not come up with a thing. Federal billed eight million dollars. I wrote their corporate ads and TV commercials. This ad, if I could think of one, would run in one hundred newspapers.

If I could think of one. What could you say about Federal that you could not say about American, United or TWA? They all served dinner and liquor. They charged the same fares.

Attitude. Attitude. The only thing the CAB did not regulate was their attitude.

I whistled a few bars from *Camelot.*

Hey . . .

I got up from my desk and got out a layout pad and a Magic Marker.

> You will hear the following funny noises
> when your plane takes off.

I tore the sheet off my pad and stuck it on my wall with masking tape. Then I just sat there looking at it.

That, by God, was a service. Explain all those funny noises that scared people. The clunk when the landing gear came up. The change in pitch when you throttled the jets back. The spoiler noise when you were landing.

Max would have loved an ad like this.

"You got a minute to talk about the Den-Test spot?"

It was an art director named Rudy d'Franco. Rudy looked as if he had just bombed the draft board. Hot dark eyes, thin bony face, angry young man. I knew what he was angry about. He was twenty-seven and he didn't have a million dollars yet.

I said, "What about it?"

"You hear we're shooting it in a warehouse? That studio must think I was born yesterday, pulling a stunt like that on me."

"What do you have against warehouses?"

"I can't control the lighting in a warehouse. What if I need an extra deuce or a keg?"

Deuces and kegs were lights. Rudy liked to talk like a cameraman. I said, "That's what the production meeting was for. Rudy, it's going to take a day just to put that set up. It's cheaper to tie up a warehouse than a sound stage."

"And that's all that matters? It's cheaper?"

"That's what the studio based the bid on and that's the bid Landum okayed."

Den-Test was one of the few packaged goods we had. It was an ancient toothpaste, an off-brand put out by Landum. Landum was one of those big places like Lever Brothers, but this was the only business we had with them. The idea was that an agency that did campaigns like Paragon's and Willow cough drops' might just pull a forty-year-old toothpaste back from the grave.

Rudy sat down in one of my chairs and put his feet on my desk and lit a cigarette and flicked the match onto my rug. "I don't like the spot, anyway."

It was a nice little spot. First you panned up the length of an old razor strop. Then over to an old straight razor. Then to a shaving mug. Then a shaving brush. Then the tube of Den-Test. Each item was going to vanish as you were looking at it. Except, of course, the Den-Test.

In the last forty years, all these had disappeared. Only the toothpaste was still there. Den-Test. Forty years with no advertising until now. Did you know how many toothpastes came out in the last forty years? Could you even guess what they spent on advertising? Forty years and millions of dollars. And they still couldn't get Den-Test users to change. Imagine that.

I said, "What's the matter with the spot?"

"It's corny."

"It's supposed to be corny. This stuff doesn't do anything that Crest does but come out of the tube."

"Yiksville. If there's one thing I don't need on my reel, it's yik stuff like this."

Never mind selling Den-Test. The big thing was to get Rudy a reel of hot commercials so Doyle Dane Bernbach would throw money at him.

"Rudy, we've had this conversation. The spot's been through legal, the client, the NAB and the networks, okay?"

"That's why we're doing crap? It got through the red tape?"

You could take so much of this guy. I said, "I don't do crap, Rudy."

"If you say so." Rudy d' Franco got up and walked out.

I just sat there. Getting somebody fired took making up your mind and gritting your teeth and it was just too much to go through right now.

That was the moment that our new president walked in.

George Brice.

I could have used a warning. Invisible for four months and then there he was. I do not know what I had expected. A phone call to go up to his office, maybe. Some sort of staff meeting. It was a little like looking up and seeing the new admiral on the base.

Well, what the hell. I was one of the colonels. "George, how are you?"

"Fine, Jim. How are you?"

"Okay."

He stopped and looked at the layout on my wall.

> You will hear the following funny noises
> when your plane takes off.

He looked a little like a druggist. Ordinary. Five feet ten, about one hundred seventy pounds. Round pale face, pale hair, light blue eyes.

He turned to me and smiled. "You do go in for the shockers around here."

"Well, George, I always wished somebody would tell me what all those noises were."

He turned back to the ad again. He looked at it for a long time. He did not move. He did not say a word.

Then he turned back to me again. "Tell me something, Jim. Did Federal ask us for an ad on this?"

"No. It just seemed to be a kind of service, telling people what to expect, you know?"

"You don't think it might turn people off?"

This was my new boss and he did not like the first ad. I said, "No, George. I think it's something they wished somebody would tell them."

"The intuitive touch. I see."

I did not answer this.

George Brice smiled and said, "Well, Jim. Tell me. How's it going?"

"Not bad. Got a nice vodka ad out of Lydia this morning. Lydia's a little spooky but she's a hell of a writer."

"Oh? What was it?"

"It brings out the taste of the ice cubes."

"Very clever. That's very clever, Jim."

I said, "Lydia makes twenty-five here, George. She turned down thirty at Tinker, if that tells you anything."

"The first thing it tells me, Jim, is that you know how to run your department." George sat down on my sofa. "Jim, what does the word *norm* mean to you?"

Norm. There was that word again.

"It's a kind of bench mark in Starch reports." Starch reports were research studies on how much attention ads got in magazines.

George said, "That's true, but that isn't quite what I meant. Jim, how much do you know about research?"

"Not very much. I read your speeches, but I couldn't get through that book you sent around."

George smiled and said, "Research people like to use big words. Well, Jim, if I had to put it in a nutshell, I'd say norm was something you tested ads against. You don't seem to do much copy testing around here."

I said, "Not very much. I guess we kind of got started down this street instead of that street, you know?"

"So I've been told." George took out a Marlboro. At least we smoked the same brand. His lighter was on the end of a mechanical pencil. He said, "Funny. The lighter works and the pencil doesn't. Jim, I have an idea we are going to need each other's help around here."

I said, "Okay."

"Now, I think, Jim, that the first obligation is mine. Gibbs & Wilson stands for something and it's going to be up to me to keep that in mind, eh?"

I said, "Can't ask for more than that."

"And, on the other hand, the kind of accounts I'd like to get in here have a few ground rules of their own. I think if your people just understood that much, Jim, we'd be halfway home already."

I said, "What kind of ground rules are we talking about?"

"Jim, they understand norms. Testing. If you want to put it that way, they'd understand my Relief commercial before they'd understand what's-her-name's vodka ad."

In no time at all, we had got to the bridge that I was supposed to defend. I said, "Well, that doesn't exactly make my day."

George laughed. "Jim, it isn't as bad as all that. Look at it from their side. The reason Relief did what it did was that we did all the right things first."

I had never done well with men who never made a mistake. I did not know how to talk to them. It was as if everything I said was something they were just tolerating to be nice.

I said, "Testing, you mean."

"As a matter of fact, Jim, we tested everything. We tested twenty-five names against Sooth-X. Eighteen names against Relief. We even tested cowboys against airplanes, tigers, rocket ships and genies."

I said, "Well, George, I'm not so sure we'd be much good at that, you know?"

"Oh? Why is that, Jim?"

"Well, we kind of have a thing we do here, you know? Look, I know what you did on Relief. It's just that what we do is something else."

"Jim, I don't believe I follow you."

I said, "Well, I don't know; I guess I'd just rather have the gut feeling of one Brook Parker than all the trailer tests on earth."

George said in a mild voice, "Why can't we have both, Jim?"

"George, you only get thirty seconds to work with. I mean, research says headache tension instead of nervous tension.

Cowboys instead of airplanes. It's like working with blocks.
There's no time left for the magic."

"You can't be creative if somebody else gives you the
direction—is that what you mean, Jim?"

"Well, I never tried to put it in words before. Something
like that, I guess."

"Still Michelangelo managed. Most of history's great art,
in fact, came from some patron's direction, Jim."

"Yeah, well, that was execution, you know? I mean, part
of the art here is the direction, George. Hell, I don't even
know if I'm making sense."

George Brice inhaled cigarette smoke. "Of course you're
making sense, Jim."

"But that isn't the way you do it, right?"

"No, Jim. It isn't. Jim, believe me, I know what we have
when a Brook Parker comes up with a Willow cough drop
campaign. I know what we have with a vodka ad like that
one you did about the mother-in-law. But, Jim, those are like
little discoveries. You might almost call them creative acci-
dents."

"Well, that's what we have, George. We kind of let acci-
dents like that happen around here."

"Pretty risky for the clients, isn't it? Hoping for an accident,
Jim?"

"Not if they get it."

George did not seem to be upset. He smoked a little more
of his cigarette and seemed about as hurried as a turtle. "Jim,
just suppose, for a moment, that I did ask you or Brook
Parker for a commercial on nervous tension. Just suppose
that we all agreed nerves was the thing to hit. Jim, I know
you aren't telling me that you and Brook couldn't come up
with something. You'd not only come up with something,
Jim—you'd come up with the best commercial on nerves in
town."

I said, "Well, I hope so. Sure."

"And, on the other hand, if that was what you spent your
time working on—time you didn't have to spend looking for
the direction in the first place—wouldn't life be a little easier
all around?"

"George, life might be easier, but the ideas might not be
the ideas clients come here to get."

George Brice smiled and said, "Jim, clients don't come to
us for ideas. They come to us to sell their products." George
got up from the sofa and walked over to the layout taped on

my wall. "Jim, suppose we could tell you people were more interested in their baggage than in funny noises. Jim, just knowing that would take at least half the pressure off your job. In fact, I think it would even make you that much surer of the ads and commercials you did come up with."

Well, there we were. I said, "George, if you're talking about sending Barry Gorner off to find out what the natives are thinking, you're just going to wind up with the world's tenth light beer."

"Jim, if I sold beer and that was the way to sell it, I think I'd be a very happy client."

"Well, we had a beer here, George, and we didn't do badly just telling people how we made it."

"Brothers beer? Jim, that was a regional brand you increased twenty-three percent in a German area where heavy beer happened to go with the demographic breakdown. That was not exactly a mass audience, Jim."

"Well, that was the product and that was the market, George, and as you say, we got their sales up twenty-three percent."

George turned back to the ad that I had on the wall. "Funny noises---I take it you're going to think about this ad for a while before you submit it. . . ."

I had done all the thinking about this ad that I had intended to, but I found myself saying, "Of course."

George smiled. "Jim, that takes a very mature attitude. I admire that kind of self-discipline very much, Jim."

He strolled out and I just sat there. I was not quite sure how he had done it, but he had got me to throw out an ad that I thought was just swell. Son of a bitch. I took the layout off my wall and threw it into my wastebasket.

On my way out that night, I stopped in our reception room and looked at the first ad Max Gibbs had ever written for Paragon. It was in a frame on the wall.

You could buy a house for the money.

That ad had started a controversy in the agency business. It was negative. It was not the way to sell cars.

Still, Bob Hope and Harry Truman had picked up the line "You could buy a house for the money." And you still had to wait four months for a Paragon.

I wondered what Max Gibbs would have said if George

Brice had asked him if he did not think an ad like that might turn people off.

But then, that was really the nub of it. I was not Max Gibbs. I had met the enemy and I was his. I went home early to take Melinda out to dinner.

You ought to feel pretty good about your twentieth anniversary. Twenty years together. Now, that is not supposed to be something you go through with clenched teeth.

Westport, unlike towns that kept getting new pizza parlors and bowling alleys, kept getting new French restaurants.

This one was called the Left Bank. It was in an old house on a little road two blocks long. It was surrounded by several other very old houses, each with big trees and ratty-looking lawns and porches that had slumped in exhaustion. The street sort of stumbled out onto Westport's main shopping center, and little stores had wormed their way in from the corner.

Melinda said, "Well, it's shabby enough to be good."

I tried to maneuver the big Lincoln around a decrepit stone wall without scraping the side of a seven-thousand-dollar silver BMW. The heat was just what you might expect for August. My sunglasses had got a little steam on them. I took them off and rubbed my eyebrows with the back of my wrist. Wasn't that something, I thought. Sweaty eyebrows. I could clear the BMW if I backed up a little to the right. I said, "It's shabby enough to be expensive."

"Don't they have a parking attendant?"

"I don't see one. Maybe they only come out for Mercedes-Benzes."

I finally got the Lincoln's nose up against a straggly hedge and we got out. I rolled down my shirt sleeves, buttoned my collar and pulled up my tie. I put on the light green linen jacket and looked at my watch. Seven o'clock. You could take your clothes off and take a bath in this air.

Melinda said, "You take longer to dress in a parking lot than I take at home. Aren't you going to lock the car?"

"How can anybody steal it if I lock it?"

"Are we going to have another evening of cryptic humor?"

The porch boards gave a little under our feet and we went inside. It was dark and cold and everything you could see looked red. I said, "It's a whorehouse."

"I think it's darling." Melinda was slight, slim and cool. Black eyes. Black hair. No bust to speak of. She was quite pretty, in a thin, intense sort of way.

A man with a black tie and formal jacket came over. "Good evening, sir. Do you have a reservation?"

"Bower," I said.

"Of course, Mr. Bower. If you'll come with me?"

Our table was in what had once been the parlor. It was a small ornate room with a chandelier that would kill you if it ever fell down, thick red carpet, complicated cream-colored molding and dark paintings in heavy gilded frames.

We sat down and Melinda said, "I don't believe this. Who'd expect a place like this inside that outside?"

I said, "Sixteenth-century French liver. What do you want, a martini?"

"In a chilled glass, on the rocks. I'll even go sit in the refrigerator and drink it."

A little blonde wearing next to nothing with a little lace at the edge came over. I told her that we wanted two dry martinis on the rocks. She went off into the gloom.

Melinda said, "That's a nice little sway she has there."

"Just advertising."

"But I noticed you noticed."

"But I didn't stare."

"Is your hair getting thin?"

"No. I don't think so."

"I found some hair in your brush. I hope you don't get bald. You don't have the head for it."

"I wonder why it's the top of your head that gets bald," I said. "Why isn't it ever your chin?"

"God. If you get bald, get a hairpiece."

I lit a Kent for her and a Marlboro for myself. For our anniversary, I had got her a dress from Lord & Taylor. One hundred thirty-five dollars. She had not worn it. She said it was a winter dress. She had thanked me, however. She said it was very nice.

I said, "This joint seems to have one headwaiter, one waitress and us."

"I hope you aren't going to spend the evening complaining."

"Just looking around and reporting on what I see. Okay, how the hell is your mother?"

"Please don't go through the motions, dear. We talk about Mother about as often as we talk about Poland."

I did not know what was bugging her. It had developed in the last year. Out of nowhere, everything was "phony." There had to be more to life than this.

I did not know how much more there was supposed to

be. All I knew was that I was making fifty thousand dollars in an ad agency and things were phony. Other people did things. They went to Africa and taught the natives irrigation or something. The word *contribution* came up a lot.

Melinda was forty-three. It had occurred to me that that might have something to do with it.

I tried changing the subject. "How would you feel, when I retire, maybe looking for a place in Virginia?"

"What in heaven's name brought that on?"

"Well, it's the sort of thing it isn't dumb to start thinking about."

Melinda said, "You don't retire until you're sixty-five."

"Only if you go by the book. I could come out with enough in my fifties to be comfortable. A little free lance in Washington to pay for the gin, what the hell?"

Melinda did not say anything. She just puffed, a bit nervously, on her cigarette.

I said, "Don't tell me. You don't like Virginia."

"I'm sure Virginia is beautiful."

Well, that was that. "What's that bartender doing? Waiting for one big order?"

She said, "They are taking a long time."

"If they have to look a dry martini up in the book, we're in the wrong place."

Melinda took another Kent from her pack and I lit it for her and she said, "Thank you."

The waitress brought our martinis. When she bent over, you could see her nipples.

I said, "Thank you."

This brought Melinda to life. She said, "They weren't all that big, you know. She had them pushed up."

"On the other hand, I would bet a fairly large sum that she isn't a boy."

Melinda drank some of her drink and made a face. "Wow."

I said. "Well, here we are, twenty years later."

"Here we are."

"Could be worse," I said.

All that this brought me was another smile and a little shrug. As anniversaries went, this party was not going to make *The New York Times*.

"Guess who just came in," Melinda said.

"Who?"

"The Matthewses and the Reynoldses."

"Together?"

"Yes."

Barlow Matthews came over. "Hi."

Every time I saw Barlow Matthews, I had the feeling he had invented himself. Six feet one. Blond towhead. Lifeguard tan. That smile alone must have cost him fifteen hundred dollars.

Barlow was the executive vice-president of a company big enough to have its own capitol and Barlow was all of thirty-nine years old.

"Hi," I said.

Melinda called hello over to the others, and Barlow said, "Are you on your way anywhere afterward?"

Melinda said, "We were thinking of going to the movies."

"Why not come back to the house with us?"

Melinda looked at me. "Would you like to?"

I said, "Sure. You can't get a drink in the movies."

Barlow smiled with all those beautiful teeth. "Fine. We'll see you back there."

He went to his table and Melinda said, "What are you grinning at?"

I said, "Barlow dolls."

"What?"

"Nothing."

"I hope you aren't going to be funny tonight."

"Not me."

It was nine when we got to the Matthewses', one of those colonials that looked as if Washington had slept in it. Kate Matthews opened the door. "We heard some moochers might come by looking for drinks."

Kate and Barlow were the same age but there was gray in Kate's hair. She was a short woman with a wide back, wide shoulders, gray eyes and swell breasts. I said, "It's only fair to warn you this is our anniversary. We came by for our presents."

"Your anniversary? Which one?"

Melinda said, "The first."

Kate said, "Well, that will give us something to drink to. Come in. Take off your coat and tie and look like a bum with the rest of us."

Barlow was wearing a blue turtleneck and looked like Flash Gordon. "Want to help me with the drinks, Jim?"

"Sure. Where are the Reynoldses?"

Barlow said. "Tom's out looking at the pool and Betty's in the girls' room."

I followed him into the study. Except in television commercials, I did not remember ever knowing anybody with a globe that big in their home before. It sat there, Barlow's world, in a big walnut stand. If you wanted to look at it up close you had to wade through an Oriental rug.

I watched him take down the glasses from a highboy. Wharton School of Finance. Harvard Business School. Golf in the low eighties. I wondered how a guy got where he was, and what he did when he did get there.

"How's the agency business, Jim?"

I said, "All right. Not bad."

There was that smile again. "I thought advertising men went around telling everybody how great it was going to be."

"I'm a lower-middle-class advertising man. I just tell people it won't be lousy."

Barlow laughed and said, "You know, I've always wanted to do a little writing myself, Jim. Did I ever tell you that?"

"How to build a corporation in the basement?"

"No. Poetry."

"Poetry?"

"There are vibrations in this country, Jim. I'd love to get it down on paper."

"What are you talking about, the kids?"

Barlow sat on one of his haunches on the edge of his desk. "Jim, they're beginning to ask questions. What are we doing, spending sixty million dollars to advertise detergents when you can't swim in the rivers any more."

I said, "Yes; well, I know the questions. It's the answers I haven't heard yet."

"You will. Jim, it's just beginning to dawn on people that it's their world. It doesn't belong to Standard Oil after all."

"I didn't think that was the way executive vice-presidents were supposed to talk."

"They'd better, if they want anything left to be vice-presidents of. Jim, do you know how exciting this is? These kids don't want things to be better for themselves. They want things to be better for everybody."

I said, "How do you pull that off?"

"Jim, that's the challenge. How do you do it?"

I said, "I don't even know who you get to break the news to Standard Oil."

I went out to the living room. Tom Reynolds had come in from the pool. Tom was forty-five. Philadelphia Main Line. Tall, bony and balding. He made about seventeen thousand dollars a year as a geologist or something for one of the oil companies. He had enough degrees to paper a room. "Ah, the fifteen percenter." Tom was also nasty.

I said, "Ah, the twenty-seven and a half percenter."

Kate asked us how we liked the crepes in the Left Bank. Melinda said hers tasted like a napkin.

Betty Reynolds came in from the john. Betty was our ex-model. Tall; long blond hair; a kind of patina of sophistication. It took you fifteen minutes to find out Betty was dumb. "Hello there, Bowers. Oh. Brandy. How about that?"

Barlow had brought the drinks in. He said, "Melinda, your husband is a born cynic."

Melinda said. "About things in general or something in particular?"

"Things in general were as far as we got. I was telling him I think the country's in for a change and he didn't think it could be done."

I said, "Leave ill enough alone is my motto."

Melinda said, "You have to understand about Jim. If it isn't an ad, it isn't important."

Tom Reynolds said, "I do not believe I've ever heard that thought expressed before."

Kate said, "What kind of change isn't Jim interested in? Maybe I'm on his side."

Barlow said, "Oh, I think the day's coming when we've got to stop taking and start putting back. The company that doesn't have anything to show for itself but black ink isn't going to have it so well."

This got us into a discussion of the responsibility of companies, and that got us into a discussion about the quality of life, and Tom Reynolds said, "You cannot put quality into another person's life. It's like trying to give somebody a sense of humor."

I said, "I don't even know what you mean by quality."

Betty Reynolds said, "I think it's every person's obligation to live up to his potential as a complete full being."

Barlow Matthews gave us that sensational smile and said, "How would you feel about a course on how to think?"

I said, "I don't know. Who's giving it?"

Barlow said, "It's a little project I've been working on."

Tom Reynolds said, "How can you teach anybody to think?"

"The first thing you do," Barlow said, "is teach them that they're not thinking now. An engineer sitting at a drawing table remembering the principles of design for a bridge is not thinking. He is remembering."

I said, "That's what I'd want an engineer to do, if it was my bridge."

"You don't want him to question, Jim? Look for new ways?"

I said, "That's how you get a bridge built of Kleenex."

"Ah, but what if a bridge built of impacted Kleenex would last a thousand years?"

I said, "Barlow, okay, you've just hired Leonardo da Vinci and he's come up with this bridge of impacted Kleenex. Is there anybody in your company who ever impacted Kleenex? Is there anybody at Kleenex who ever impacted Kleenex?"

"What's your point, Jim?"

"Thinking is bad for you."

Melinda said, "God, we're funny tonight."

Barlow said, "Ah, but Jim's right. What Jim is saying is that we do not have people who can keep up with a da Vinci. But that, Jim, is what this course is for. I don't want department heads who confuse doing the same thing they did yesterday with managing. I want men who aren't satisfied with yesterday."

Tom Reynolds said, "If those are your department heads, you ought to start with your personnel department."

I said, "Oh, Christ, Tom, those are all department heads."

After a while, Kate turned on the stereo system and I asked her to dance. Kate was wonderful to dance with, all breasts and belly and warm and friendly. I said, "Every once in a while I get the feeling your husband's running for office."

Kate said, "This is a new one on me. I didn't know he was working on anything like that."

I said, "Well, I think he's got his first recruit. Melinda really digs that stuff."

Melinda and Barlow were sitting on the sofa. Melinda seemed to be doing all the talking. Barlow just sat there and smiled.

Kate said, "What stuff is that, Jim?"

"Oh, she's had this thing about saving the world ever since she got out of college. Just tell her she's contributing and off she'll go like a goddamned lemming."

There were quite a few more drinks and I found myself dancing with Betty Reynolds, who danced with her pelvis and said, "I love talking about things that mean something, don't you?"

The last that I remember of our twentieth anniversary was sitting on the floor in a corner with a drink, watching Melinda dancing with Barlow. It occurred to me, in a fuzzy sort of way, that it was going to take surgery to separate them.

wednesday

It was one of those hot, soggy days of August. Between the city and the sky was a layer of grime. It had been there for a week. There had been no wind. Here and there thick black smoke came out of stacks and joined the grime. If you got out of a plane at just the right altitude, you could have walked on it.

In my office the poison was pretty much trapped by the spun glass filters of the free-standing General Electric air conditioner. The machine stood in the hall and reached into offices with pale gray ducts. This manufactured breeze made my vertical blinds rustle. Blue-white light from two banks of

Sylvania fluorescent tubes lit the room. The carpet was blue Chemstrand nylon, heat-texturized. The crimp bounced back after you walked on it. You could barely breathe in God's world outside. We had made a world of our own.

Eleven copywriters worked for me. I had had a hand in deciding how twenty-three corporations spent fifty million dollars. I had nine hundred dollars in my checking account at Bankers Trust and forty-five hundred in my savings account in Westport, where Melinda could get at it.

I also had an option on three thousand shares of Gibbs & Wilson stock. The option price was nineteen dollars a share. The current over-the-counter asking price was fourteen dollars. Buying it at the moment would be like buying a debt.

I also had eighty thousand dollars in company insurance and a tidy amount in my pension and profit-sharing plans. There was a little booklet that told you how much of this you actually got if you quit, got fired or dropped dead, but I had never been able to figure little booklets like that out.

If you could call them assets, we also had a swimming pool that did not work and a boat that we were still paying for. The boat was a two-year-old Bertram that I had bought for ten thousand dollars. Work on the outdrives had cost me eleven hundred dollars in May alone. Melinda took a more positive approach. "If we'd bought the boat new it would have been fifteen thousand."

I had said, "So we saved five thousand. Let's use it to pay for the outdrives."

There was a faint rumble in the floor of my office. Ten stories below, a New Haven diesel had begun to pull six cars from their snug burrow in Grand Central out toward the sunshine in East Harlem for the run to Stamford. One of these days the whole damned city was just going to fall down.

I had been through my mail already. There had been a letter from Young & Rubicam and a letter from Benton & Bowles. Both had been signed by vice-presidents. One wanted me to send money to the blind. The other wanted money for research for some blood disease. Both letters had had little three-inch-by-five-inch pamphlets enclosed.

Letters like this, for some reason, did not move me. There seemed to be something manufactured about them.

What did get me was a letter from a man looking for a job. "Experience is the link between ad copy and product action—and experience is the plus that my thirty years in the trenches can offer you."

You could not get cornier than that.

The poor bastard had been a vice-president at one of the 4-A agen ies and was now fifty-five years old and had probably been canned. I pressed the button on my phone and my secretary came in.

I said, "Edna, drop this guy a note and see when he can come in."

"Should I get papers from personnel for him to fill out?"

"God, no. We're not going to hire him."

"Then why waste your time and his telling him no?"

I said, "Honey, when you've been somebody for thirty years and they kick you out, somebody ought to talk to you."

"And then you'll wonder where the day went and why you don't have time to get anything done any more."

I said, "You know what? There those guys are in Houston, trying to make that mechanical heart work, and here you are in New York keeping it a secret."

She shrugged this off and said, "Barney Marker wants to see you."

"He'd better have an ad with him."

She went ba k to her desk and I just sat there. When you've done something for thirty years, there ought to be more waiting for you than an interview for a job.

Our newest vice-president, Barry Gorner, came in. White silk suit, navy blue shirt, pale gray tie. Every curly hair was where it was supposed to be and his grin was bright enough to read by.

I said, "Don't tell me. Research has come up with a headline-writing machine and you're here with my notice."

"Wrong. I am here with news."

"Do I want to hear it?"

"Tonight your research department launches a massive attack on the flying public and you're invited."

"What are you talking about?"

"In-depth interviews with business travelers."

"You're kidding."

"It's called 'focus interviewing.' Do you know how it works?"

"You aren't kidding."

"Once a week, we get six or seven guys in for a round-table talk about flying. Not here in the agency. Senser Research is setting it up. Figure two hours a session, with Aaron Senser steering the discussion. Aaron's very good." Barry Gorner took out a pipe and pouch and began to load up. "You sit in the next room behind a two-way mirror. You can feed in questions of your own, of course. Aaron will work them in."

"What are we doing all this for?"

"You didn't read my report."

"Of course I didn't read your report."

"Okay. Leading you by the hand, it goes like this. Step one. We hold a series of sessions like tonight's. Everything they say will be on tape. Next, an analyst, one of Aaron's guys, will summarize every point that comes up. Airline food, reservations—we now begin to get a fix, right?"

I said, "Maybe you get a fix, but don't drag me in on it."

"Jim, I've already had George Brice's promise of your intense interest."

"Swell."

"Now then. Step two. We check every high point that comes up. We work up a statement—not an ad, just a statement of fact. Federal stewardesses get five weeks' training. Like that. Then we take these statements out into the world and see what people have to say about them. You still with me?"

I said, "For Christ's sake."

"We are now ready for step three. I deliver to you the list of winners."

"What am I supposed to do with it?"

"Parcel out ads or TV spots on each of these points. Maybe you'd write a couple yourself, give a couple to Percy Holland and Lydia. We then have a pool of commercials ready for testing."

"Barry, if you absolutely had to, you could hold this soiree without me, right?"

Barry stopped grinning. "George seemed to think you ought to be there, Jim. Federal's the first account he's trying this on. A success on Federal is kind of important to him."

"A success on Federal? What in hell does he think we've had ever since we got the account? Federal was a success before George Brice ever walked in the door. He didn't do it. I did. I don't even understand all this jazz."

"Well, can I tell him you wanted to make it but I didn't get to you in time? I mean, what the hell, Jim."

I said, "Sure. Tell him anything you want to."

"Give me a ring tomorrow and I'll play the first tape for you."

I said, "For two hours? Get out of here."

Next, Barney Marker came in. Barney was a little guy with hair piled on his head like hay and a pouty mouth underneath. He lived in the Village and was wearing a tight mod checked suit and a button that read DOWN WITH.

Barney had a rough layout with him. "I don't suppose Federal has the guts to run this."

I said, "Let's see."

Barney put the ad on my desk.

We've wiped Syracuse off the map.

I said, "What's the story?"

"They want to announce a new nonstop flight to Buffalo."

"This doesn't announce a nonstop flight to Buffalo."

"Sure it does. They don't stop at Syracuse any more."

"That doesn't tell me anything about Buffalo."

"It will when you read the copy."

"Barney, if I want to go to Buffalo, why would I read an ad about Syracuse?"

His mouth got a little poutier. "How could anybody see a headline like that and not read it?"

"Barney, the papers are full of cute headlines. If you want people who are going to Buffalo, what you say is Buffalo."

Barney shrugged. "Anybody can write 'New Nonstop to Buffalo.' " I knew what Barney was thinking. They ask you to be creative and then they throw stones at you.

I said, "What do you want me to say? Federal isn't running an ad to keep it a secret."

"Okay, but it will be dull."

"Do it so it isn't."

The brave little mod suit left the room with a crumpled spirit in it, and I lit a cigarette and thought, Barney Marker and the creative process.

My intercom buzzed. Edna said, "Jeff Sermon's on the phone. Do you want to talk to him?"

"No, but I guess he wants to talk to me."

Edna said, "He's coming on a little strong, yes."

Jeff Sermon always came on strong. He was like a truck trying to frighten the rest of the traffic. Jeff was tall and fat and important, and had been the account executive on Federal Airlines for two years.

I pressed the button that put him on. "What's up, Jeff?"

Jeff Sermon said, "I'd like to know why Federal doesn't have an ad on Buffalo."

I said, "Barney Marker's working on one now, Jeff."

"And what am I supposed to do, tell the client he'll get something when inspiration comes to Barney Marker? It's standing policy on Federal, new flight announcements start three weeks ahead. Barney Marker isn't making it with me, Jim."

I said, "As long as he makes it with me, he doesn't have to make it with you."

"Jim, this is an eight-million-dollar account. I can't make free with billing like that."

I said, "Sure you can."

"I know you don't mean that, Jim."

"Yes. I mean it. Barney's killing himself trying to come up with something people will read and you're just standing there with a stopwatch. Promptness doesn't happen to be next to godliness around here, Jeff. We aren't doing any dull ads just because you're in a hurry."

Jeff Sermon said, "Nobody asked for a dull ad, Jim. You know I'd never ask for a thing like that."

"You just won't give us time to do anything else, right?"

"Damn it, Jim, after Max died, George Brice told Federal we could live with their deadlines. They still weren't all that sure we could handle an account like theirs and George made a goddamned speech about it. I'm just a colonel here, Jim. The general made the speech."

I said, "Well, he didn't make it to me."

"Well, he will if I don't."

I said, "Fine. Give me a general any day."

Jeff Sermon said, "Okay. If that's the way you want it."

"That's the way I want it, Jeff."

I got the speech just before lunch. Edna buzzed me and said, "George Brice is on the phone."

I said, "Swell." I pushed the button. "Yes, George?"

"Jim, can you drop up here for a moment?"

"Sure."

"Thank you." Click.

George Brice looked as if he had just taken a shower. You had the feeling he was wearing a thin layer of softness on his body like a skin diver's wet suit. He also seemed to have five more teeth than anybody else and all of them were shining at you when he smiled.

"Sit down, Jim."

"Okay."

"I'll be with you in a moment."

I sat there while he looked at a research report. His desk was clear. Just the report and a copy of *Drug Topics*. Behind him on the wall, showing no interest in *Drug Topics* at all, was an enormous picture of Alexander Hamilton.

"Well now, Jim. Tell me about Barney Marker."

"What about him?"

"Jeff Sermon doesn't seem to think he's pulling his weight."

"Yeah, well, Jeff's idea of getting an ad out is to tell some kid we'll lose the account if he doesn't have something by three o'clock."

"Jim, if an account man can't go to you when he has a problem, who can he go to?"

I said, "He can come to me, George."

"And get the sort of answer Jeff got?"

It was hard to talk to George Brice. You had the feeling that inside his head all these little transistors were whirring away.

I said, "When he's unreasonable, George, sure. Barney's a trainee. Hell, he's only making seventy-five hundred. Jeff pulls stuff like this now and then, just to see if he can get away with it."

"Still, Barney Marker's had a week, Jim."

"George, there are ads it's taken me a month to do."

"A simple flight announcement? Jim, if he's been having trouble with the ad, why didn't you give it to somebody else?"

I lit a cigarette. "Well, George, I guess we just think that's a rotten thing to do to a writer."

George Brice said, "I'm afraid I don't follow that, Jim."

"One ad, one writer, George. We figure you give a guy a job and you trust him to do it. You don't take it away from him or put two other guys on it, too. That's just saying you don't trust any of them."

"And that's the only ad on the subject the client sees from us?"

"That's right."

"What if they turn it down?"

"Then we do another one."

George Brice did not say anything for a moment. Then he said, "Jim, when I was on the client's side, the agency always came up with at least three approaches for any given campaign."

I said, "A lot of agencies work that way, yes."

"But not this one."

I said, "Well, George, Max used to say one swell idea was

all you could expect on any subject. Asking two other guys to come up with something just so you could show the client three pieces of paper isn't the way Max did it."

George Brice smiled. "You miss Max Gibbs, don't you, Jim?"

I said, "What do you mean?"

"Oh, I think you know, Jim. It must have been pretty nice, being a writer for Max Gibbs. The writer's Renaissance, eh, Jim?"

I said, "George, take away the fun and put in a time clock and this is just another advertising agency."

George Brice laced his slightly fat neat fingers together on the top of his desk. "Jim, this is just another advertising agency."

So that was the way it was going to be.

I put my cigarette out. "George, that isn't what we have the reputation for. We do things a certain way and certain things happen."

"Synergistic action? One plus one makes three, Jim?"

"That's the way Max put it, yes."

"Well, Jim, I'm sure all this is very advanced as far as child therapy goes, but I can't say it's any way to run a railroad."

I did not answer this.

George Brice took a shiny little ring puzzle from his desk. He did not say anything for a moment. He just studied the rings.

Then he parted them. Then he changed the subject. "Jim, tell me what you think of something."

"If I can."

He took from a drawer several ads. On top was our latest ad for Paragon.

How I lost my license
in second gear.

"Think this is a good ad, Jim?"

"Sure."

George Brice was not looking at me now. He was putting the puzzle back together. "The word *negative* didn't come up?"

"No. I don't think that ad's negative, George. Negative is just a label."

"Do you know what I get from this ad, Jim? I get the idea I can't drive that car in this country."

"Well, George, I think that ad tells you what the Paragon's all about."

"I see. Well, how about this one? Did you see this before it went out?"

It was an ad for Manhattan National Bank.

> This city's full of crooks.
> You look a little shifty yourself.

"Sure. I saw it."

"And I'm sure you think this is a good ad, too, eh?"

I said, "George, every bank in town has a check guarantee card. How do you do an ad on it without sounding like everybody else, you know?"

"And this was the only way to do it. I see."

George Brice turned over another ad. This one was for Mountainaire air conditioners.

> Did your father ever tell you
> someone would try to sell you
> a box of air for $3,500?

I said, "That ad never ran."

"I know it didn't, Jim. I'm wondering how it ever got plated."

"We thought it was a good ad. Percy Holland wrote it. Percy's one of the best writers in the place."

"The president of Mountainaire asked me what I thought of it, Jim."

"And you thought it was negative, eh?"

"Negative doesn't begin to cover it, Jim."

The next ad was for Federal Airlines.

> Our new 25%-off plan.
> Maybe you could do better.

I said, "Yeah, well, all the airlines were coming out with the same thing. Federal's got all these other plans, too. We thought we'd kind of turn the announcement around into a service."

"That's quite a service, Jim. Telling people they could do better on American or TWA."

"That isn't what it says, George."

"Isn't it? That's the way I took it, Jim."

It was not the way he took it. It was the way he wanted to take it.

The last ad was for 19th Century vodka.

It's better than air pollution.

I shrugged.

George Brice just smiled. "Jim, did you ever hear of Benefit?"

"No."

"It was an effervescent that General Drug came out with. You take it for upset stomachs, like Bromo and Alka-Seltzer."

I did not know where he was going so I did not say anything.

"That isn't how we advertised it, though. We advertised it for headaches. Now, Jim, why do you suppose people would take an effervescent for headaches instead of an analgesic, like Relief or Excedrin?"

"Some copywriter told them to."

"No, Jim. That isn't why. But I think you should know why."

For a moment we had complete silence.

Then George Brice said, "The agency's research department made that decision for us, Jim. The analgesic market was worth half a billion dollars. The upset-stomach market—effervescents—only did about ninety million. Now, what would you do, Jim? Go after a little share of the big market, or try and establish yourself in with the other effervescents?"

I said, "I don't know."

"But isn't that the kind of decision you take on yourself every time you do ads like these? Jim, I'm not trying to gang up on you, but these are just grandstand stunts with the clients' money. No research. No copy strategy. No direction at all. We'll just make ads and have fun."

It seemed silly to point out that that was what we did here. It was why clients came to us. George Brice knew that and he still did not like it. I said, "George, what can I say? You're talking about some of the best advertising in the business. Paragon. Federal."

"Best by whose yardstick, Jim? Oh, I'm sure ads like these have a certain sophisticated following. I imagine there are copywriters all over town who get quite a kick out of our ads. But I'm afraid, Jim, that you don't sell a product like Relief to a small sophisticated audience. Jim, do you see what I'm talking about?"

"No. Not yet."

George Brice took a tiny auto engine from his drawer. It was no bigger than his thumb. "This thing actually runs. You put the gas in with an eyedropper. Jim, when I took this job, a friend of mine at Proctor & Gamble told me I was taking over a zoo. They're afraid of us, Jim. The accounts I'm supposed to bring in here are afraid of us."

I said, "George, I just don't get that."

"Don't you, Jim? We're starting focus sessions tonight on Federal. I understand you can't make it."

I felt my face get hot. "Well, George, that's kind of Barry Gorner's show."

"All right, Jim. You asked me why they were afraid of us and you've answered your own question."

"George, I'm sorry. I don't follow you."

"Jim, I'm supposed to bring in accounts like Relief. Now, just how am I supposed to do that if we don't believe in the things Relief believes in?"

"George, what does one thing have to do with the other? What's that got to do with these ads?"

"Is it really that hard to understand, Jim? You can lose your license in second gear? You look a little shifty yourself? That's what we do here, right, Jim? Ads by the seat of our pants. I'm going to tell you something. Every time a product manager sees ads like these, he gets this little nightmare where the management just assigned his brands to us."

I said, "Then they're fools."

"Are they, Jim? Relief bills twenty-two million dollars a year. Would you give it to an agency that won't even ask people what they want in a headache tablet?"

This talk was not going well. This guy stood for everything that was wrong in this business and there was still no way you could argue with him. I said, "George, yes. I would. If I was the product manager on Relief, yes. I'd give it to the agency that did the Paragon campaign."

"Where the account men have no control over creative? An agency that won't even listen to the clients? Jim, we come up with wild ideas they can't use, and we're even late with them. Jim, I was the executive vice-president of General Drug, and I wouldn't give Relief to a place like this. And I think,

Jim, that I am a little more qualified to discuss product managers than you are."

I did not know how to handle this. I said, "Well, George, I'm not even sure what it is that you want."

"I don't want another ad like these going out that door, Jim."

"George, you can't do that. That's just saying let's don't do our best for Paragon because it might keep us from getting General Drug."

"I didn't say that, Jim. I resent the implication that I did."

"Well, then I don't know what you are saying, George."

"I'm saying we've done great ads for every account we have without being negative at all. I'm saying, Jim, that there's no need for ads like these. That ad of yours—*Tell your mother-in-law it's potato soup.* That certainly isn't negative and it's one of the great vodka ads. Jim, don't tell me a great ad has to stick a thumb in somebody's eye. I've been over the ads here. That just isn't so."

I said, "George, we don't even agree on what's negative and what isn't. What do I do when a kid comes in with an ad I think is swell and you might not? Bring it in and talk to you about it?"

George Brice said, "Why, I think that would be just the way to handle it, Jim. I think that that might work very well."

He was the president. I said, "All right."

"And, Jim? I think it might help a little if you didn't do so much of the writing yourself and concentrated a little more on supervision. This Barney Marker thing with the Buffalo ad. We don't have any business being late on a simple flight announcement."

"It isn't late yet, George. That's just Jeff Sermon expecting it to be late. I checked the requisition."

"But you will keep an eye on it."

"Sure."

"Fine; Jim, that's just fine. Believe me, I know what you mean about the creative climate around here. I don't want to change that and I don't want you to let me change it."

I did not know what to say to a thing like that. I said, "Okay."

George Brice said, "I'm glad we had this little talk, Jim. I think we both got a little something out of it." George Brice smiled at me with all his teeth. I could even see the ones in back.

I returned to my office and found on my desk the layout for a Mountainaire air conditioner ad.

> For 9 months a year,
> you'll wonder why you
> spent the money.

"What ho."

It was Alex Mayberry, the copywriter on the international end of Mountainaire.

I said, "What what?"

Alec came in and sat on my sofa. "I understand," he said, "you have been up conversing with the Establishment."

It was the sort of crack you expected from Alec. He had lived in Europe for a few years and was as sophisticated as the Ivy League could make you. He wore a scarf at his throat.

I said, "You do this?"

"I did. You like?"

I said, "What are you doing on a domestic ad?"

Alec grinned. "The domestic ad writer is on vacation."

I looked at the layout. I said, "Now I know what you're up to. You're trying to kill me."

Alec lit a cigarette and said, "Jim, you cannot possibly sit there and tell me you don't like that ad."

I gave a sigh. I said, "I can sit here and tell you the president of Mountainaire won't like this ad."

Alec draped one long leg over the arm of my sofa. "Why, hell, Jim, neither would the president of Gibbs & Wilson, right?"

I said, "Probably not." You couldn't con a guy like Alec Mayberry. Alec had a kind of built-in infrared device that spotted phonies. I suppose it was the sort of thing you got when you were bright and had the kind of background that he had.

Alec said, "And that, I believe, brings us to you."

I said, "Don't go too fast for me. I have trouble with subtle people."

Alec said, "Georgie Porgie wouldn't like it. Mountainaire won't like it. So what we have here, ladies and gentlemen, is a perfectly splendid concept with no mother or father."

I said, "That's what we have here."

Alec inhaled and blew out cigarette smoke and said, "Okay, Jim. If that's the way it is."

I said, "I didn't say that was the way it is. I said that's what we have here."

"Then what do I do with it?"

I rubbed the back of my neck. This was the sort of thing that I had just promised George Brice I would discuss with him.

I said, "Take it to the account man and tell him I think it's swell."

"Will you get in trouble?"

I shrugged. I said, "If the question comes up, you might say you showed it to me yesterday."

"Ah, so."

I said, "There are those abroad in the land who would say this is negative."

Alec said, "Reading between the lines, I take it you've had a little talk about this sort of thing with our fearless leader."

"Alec, don't be clever, okay?"

"Jim, I speak from admiration."

"Knock it off. We aren't going to start any little let's-talk-about-George clubs around here."

"As you wish, *mon ami*."

"Don't leave without your ad."

Alec had got up and now he looked at me, one eyebrow cocked as though he was about to say something else. Then he just shrugged and picked up the layout.

"Okay, Jim. Thanks."

"And don't thank me. That's a swell ad. We're supposed to thank you."

"Right." Alec left, nodding his head a little as if to himself. I just sat there.

The main question, I realized, was how long it was going to take George Brice to kill me.

I had often wondered what would happen if the businessmen took over. Now I knew.

Couldn't we screen out the controversial ads?

Was there any excuse for a negative idea like that Paragon ad ever getting out the door?

George Brice would be very nice about it. He was going to understand just what we stood for. He'd understand why clients came to us and why it was important to do the kind of ads we did.

Then he was going to kill me, surer than hell.

The nice thing about going home to Westport every night

was that it was just the opposite of the city. You were through with George Brice for the day. You were out in the country.

At least, everybody thought of it as being out in the country. I wondered why I didn't.

The evening started out rather nicely as evenings were going these days. Melinda had lamb chops and mint jelly and macaroni salad for dinner, and had bought me three polo shirts. "I asked for medium. That's right, isn't it?"

"Honey, I'm so medium I could get a job on a chart. What time are we due at Helmut and Ina's?"

There was no hurry. We could have some more coffee. Oh, Fortunato was going to have to be talked to. We had paid for topsoil last spring and all he had done was lime, seed and fertilize. You could look at the lawn and see he had not put any topsoil in. I said that August was kind of late to complain about that. Melinda supposed that it was, and we sat there being nice.

Wasn't that a nice time we had had at Barlow and Kate's last night? I did not think I had had all that nice a time particularly, but I saw no point in saying so. "Yep. That's a nice place they have there."

She did not like Tom Reynolds very much. "He picks up everything you say."

"Yeah, well, he's got all those degrees and no money, you know?"

We drove through the hot sticky evening to Helmut and Ina Cross's. It was a big stone ranch on three acres on Long Lots Road. Big maples stood around it like a gang talking things over.

I said, "I wonder if Helmut rents this place out for wars."

"It does look like a fort, doesn't it."

"If Helmut ever takes up fishing, I'll bet he buys a destroyer."

There were several cars already in Helmut's turnaround. I recognized Barlow and Kate Matthews' white Ford LTD, the Vans' Buick and the Slatterys' Plymouth. A tan Chrysler station wagon was parking next to Helmut's Porsche as we pulled up.

Melinda said, "Is that Jean and Slim? I thought he was in South America."

Slim Hawes' real name was Ed. He was fifty-two, six feet three, and had been a cowboy once. Now he was a construction engineer and always seemed to be coming home from some dam or bridge in Peru. I liked Slim. I had always wanted to be a cowboy.

"Hello, Jim," he said as we got out. "Hey, Melinda, can't one of those committees of yours get this town air conditioned?"

I said, "Slim, they keep deporting you and you keep coming back."

"Well, I picked up a bug down there and I just figured I'd bring it home to my friends."

Jean Hawes said, "Isn't this something? All the mercury's up at the top of our themometer trying to get out." Jean had grown up with Slim in some little place in Montana. She was pretty, a bit plump, and she knitted.

Helmut Cross met us at the door. "You all found places to park, I hope?"

Slim said, "Oh, sure. I just backed over a little Porsche out there. Plenty of room."

Helmut said, "The doctor over there will give you your shots. We will then reconvene for the oral examination."

Helmut often had a bartender. He owned seven chemical plants and looked like Theodore Roosevelt and climbed mountains and did other odd things.

I met Barlow Matthews at the bar. "Jim, we seem to be meeting these days."

I said, "If you're here, this must be my chance to get Kate alone."

Barlow kept on smiling but seemed to blink at this. It occurred to me that our regular guy was bewildered by little jokes. "She's right over there, Jim. . . ."

I brought Melinda a gin and tonic and said to Helmut, "Where's Ina? I came here to see Ina."

"Ina's in the kitchen, Jim. She isn't housebroken yet."

I took a Scotch and soda out to the kitchen. "I came out to see my favorite blonde."

"Lover!" Ina was five feet ten, blond, athletic, sensational bust. She had been an Olympic swimmer once. "Let's have a drink and lose our heads."

"Ina, I can't think of a better way to go."

"How about you and Melinda coming to Saint Thomas with us this winter, lover?"

"Don't think we can afford it, Ina."

"Lover, you're our guests. Helmut writes it off."

"Ina, I only sponge liquor."

"God. I knew the dollar was in trouble but I didn't know you couldn't give it away."

I got Melinda another drink and there came Joe and Nora Slattery. Nora was dumpy, sweet and believed in heaven. I liked the Slatterys. Nora said sweat instead of perspiration.

Joe said, "Jim, old buddy, how's your sex life?" Joe Slattery was fifty-six and Joe was getting heavy. Knights of Columbus. District sales manager. Ex-marine.

Nora said, "Joe, the way you talk, people will think you have a dirty mind."

"Well, I do, honey. How about that, Jim? Want to borrow my mind for the weekend?"

I said, "Sure, if you aren't using it."

Melinda said, "I love your hair, Nora."

"Any more spray on it, I'll break my neck."

I left this and stopped to say hello to Neil and Harriet Van. Harriet was a tiny blonde and Neil was tall, thin and pale. They were in their thirties and a little spooky. They never seemed to talk to anybody and if you didn't know better, you would think they were living wallpaper. I knew better. Harriet was the dirty girl on the block.

I said, "How do the kids like the sailing class?"

Neil said, "Leslie's the only one who took it. I guess she liked it all right."

Harriet said, "She kept getting in irons. They say a Sprite is the easiest thing to learn sailing in, but every time she made a turn she lost the wind."

I said, "That's my kind of girl."

I found Slim Hawes on the sofa. The ex-cowboy was alone with a shot of bourbon. I said, "Well, how does Westport look after the jungle?"

"Jim, while I was gone, a real estate fellow came around and told Jean he could get us twice what we paid for our place. You know we only moved here five years ago?"

"Don't knock it."

"I'm not knocking it. It just seems a little indecent, that's all."

I said, "I only think it's indecent when I have to pay it."

"Well, it might not be a bad thing at that. About time I went back where I belong, old friend."

"Peru or Montana?"

"Montana. Got an uncle with a little ranch out there."

"No more dams and bridges?"

"Jim, the time comes when a man has to make the move."

"Hell, Slim, between Westport and somebody to talk to and Montana and a lot of cows, I'd take Westport."

"Well, maybe you speak the language around here, Jim. I sure don't."

"What language is that, Slim?"

"This is a funny place, Jim. You go to one of these parties, if it isn't somebody telling you marijuana's better than whiskey, it's somebody talking about free love. I guess that just isn't the way I was brought up, old friend."

"More people talking about it than doing it, Slim."

"That's still one funny way for people to be. Jim, as far as I can see, if you happen to think a little favorably about your mother, God or the American flag, people around here think you need a psychiatrist. I can't help it, Jim. I think half the people in this town ought to be in cages."

"Get you another drink?"

"I'll nurse this one awhile, Jim. Got to watch the liquor with this bug I picked up."

I went on to the bar and a whispery voice at my elbow said, "Buy you a drink?"

It was Harriet Van, the silent little blonde.

I said, "Somebody'd better, and you're prettier than anybody else."

Harriet said in a very quiet little voice, "I know what I am and you know what I am. Perhaps we had better start from there."

The thing with Harriet was to keep a crowd around. Once she had reached right out and put her hand against my trousers. You had to assume Harriet meant everything she said.

I said, "Sorry. I think I got into the wrong room."

"That would be interesting." She smiled and looked sweet. "I'm afraid I'm not a very nice person."

"Nobody's a nice person. Don't worry about it."

"You know what? You're a scaredy-cat."

I said, "I'm a drunk and I have to keep in practice."

I went off and found Joe Slattery. "Joe, tell me all about business."

The big marine said, "How does 'Sales Allotment Time' grab you?"

"What is it?"

"New chart the management came out with. How much time you're supposed to spend with a customer." Joe lit a cigarette. "I asked them why they didn't just fire the field men and send customers the chart."

I said, "I never heard of a thing like that."

"Jim, one of my customers came in just the other day. Wanted to know what I thought of a fabricator they were using—one of those outfits that build pressure vessels? Well, Jim, I spent two hours with the guy. Told him their welders were lousy and who to look up if they wanted a good job. Now, Jim, that's a service and maybe the next time we'll get the job ourselves, and how do you put that down on a goddamned chart?"

I said, "I didn't even know there were good and bad welders."

"Finding any welders at all is something. You want good ones, you go to a fortuneteller. Well, keep the old pecker up, kid. It's the only thing in life that's free any more."

I had a drink with Kate Matthews, Barlow's graying wife. I learned they had had their trees sprayed and that one of their kids had trapped a squirrel on the porch and that their oldest boy had had a cyst taken out.

After this I stopped to talk to Jean Hawes, Slim's wife. "I hear you're going back to Montana one of these days."

"That's what the big fellow wants."

"Too bad he doesn't like the neighborhood. We like him."

"He doesn't like the East, Jim. This isn't the way it's supposed to be."

"What isn't?"

"Oh, you work hard. You're loyal to your company. And when you've been with them twenty-five years, they trade you to another ball club."

"Trade him? Christ, Slim wasn't fired—?"

"They're pulling out of South America, Jim. They don't need him any more."

"You're kidding."

"Jim, two years ago he was offered twice his salary to go with somebody else, and the company said they'd make him a vice-president if he'd stay. Wasn't that nice of them?"

"And then they let him go?"

"That's right."

"Nice world we have here."

I wandered around the room thinking about this. How could you fire Slim Hawes? Slim Hawes was Gary Cooper.

At the door, I found Neil Van looking out into the night. I said, "Neil, you look like the lookout."

"I am the lookout."

"Any sign of them out there?"

"They're waiting for dawn. They never attack at night."

"Then why don't they go home and get some sleep?"

"It isn't done."

I wondered what I was doing here. There was a good ball game on television. I went outside and walked across the grass. The big maples blocked out the moonlight.

The woman's voice said, "I don't know. They say there's good and bad in people, but the bad always seems to be what comes out."

The man's voice said, "Good's no fun and bad is."

"And we're all just so many animals. We just pretend we're something else."

"People are people. You can get good out of them, if you know how and want to enough."

"You want to, don't you?"

"There are worse things to do with your life."

"Do you know something funny? I couldn't even talk like this to Jim."

"Don't blame Jim. The ad business doesn't leave you much time for anything else."

"Neither does your business, but you're doing it."

"Well, I'm a little luckier than Jim."

Barlow and Melinda.

Now, if they wanted to talk about life, why did they have to do it in the dark?

That little question answered itself. I went back in to the bar.

"Two Scotch on the rocks. Put them in the same glass, will you?"

thursday

I came up from Grand Central and got into a cab in front of the Biltmore and took out a piece of paper I had torn off a lined yellow pad and gave the driver the address of a warehouse in the West Sixties.

The West Sixties made me think of St. Louis on a hot summer day. I did not know why. I had never been in St. Louis.

The studio had rented the warehouse and put up the set, a bathroom from the 1920s. Carpenters, grips, prop men and electricians were swarming about—ignoring completely a fine brawl between our producer and our art director.

"No, it wasn't on the board and we aren't shooting it."
Mel King. Our producer.

"Don't tell me what was on the board, I did the goddamned
board." Rudy d'Franco, our art director.

The fight was inevitable. Mel King had over fifteen years
in the business. Assistant cameraman. Editor. Cost analyst.
Producer. In most agencies, the producer is in charge of the
shooting.

Not in our agency. The creative team was in charge. Rudy
and I.

The trouble with Rudy was that "in charge" business. He
had gone to Pratt and had made a sixteen-millimeter film on
his own and what else did you need? These days, everybody
knew the art director was a genius. Rudy was going to be in
charge no matter what.

I called my office. "Listen, I'm being held prisoner in this
dungeon. Anybody looking for me?"

Barney Marker was looking for me. I asked Edna to switch
me to him.

"Jim? Are you ready for our sixth ad for California?"

"I'll tell you after I've heard it."

"Well, we have the sun going down over the Pacific. Big
ocean sunset? And what it says is, *When it goes down in the
West, you ought to be in the West to see it.*"

I closed my eyes and tried to see this. "You can't put a
palm tree or something against this sunset, can you?"

"All the stock shots we have are palm trees against white,
Jim. You won't see the sun at all."

"You get a good sexy sunset?"

"Pretty good. We want to retouch it."

I said, "Okay. Give it a try."

I hung up and went over to the coffee urn. The crew call
had been for eight. Most of the cardboard cups had cold
coffee in them.

Mel King came over. "I'm going to kill that little fart."

"What's he want to do?" I asked.

"Backlight the toothbrushing."

There was a sentence you hardly ever heard. "What does
he want to do that for?"

"What do you think? He saw somebody else do it."

I was not surprised. I remembered the day Rudy and I
first worked together on Den-Test spots. That had been six
months ago. It was Rudy's first TV assignment. He thought
he was Howard Hughes.

"We open on this surrealistic dentist's office. It's the year two thousand and this is the kissing clinic. Big atomic drill. X-ray machines. Electronic filling dingus. Fish-eye lens stuff."

I had said, "You're talking about a thirty-thousand-dollar set."

We had been in his office then. He had cocked his fifty-dollar chukka boots on his desk. "You ever see anything by Fellini?"

"What's that got to do with it?"

"I just wondered if you knew what they're doing these days." The kid's first commercial. He wondered if I knew what they were doing these days.

I said, "Maybe you'd better tell me."

"Well, they aren't doing sinuses and nasal passages."

"Let's see if I follow this. If we don't spend thirty thousand dollars on a set, we have to do nasal passages?"

"Look, if you don't know what I mean, I can't tell you."

"So far, I don't know what you mean, no."

"Look, it's a kind of feel for things. Ambience. You don't have that, forget it. Maybe I'd just better get Brook Parker to give me somebody I can work with."

"Somebody who knows what they're doing these days . . ."

"Look, they put me on this account because I know film. I can't work with anybody who doesn't know how I do things."

This kid was something. I said, "Rudy, before you say anything you don't want to say, talk to Brook, okay?"

Brook Parker took Rudy aside and told him that I had only taken on the Den-Test job because it was Rudy's first crack at television. We wanted to help him over the rough spots. I think that Brook also told him to shut up. At any rate, Rudy went off and sulked for a day and then turned up in my office saying, "Okay, let's give it another try."

We had finally come up with some nice commercials. Why not take people back to knickers and iceboxes and the razor strop in the bathroom? Den-Test had been selling all these years without any advertising at all. The customers must know something.

We had two spots on the air. This was our third. Rudy was a veteran. He had told me he was thinking of writing a book.

It was harder on Mel King. Mel had to keep catching Rudy before he fell off cliffs. It was Mel who told him you had to have a second and a half bumper of silence at the head. And that if you skip-framed on a zoom-in you got a jump in the picture. And that if the music was too thin, you could over-dub. After every tip from Mel, Rudy thought he now knew everything.

I looked out at the set and said, "Oh, Jesus."

Rudy was going at it with Joe Siro, the cameraman. "I didn't ask you what you thought of it. I told you what I want and nobody's doing anything."

Joe Siro was fifty, a tall, vast, blond man with a tall, vast face. "Son, we don't have a drawer we pull backlight out of. You want to backlight something, you have to know how to do it."

"Never mind. I'll do it myself. Hey, you. Pull those cables out of the way while I move these kegs."

The "hey you" Rudy said this to was the gaffer, the lead electrician, short, bald, raisin eyes, a round red face and a cold cigar. At Rudy's words, he did absolutely nothing.

Rudy had begun tugging at the high metal stand for one of the lights.

The gaffer said, "You got a cameraman's card, young fellow?"

Rudy wiped sweat from his forehead with his wrist. "Are you going to get that cable out of the way or aren't you?"

"Mister, nobody tells us what to do with the lights but the cameraman."

"Okay, Pops, back to the barn. We don't need you today." Rudy got the stand turned a little and now he was dragging it.

"Take out the lights, boys."

A hush fell on the set. Rudy looked around, angry and now a little frightened.

I said to Mel King, "Yes, sir, folks. Everything's happened here today." I walked out onto the set and said, "Is this where I come to see all the movie stars?"

Rudy said, "What's the matter with everybody?"

I said, "Rudy, don't help any more, okay?" I turned to Joe Siro. "Joe? Do you have a minute?"

The big cameraman walked off the set with me. I said, "Come on, Joe. You've backlit scenes before."

"That little brat needs his ass kicked."

"Can't we leave that to the ass-kicking department and get the job finished?"

"You know the union rules. Nobody moves the lights unless I tell them to, and nobody but an electrician moves them at all."

"Yes, well, I think that just got through to our friend.

Come on, Joe. You're talking about a day's out-of-pocket, you know?"

"Well, I don't want to see Mel get in trouble." Joe Siro gave a big sigh and walked back to the set and talked to the gaffer for a moment, then he said, "Okay. Let's see what we can do with these lights."

I sat down in one of the director's chairs with Rudy. Rudy said, "Did he ever shoot a commercial before?"

I said, "He was a cameraman in the war before you were born."

"Well, I never heard of him. And that fat squirt—I want him fired."

"That fat squirt is the lead electrician and you can't get him fired. The union will put out everybody in town who knows what a wall socket is." I lit a cigarette and said, "You almost cost the agency a day's out-of-pocket there, friend."

"This job's just been one big botch from start to finish. I'll tell you something—I've had it with Mel King, too."

"Rudy, do you know how many times Mel King could have let you hang yourself just by keeping his mouth shut? He's been doing this stuff fifteen years and you've been doing it six months, okay?"

I guess this was not what Rudy wanted to hear. For a moment, he said nothing at all. Then he got up and said, "Well, I've got a phone call to make. I'll be back when the lights are straightened out."

Bob Coleman came in. He was a senior vice-president now, over Paragon, Den-Test, Mountainaire and 19th Century vodka. He almost never turned up on the set.

I said, "Sit down. Have some coffee. If you have worms, you'll never have them again."

Bob Coleman was now forty-six. Same white hair. Deep tan. "Now I know why you come to shootings like this. You don't want anybody to find you."

I said, "Who ratted?"

"Jim, we just got the Nielsen on Den-Test."

"And?"

"It's off half a point. And that, Jim, comes to one and a half million dollars."

I looked at the men on the set. That was why commercials cost so much. All those guys moving lights.

"I don't get it. If they sold nine million bucks' worth of the stuff without any advertising at all, how could they lose a million and a half now?"

"Everybody who uses the stuff is dying."

"From brushing their teeth?"

"Age. The average age of the Den-Test user is sixty-one."

"What did they do, just have one good year forty years ago?"

"Just about. Jim, they haven't done any advertising since 1933."

On the set, Joe Siro looked through the Mitchell. "I'm getting flare."

I said, "What do we do now?"

Bob Coleman said, "Landum wants to cancel everything. I'm trying to talk them into one more chance."

"Do we have a solution?"

"That depends on how fast you come up with a new idea. Landum won't go network with a loser again. We show them something in test market or we're dead."

On the set, Joe Siro said, "You sure you sprayed that mirror?"

A little man in a T-shirt said, "Any more spray, we'll pull the screws right out of the wall. Maybe it's from the sink."

The set was a bathroom the studio had bought from an old house in Bedford. They had even taken the tile floor.

I said, "Christ, maybe Landum's right. A forty-year-old toothpaste. It doesn't have stannous fluoride. There isn't a dentist alive who even knows it exists. What do you say? No secret ingredient, folks. It's all toothpaste."

Bob Coleman had a quick white smile. "I like to think you and Brook will come up with something."

"Brook? I'm working on this with Rudy."

"Now you're working on it with Brook."

"Kind of a slap in the face for Rudy, isn't it?"

"This is the only foot we have in Landum's door, Jim. The hell with Rudy."

"You going to stay around and tell him the good news?"

"Where is he?"

"Out making a phone call."

"There's a phone over there. Why didn't he use that?"

"He's surrounded by assassins."

"You talk to him, Jim. I have to get over to Landum. Tell him to finish shooting but not to cut it."

When Rudy came back, I said, "Bob Coleman was by. If you've scheduled time to cut this spot, forget it."

"What do you mean?"

"Den-Test is off half a point. They want to drop the line."

"Where's Coleman now?"

"On his way over to Landum. He's trying to get them to give it one more chance." I lit a cigarette and took a deep breath. "Listen, we're just hanging on by our fingernails to the only Landum business we have. Coleman wants Brook Parker to work on this."

"Brook Parker?" Rudy's face looked as if it had been set in cement.

"Be happy. Rudy, this is a born loser. You don't want to be the last one to see it alive, you know?"

"You working with Brook?"

"Yes."

"You guys are cute, aren't you? Account in trouble? Let's blame it on the kid."

I said, "Why don't you grow up."

I got a cab at Ninth Avenue. By then, I was wringing wet. The driver told me the mayor was giving the city away to the niggers. He did not call the mayor by name. He called him "that commie we got."

Brook Parker was bent over his drawing table when I walked in. I said, "What are you drawing?"

"Helipad."

"What, for helicopters!"

"What else do you use a helipad for?"

"Okay. I'll start over. Why are you drawing a helipad?"

"I felt like it."

"Well, it looks like a helipad, I guess."

"A thing ought to look like what it is."

"Then why don't you just trace one?"

"Make this with edge-lit Lucite and you could light it up at night and you wouldn't get it confused with the top of an apartment."

"Will Lucite hold a helicopter?"

"That's somebody else's problem."

"We're about to lose Den-Test."

"Good. We ought to lose it. The whole world ought to lose it."

"Coleman thinks if you and I come up with a new concept, we might still have a chance."

"Why doesn't Coleman come up with one?"

"I'm sure he's itching to. This is our last chance at any more Landum billing."

"So?"

"Landum has a lot of money."

"And what's more important than money, eh?"

"If somebody's going to get it, I'd just as soon it was us."

Brook Parker said, "Do you know what Landum is? Landum is a giant computer with all these nice little people in it. Do they ask if the world needs something? Do they ask if a thing is good or bad? Not Landum. They don't have anybody in charge of questions like that. They just have nice clean little men in charge of consumer studies and market projections and anything else you can express in numbers. I thought you were working with Rudy d'Franco on this."

I said, "I was, but Coleman wants you."

"How does d'Franco feel about it?"

"He doesn't know whether to cut my throat or his own."

"He'd be better off if he cut his own. It's a swell thing to do."

"It gets all over everything, though."

Brook Parker said, "I saw the spots you did. They're very nice. I think that's what's wrong with them."

I said, "It seemed like a good little campaign at the time."

Brook Parker turned back to his helipad. "You don't know what it's all about, Jim. You go home to Westport every night and miss the show."

"I get tired every night."

"I don't know if I want to work on Den-Test." He wasn't even looking at me now. He was drawing. "Maybe you'd better get Coleman to get somebody else. I don't like products like Den-Test."

"Think about it. The challenge will get to you."

He didn't answer. He just went on drawing.

I left. He'd work on it.

Jeff Sermon, the fat account man, was waiting in my office. "Jim, am I glad I caught you."

"What's up?"

"Jim, we need a spot right away."

"How soon is right away?"

"Federal wants to be on the air with it next week."

"Next week? Six weeks. How would they feel about six weeks?"

"Next week, Jim. This one's my fault. They told me about it last month. Can't you do something on tape?"

It took four to six weeks to do a commercial on film. On tape you could have it the next day.

I did not like tape. You shot everything the same day and

saw everything played back instantly and by nine at night, you thought shots were better than they were.

I said, "Explain the importance of next week."

"End of summer. They want to be in there early for business travel."

"What about some of the spots we ran last year? If you're in a sweat, run one of them."

"Jim, any other time I could, but right now Federal's getting picky about things."

"What's the matter with them now?"

"The Buffalo ad, which they still don't have. The California ad."

I said, "Barney Marker called me at the studio with the California ad. Did you take it over?"

"That's where I just came from. God, those kids. Do you know they wanted to spend a whole day retouching?"

I said, "What's wrong with that?"

Jeff Sermon sighed. The world was too heavy for him to carry alone any more. "Jim, that ad has to be in the papers the day after tomorrow. Forty-eight hours to plate and ship. Federal's got the old needle in me, Jim. Do you know they have a bet on we'll miss the insertion?"

"What's eating them these days? They keep killing ads and then asking us where the ads are."

"Oh, we're over budget and I didn't tell them about it. They wanted a spot on the Late News and we screwed up on that. I don't know what's eating them, Jim. You name it; it's eating them."

"Yeah, well, what's this California ad going to look like if we don't retouch it?"

"It's a sunset. It's beautiful. Don't worry about it. Jesus, there I am going down for a third time and that kid wanted to have a rough layout set in type. Anyway, that one's in the works. What I have to have now, like before Federal goes home for dinner, is a commercial."

I said, "Okay. What's the story?"

"There isn't any story. Chicken or steak. You want me to get Barry Gorner?"

"What the hell do I want Barry Gorner for?"

Jeff shrugged his fat shoulders. "He's got tapes on three of those focus sessions, if you want to listen to them."

"He's done three already?"

"George Brice wants something as fast as he can get it.

Barry's already got a kind of preliminary sheet done on it. Do you want me to get it?"

I said, "I do not. You want a commercial before five o'clock? I'll give you a commercial."

I took a small layout pad and a Flair pen and drew a face. I sat there looking at this for a while, and then I lit a cigarette and looked at it for a while longer.

Jeff Sermon said, "Can I get you some coffee or anything?"

I said, "You know what I like to do when I have to do something in a hurry? Just take one thing and see what you can do with it. If we were just on one man's face for thirty seconds . . ."

Jeff Sermon said, "If it helps any, we have miles of airplane footage we can transfer to tape."

I said, "Jeff, I can't think of anything more dramatic than miles of airplane footage."

Under the face, I wrote:

Passenger keeps turning head, trying to stop stewardess we do not see. We hear announcer voice over, and man calling girl.

V.O.:	"You're traveling on business, right?"
Man:	"Miss?"
V.O.:	"It's hard enough to concentrate when you're traveling."
Man:	"Miss?"
V.O.:	"So little annoyances aren't little to you."
Man:	"Miss, I asked for steak. This is—Miss?"
(Zoom in very tight on face. No expression.)	
V.O.:	"If you wish there was a Federal law against little girls like this, there is. We stop them at the Federal Airlines Stewardess School. They never get as far as the plane."

I showed this to Jeff and said, "If they'll buy the idea, I'll do a little more with the copy. It's a little rough."

"We just stay on this guy's face, right?"

"Yep."

"Jesus, I like it. You know what I'm going to do with this?"

"Have it framed. I'll autograph it for you."

"I'm going to take it over this way."

I said, "Well, we can do a little better than that for you.

Why don't I type it up so it doesn't look like I did it on the bus?"

Jeff Sermon said, "Not this time. I'm going over there and tell them you did this in fifteen minutes. They dig this stuff, Jim. It's the envelope Lincoln wrote his speech on."

I said, "Just make sure they can have a couple of airline seats in that studio."

Jeff Sermon said, "God bless you, Tiny Tim."

I said. "On your way out, go to hell."

Almost the moment he was out the door, our president, George Brice, walked in.

I thought, Oh oh.

Barry Gorner's research department had already held three of those damned depth-interview sessions and I had not made one of them. Was I going to have my wrist slapped or my ass kicked?

I said, "Hello, George. I just got in. We were over shooting a Den-Test spot."

George Brice said, "Jim, I'm sure you've seen this." He was smiling which was not a good sign, and he had a layout with him which he now tossed on my desk.

It was Alec Mayberry's Mountainaire ad.

> For 9 months a year,
> you'll wonder why you
> spent the money.

That took care of that. I was going to get my ass kicked. I had promised George not to let anything out the door again that might frighten all the little brand managers at Landum and General Drug. I said, "Yes."

Smiling George Brice said, "If you're wondering what I'm doing with it, the president of Mountainaire called me about it. He wanted to know if we'd lost our minds."

I said, "George, that guy used to call Max Gibbs twice a week."

Today, however, George was trying a different approach. "Jim, don't you ever get tired of all this?"

I said, "Well, tired of what, George?"

"Oh, the fight. The frustration. It must be pretty hard on the stomach to have to live with this sort of thing day in and day out." George Brice crossed his legs and lit a cigarette and went right on smiling. "Jim, what are your plans in this business, anyway?"

I said, "I don't know that I follow you, George."

"Why, nothing stands still, Jim. We're all either moving ahead or moving backward."

I had the feeling that this was going to be more than a friendly little talk. I said, "I can't say I've given it much thought, George."

George Brice said, "Oh? That's surprising, Jim. I would have said that you were the sort who would have figured out just where he was heading."

I said, "No. Not really."

"I see. Jim, tell me something. Have you ever given any thought to account work?"

"No, George. I can't say that I have."

"It's occurred to me that you ought to be very good at it. You know the business. You have a very clear mind, and you're certainly articulate."

I said, "I guess I've just never given it much thought, George. Were you asking for any particular reason?"

George's shoulders moved in a little shrug. "Oh, just wondering where the copywriters go when they get tired of the grind, Jim."

"Well, George, I don't really think any dry rot's set in yet."

"I'm sure it hasn't, Jim. And yet, I see something like this and I have to wonder just how flexible a man can be when he's been at the same old stand all these years."

"George, what can I say? You think that ad's over the line and I don't. I mean, that's one of the things you're paying me to make decisions about."

"Jim, believe me, I am not here because you sent an ad out behind my back. I don't really have time for that sort of nonsense. What I have to ask myself, Jim, is how adaptable you can be to a new way of doing things. I'm afraid, Jim, that I'm not at all convinced that you can adapt."

"I told you I'd cooperate with you, George."

"I know what you told me, Jim. The fact remains that you were over shooting a commercial when I asked you to spend more of your time on supervision. The fact remains, Jim, that we did have a discussion about ads like this and I see they are still going out. What am I to make of all this, Jim?"

I said, "George, when Barry Gorner's got the winners and losers sorted out in that horse race of his, we'll give it a whirl. We've still got ads to get out in the meantime, you know?"

George Brice sighed. "Jim, Barry's got a preliminary report on paper already. Have you bothered to look at it?"

"Not yet. I just got back from the studio, George, and Jeff Sermon had to have a commercial over to Federal by five o'clock or the sky would fall down."

"All right, Jim."

I did not know what that meant. I finally said, "Well, anyway, he got the commercial."

"I'm sure he did, Jim." George Brice gave me a very nice smile. "Don't expect me to be surprised because you pulled a rabbit out of the hat. I've seen your work, Jim."

I lit a cigarette and said, "Well, anyway, it's been a day, you know?"

"Jim, I won't keep you from whatever you're doing. I really just dropped around to say hello. I do hope you find the time to get a little more involved in the focus sessions. I'd like to think we were working together on this."

"We're working together, George. We're just working together on different floors."

George Brice got up, smiling away. "Okay, Jim."

When he was gone, I just sat there for a while. He had not just dropped around to say hello. He had dropped around to let me know he had seen the Mountainaire ad.

That night started on the five twenty-five's bar car. First it was Joe Slattery. The big marine was a little down. "Guy in our place dropped dead today."

"What was it, the heat?"

"His heart, probably. Jim, they had him out of there in an hour. Christ, if they fire you, they give you two weeks."

We had begun to move. Pale naked bulbs went by in the murk in the tunnel under Park Avenue.

I wondered how the ice in my drink had melted so quickly. "Is that air conditioning working? I think my skin's getting wrinkled."

"What are you drinking, gin and tonic? Stay put. I'll buy." Joe headed for the bartender.

A voice said, "Jim, boy, just the guy I wanted to see."

I said, "Hello, Jack."

I did not want to see Jack Thompson. Jack made me nervous. It was as if he went through life trying to find the handle. He had tried dancing lessons, weight lifting and some of those books that are supposed to set you free. "What you do is read *Cybernetics*," he had told me one day on the train.

"I always used to worry about things, you know? Crazy things that keep you from seeing life the way it is. Jim, this book showed me the way. There isn't a thing on earth that can bother me now. It's learning to cope, Jim."

I had said, "Good for you."

"You ought to try it, Jim. I'll lend you the book, if you like."

"I don't think so, Jack. I'm kind of used to worrying about things."

"No, I mean it, Jim. This is an experience. Just try the first three chapters."

"Jack," I had said, "it might start me thinking and then where would I be?"

"You oughtn't turn your back on things that way, Jim."

The best description of Jack Thompson came from a gray-haired woman at a cocktail party once. She had said, "What's that jerk doing now?"

What he had done was jump into a swimming pool with his clothes on. I suppose he wanted to show everybody he was a good sport. He had yelled, "Hey, everything's shrinking." It had got him a laugh and he would not go home to change after that. I remember his wife's just looking at him. He had ruined his suit and a gold watch but he had got a laugh.

The word got around that Jack Thompson had bought a house he could not afford and that he had run up some bills in town he had not paid. You would not know it to look at him. He was in his forties, a big, good-looking guy. Tonight's suit was Italian silk.

He sat down and said, "I'd been meaning to call you for lunch."

I said, "Joe Slattery's sitting there, Jack. He just went to get a drink."

"Jim, how would your agency like to get in on something big?" Jack Thompson took out a gold and silver cigarette case, took a French cigarette out of it and lit up with a gold Dumont lighter that looked like a small safe. "The moment I thought of this, I thought of you."

"It isn't my agency, Jack. I'm just a copywriter for the place."

"It's a new book I'm putting out. 'How to Stay Home and Live.' Tips on things like fuses and gas furnaces and what to do with electric outlets. Stuff not one guy in a hundred knows anything about." On his little finger, a ruby gleamed at me.

I said, "What would we do with it?"

"Are you kidding? As a giveaway for one of your clients? What about Federal Airlines? Jim, if they'll sign up for half a million, they get an exclusive and I'll see you're in for a good cut yourself."

"Federal isn't giving out any books called 'How to Stay Home and Live,' Jack."

"That's just the name, Jim. We can change that. All the family plans the airlines have these days, this is a family giveaway if I ever saw one."

"I don't think so, Jack."

Jack Thompson began to fidget. I wished Joe Slattery would come back so he would go away. Jack said, "I'm not kidding about your cut in this, Jim."

"Well, that's nice of you, Jack, but I don't think so."

"I wasn't thinking of anything you'd have to do yourself, of course. All you'd do is tell Federal about it. I mean, they expect you guys to come up with ideas like this, right?"

I said, "Jack, that isn't how it works. They tell us their problems and we tell them what we think they ought to do. We don't go over with solutions and ask them if they have any problems for them, you know?"

"I didn't mean I wanted you to recommend it, Jim. Just tell them about it in case they're interested. . . ."

"What can I say, Jack? They aren't interested in anything that doesn't have anything to do with travel."

For a moment, he just sat there. Then he took off his ring. "Jim, boy, did I ever show you the Princess?"

"Very nice," I said.

"That's a star ruby. You don't see stones like that every day."

"I guess not."

"That's the down payment, Jim." He held the ring out. I got out a little laugh. "Jack, I don't want your ring."

"Just one word, just to get me into Federal. Go ahead, Jim. Win, lose or draw, the Princess is yours." He tried to put the ring in my hand.

"No. Okay? No, Jack."

"Well, why not?"

"Come on, Jack."

"Take it as a present, then, Jim."

"No!"

"Okay. Far be it from me to force riches on a friend." Jack Thompson put his ring back on. "Oh, say, Peg and I had been meaning to have you and Melinda over. How are you fixed for Saturday?"

God in heaven. I said, "I think we're busy, but let me check her, Jack. I'll call you."

Jack Thompson got up and slapped me on the shoulder. "You're looking good, Jim."

Joe Slattery came back with the drinks. "Was that who I thought it was?"

"Jack Thompson."

"What brought him over? You spill some syrup on yourself?"

The tide was out when the train got into Westport. You could smell the bottom off Stony Point. We had a seven-foot tide and I guess anything that spent part of the day under seven feet of water had to smell when it got the chance to.

I found Melinda on the porch with a pitcher of martinis. I said, "Is that all yours or is this a share and share alike day?"

"Kate Matthews asked us over to share their pool tonight. Your trunks are on the bed."

It was getting so that a night did not pass without Barlow Matthews turning up in our lives. I said, "Okay."

"The reason you don't have a twist is we're out of lemons and the reason you don't have any onions is we're out of onions."

"How is it possible to run out of onions before you run out of gin?"

"Just put it down as another demerit."

Whatever was wrong was not getting any better, but I did not know what to do about it. I said, "Oh. Jack Thompson wants us over for dinner Saturday."

"Jack Thompson? Oh, God. Not Jack Thompson."

"Well, you've got the right Jack Thompson."

"How did you get out of it?"

"What do you say we go?" I did not know what made me say this. I thing it had something to do with helping the lepers.

"Go? What in heaven's name for?"

I lit a cigarette. "Just because I don't think anybody else would. How does that grab you?"

"You can go."

"It's just for one evening. It won't kill you. Look, his wife's name is Peg. Will you call her?"

"I know his wife's name. You call her."

"It would be nicer if you did."

"And we must be nice, mustn't we? God." Melinda went out to the kitchen. We had an extension in the kitchen.

Presently she came back. "Peg Thompson didn't know anything about it."

"Then we aren't going?"

"Of course we're going. Once I asked her, she had to ask us. She hopes we won't mind taking pot luck with them. I gather they've had a lot of expense with some horse."

"What the hell did the guy ask me for, then?"

"I take it the words *social acumen* are foreign to you."

"The man came up to me on the train and asked me."

"Social acumen is what you have when you have the sense to say no. It's also known as the sense God gave geese. Well, now we can scratch one Saturday from the summer. We'll be spending it at the Thompsons' and we'll all be very nice."

I said, "If you plan on being nice for a whole evening, you'd better go into training."

We got to Barlow and Kate Matthewses' at about nine. I said, "Do they have a cabana or do we change behind the hedge?"

Melinda said, "Why don't you change on the diving board? Give everybody a thrill."

We walked around the house on the grass and came to the pool. It was forty feet long and had a light green tile walk around it. Kerosene torches on high white wooden posts stood like sentinels on the far side and yellow electric bulbs on a wire near the house lit up the evening's bar.

Barlow was wearing tan trunks. Barlow had a very nice build. You wouldn't find anybody kicking sand in his face.

"Jim. Glad you could come over. Scotch? Gin?"

"Hi. Scotch, I guess."

"Melinda?"

"Gin and tonic."

Helmut and Ina Cross were in the pool. Slim and Jean Hawes and Neil and Harriet Van were sitting in chrome-and-canvas camp chairs.

I sat down beside Slim and said, "Slim, I've been thinking. What we ought to do is swap jobs. I'll go down to Peru and write an ad for that dam and you go into the agency and see how far a little common sense will get you."

The cowboy was in his swimming trunks, tall, lean, deep-chested. His face and arms were almost black, his body dead white. "Well now, Jim, a good ad may be just what the dam needs. What would you say about it?"

I said, *"Be the first on your block.* How long does it take to build a dam, anyway?"

"You want a big dam or a little dam?"

Jean Hawes said, "Start with a little one. It's easier to bring back if it doesn't fit."

Beyond the lights of the pool, the night seemed black. You could not see Barlow's lawn or trees at all. We were all on an island.

Ina Cross climbed out of the pool. Somehow, I knew Ina would have on a white suit. Some suit. It barely got over her nipples. "Gin and tonic, Barlow, please. Jim, how's my favorite fellow?"

"Holding together."

"I hope we're going to get you into a suit. I'm dying to see your legs."

Kate Matthews said, "Go ahead, Jim. We all want to see your legs."

Harriet Van said, "I hope they're thin. I love thin legs."

I said, "I like to think I have the legs of a thinker."

Melinda and Barlow had walked down to the end of the pool with their drinks. Getting away from the crowd was getting to be a thing with Melinda and Barlow.

Ina Cross said, "Come on, Jim. Off with your clothes."

Kate said, "There's a john in the basement, Jim."

Harriet Van said in a quiet little voice, "Do you need any help?"

The basement was finished in wormy cypress. Ping-Pong table. Pool table. Bobsled. Rack of fishing rods, two light ones with Garcia 300 reels, two big ones with Penn reels, an Exercycle all set to go nowhere, white water skis. Abercrombie and Fitch was not as well stocked as Barlow's basement.

I changed into my trunks and went back out. Six feet, one hundred sixty-seven pounds, and I was losing my hair.

Ina Cross said, "It's a bird. No, it's a man. No, it's a bird."

Kate Matthews said, "I like his legs."

Helmut Cross said, "Jim, at least they match." Helmut, in a bathing suit, looked like the front of a rhinoceros.

Slim Hawes said, "Don't just stand there, Jim. You ought to start out with a double gainer."

I said, "I thought a double gainer was a drink."

Kate said, "Come on, Jim. Into the pool."

"These people who force their algae on you."

I dived in. The cold water was a shock. When I came up, there was Kate beside me, her hair in wet strings around her face.

I said, "What's the matter, didn't the house come with a shower?"

"I think Barlow writes part of it off as a business expense. The kids love it."

"Of course they do. What do kids know?" I got hold of the side of the pool and said, "Enough health. Let's get out of here."

"You'll never get to be big and strong that way."

I climbed out and dried myself off and made a new drink and Barlow and Melinda were nowhere in sight.

I lit a cigarette.

Kate came over. "Make me one, too, Jim?"

"Sure. Bourbon?"

"Please. Neat." Kate was looking at the darkness that covered the lawn.

"One bourbon."

"Thanks." She looked at me with a little smile.

Harriet came over. "Come find the drainpipe with me."

"Just at the moment, I don't want a drainpipe."

"Look for a drainpipe and you never know what you'll find. Serendipity."

"Jim!"

It was Helmut Cross. He was standing over Slim Hawes' chair.

I said, "What's the matter?"

"Is the top down on the Lincoln?"

"Yeah." I went over. Slim's face was shiny with sweat. He seemed to be grinning. "What happened?"

Helmut said, "I think it's his heart. You and Neil get his feet. I'll get his head. Jean, tell Kate who your doctor is. Kate, you call him and tell him to meet us at Norwalk Hospital."

Ina said, "Shouldn't we call an ambulance?"

Helmut said, "I don't know if the ambulance has oxygen. We'll get oxygen for him faster if we take him ourselves."

By the time we got Slim to the Lincoln, Kate had already

gone into the house to phone. Helmut said, "Slim, you're in the back of Jim's car. Just take it easy. Everything's fine."

Slim looked at us but did not answer. His mouth was open.

Jean and Helmut got in front with me. I turned onto the Thruway at exit 18 and got the Lincoln up to 85.

At exit 15, I turned down the ramp, went through a red light and drove up the hill to Norwalk Hospital.

They let Jean go along with Slim.

Helmut and I sat in the waiting room. Helmut said, "I wish I'd brought my cigarettes."

A young black attendant took out a pack of L&Ms. "Here. If I don't see you, I can't stop you."

Helmut said, "Thank you."

I said, "So that's the bug he had."

"He should have said something. A heart attack is nothing to be ashamed of."

"You know Slim. Sign of weakness."

Jean came back after a while. "They think he'll be all right for the night. . . ."

"Jean, I can drop you off and bring your car over for you."

"I'll take the car home, Jim. Let's go back. I'd like a drink, anyway."

"Fine."

The first thing I noticed when we got back to the Matthewses' was that Barlow and Melinda were among the present again. Melinda said, "How is he, Jean?"

Jean said, "He's holding his own. Barlow, may I have some bourbon and ginger ale?"

"Of course," Barlow said.

Jean said, "It's funny, isn't it? I suppose companies can't allow themselves to think about people."

Barlow said, "What do you mean?"

"The company is phasing out their South American business. Slim said it was the graft. That was Slim's last job, Barlow."

Barlow said, "Jean, Slim can name his own ticket with his experience."

"The thing is, he was offered another job and they begged him to stay. Do you know what they said? They said they stood for something. Slim stayed with them because they stood for something."

Barlow said, "Well, for what it's worth, Jean, I'm sure they meant it at the time. I know Slim's company."

Jean gave him a sunny smile. "But that isn't quite the same as meaning it, is it?"

Barlow said, "Well, Jean, I know how you feel."

Jean said, "Why, no you don't, Barlow. You really don't know how I feel."

Melinda did not have anything to say on the way home. She was not even nasty. She did not say anything at all.

friday

When I got in, Edna told me that Bob Coleman wanted to have a meeting about Den-Test with Brook Parker and me. She told me that Barney Marker had also been around, and that the unemployed vice-president with thirty years in the trenches had called for an interview.

I said, "Call Coleman's secretary and ask her if she reached Brook yet. I don't want to sit up there cooling my heels until Brook gets in."

"That's a nice double standard we have here. You get in at nine and Brook Parker gets in at ten-thirty."

I said, "The world needs double standards. Man doesn't

live by bread alone. Man needs something he can hate. What did Barney want?"

"What does he always want? I think he wants to talk to you about what it all means."

"Christ."

"What about the welfare case?"

"The what?"

"The unemployed gentleman."

"Tell him to come in Monday. Tell him we don't have any openings but we'd like to talk to him anyway."

"Isn't that just stringing him along?"

"Sure. When you're out of work, it's nice to find somebody who wants to talk to you. Most people don't."

"You're the boss."

"I knew that would get through to you, sooner or later."

I went into my office and the phone rang. It was George Brice's secretary. "Mr. Brice would like you to come up to his office, Mr. Bower."

"Sure. Be right there."

"Thank you." Now there was a woman with a cold voice. She sounded as if she had been made by the telephone company.

I went up. George Brice said, "Good morning, Jim."

"Hello, George."

"I thought we might have a little talk about things, if you have a few minutes."

"Sure." We had just had a talk about things yesterday. We had also had a talk the day before yesterday.

George Brice smiled with all those teeth. "How's the heat been, up in Westport?"

"About the same as it is here."

"We have friends in Westport. It must be nice, going home at night and having the water right there."

I said, "Well, some guys get off the train and go down to Compo for a swim. I don't get that athletic myself, but it's good to know the water's there."

"I've always thought it would be nice to live near the water and have a little sailboat to go out on. Do you sail, Jim?"

I wondered what all this was leading up to. "No, but we have a powerboat we keep at Longshore."

"Do you? What kind of boat do you have?"

"Bertram. Get it up to four thousand rpms and it lands on the moon."

"A Bertram. I've heard of them, Jim. That's a lot of boat."

"Well, it's a lot of money."

George Brice began to turn what looked like a class ring around and around on his finger. He watched this with what seemed to be great interest. "Jim, I had a funny discussion this morning."

Now what? I wondered.

"Ed Farrel. Did you ever meet Ed Farrel, Jim?"

"Once or twice." Ed Farrel was the president of Federal Airlines.

George Brice said, "I think I told you, Jim, that Federal knew about Barry Gorner's project."

"Yes."

"Well. Jim, the strangest thing seems to have happened. Yesterday I had a messenger bring over Barry's preliminary report. Not conclusive yet, but still three sessions and twenty-one depth interviews did turn up something of a pattern. You didn't see that report, did you?"

I said, "No."

"I understand Jeff Sermon offered to get you a copy."

I said, "Jeff Sermon also wanted a commercial immediately."

"I know. That's one of the things I wanted to talk to you about. Jim, so far, Barry's research turned up a number of areas worth exploring. Baggage and reservations seemed to head the list. Airline food and ground service, of all things, came next. After that I think the two-drink law was all by itself, and after that was information, carry-on baggage and ticket transfers, whatever that is."

I said, "That's interline. You have a round-trip ticket on Federal and when you want to come back there's a United flight at a better time. You can use your Federal ticket on United."

George Brice said, "Jim, would it surprise you to know the two items at the bottom of the list?"

"What?"

"Movies and stewardesses."

I found myself taking a deep breath. I did not say anything.

George Brice opened his drawer and took out a little gold pistol about the size of a tie clasp. He broke it open and dropped in a tiny cartridge. He pointed it at his window. Boom.

"Damnedest thing, isn't it? You wouldn't think it would make that much noise. Well, Jim, what do you suppose Ed Farrel wanted to talk to me about?"

I said, "Well, I did a quick commercial for Jeff yesterday. . . ."

"That's right, Jim. You did a quick commercial for Jeff yesterday." George Brice broke open the little pistol and let the empty shell fall into the hollow back of his glass swan ashtray. "I sent Ed Farrel a report saying the last thing to concentrate on was stewardesses and you sent over a commercial about a stewardess."

I said, "That's what I did."

"Of course," George Brice said, still looking at his little pistol, "it wasn't just a run-of-the-mill commercial about stewardesses. It was our kind of commercial, right, Jim?"

I said, "What do you mean?"

"Why, Jim, when we do a commercial about a stewardess, that stewardess is going to be rude, arrogant and just as unpleasant as we can make her, isn't that right?"

I said, "Well, George, who wants to watch thirty seconds of a stewardess smiling at you?"

George Brice said, "Why, all right, Jim. If you want to put it that way, who wants five and a half hours of a stewardess who won't speak to you at all? That's what your commercial was all about, wasn't it?"

I said, "The kind of stewardess we don't have on Federal."

George Brice said, "Oh? Ed Farrel was under the impression she was a Federal stewardess, Jim."

I said, "That's ridiculous. What the hell would we do a commercial about a rude Federal stewardess for?"

"I wouldn't know, Jim. As a matter of fact, I didn't even know what to tell Ed Farrel when he asked me that question."

I said, "I don't know how he could have got the idea at all."

"Why, Jim, perhaps he got the idea because it was a Federal commercial about a rude stewardess. Wouldn't you say that was possible?"

I said, "He'd have to be nuts to get that out of it."

"Whether or not Ed Farrel is nuts is conjecture, Jim. What happens to be fact is that he's the president of Federal Airlines and he came in personally this morning to find out what on earth we're doing here."

I could feel my face getting hot. I said, "George, yesterday I was at the studio shooting one commercial and in my office writing another and I don't even know where I was supposed to find time to look at Barry Gorner's report. Jeff was bleeding to get something over to Federal before five. What was I supposed to do, spend the time reading a report or doing the commercial?"

George Brice said, "I wouldn't know, Jim. Yesterday I spent the morning with a Paris agency and the afternoon with some people from Lever Brothers and I seem to have found the time."

George Brice tossed the little gold pistol back into his drawer and made a steeple of his fingers and sat there smiling at me. He looked at me, smiling away, and said nothing at all.

I said, "George, did you ever consider the possibility that that commercial will make stewardesses important?"

"No, Jim, I didn't consider that possibility. Ed Farrel didn't consider that possibility and I didn't consider that possibility."

I said, "Okay. Where does that leave us?" I lit a cigarette. My hand was trembling a little. "They still need something on the air next week."

George Brice said, "Why, Jim, once again I seem to have found myself in the position of saying we couldn't do it. There will be no commercial written for Federal until we've reviewed Barry Gorner's report and decided on the direction to go in. I say 'once again,' because I understand they still do not have an ad on Buffalo from your young friend Barney Marker."

I said, "Yeah, well, that's because they had to have another ad on California from Barney Marker. They keep turning ads down and then throwing rocks at us because we don't have the ads done, you know?"

"Jim, this afternoon the people from Powell Power are coming in. You'll keep yourself available, I trust?"

"Powell? The power saws and stuff?"

"They particularly want to talk to Brook Parker. Can you tell me how Brook is in a new business presentation, Jim?"

"Brook? Brook's fine."

"I hope he is." George Brice took out a Marlboro and opened his desk drawer. I wondered what was coming out this time.

It was an inch-and-a-half-high grandfather clock. George Brice turned the clock part down with his thumb and it turned into a cigarette lighter. "Real clock, believe it or not. I asked you about Brook, Jim, because I have the feeling that you and Brook Parker do not wholly appreciate my efforts here. I would not care to see a client presentation scuttled in the name of—shall we call it artistic integrity?"

I said, "George? We aren't fools, okay?"

George Brice got up and walked over to a teak cabinet and sat on it, his feet dangling above his gold rug. He looked at his shoes. They were a dull gray. "Elephant. Decadent, isn't it?"

I did not say anything.

George Brice said, "Powell bills just about six million, Jim. I don't know these people, but I have an idea they wouldn't really appreciate any commercials about somebody's cutting off his arm."

"George, is that really the only thing you think we can do here?"

"I hope not, Jim. I wonder where I ever got the idea."

In my office, I started work on a Federal ad. Some copy chiefs do not write ads themselves. They supervise. I did not do this.

I think that writing is something you have to keep doing. I was afraid if I was just a supervisor, I would not be a very good supervisor for very long.

The ad was about the three-and-two seating in coach on Federal's Altojet. The picture had two seats just sitting there on the white page. There was a gap between them.

One of our coach seats is missing.

The client had bought this. Now I had to write the copy. I tried the first paragraph.

It's easy enough to find 2-abreast seats on a plane. All you do is buy a first-class ticket. Finding 2-abreast in coach is something else again.

I sat back and looked at this. We could do better than that.

Coach seating on Federal's new Altojet is 3-and-2, which means one side of the cabin gets first-class elbow room.

I did not like this, either, and I wrote still another first paragraph.

We've taken some of the togetherness out of coach.

I liked that and lit a cigarette to put off figuring out what I was going to say next.

"Jim?"

It was Jeff Sermon, six feet four, whatever size jacket barrels wear.

"If you want another commercial to get yourself out of a jam, beat it," I said.

"Jim, I didn't know what was in Barry's report."

I said, "Fine."

He did not go away. He said, "What do I do with this?"

It was a bill from Sigori Studios. Sigori was a photographer.

"What about it?"

"This is for eleven hundred dollars. Jim, we agreed on seven fifty for all destination photography."

I looked at the bill. I said, "It's still for seven fifty. The rest is for flying out to Los Angeles. What did you want him to do, take the subway?"

"Jim, we agreed on this. The art department said seven fifty would be the top price. The client didn't even want to pay that."

I said, "For Christ's sake, Jeff. Expenses go without saying."

"Not to the client, they don't."

I said, "Jeff, two weeks ago Sigori spent half a day shooting a 727. Do you think seven fifty was all Federal paid for that? Do you know what it costs to keep a 727 on the ground?"

"They didn't keep it on the ground. It was on the ground anyway."

"Jeff, don't be silly. Okay? Just don't be silly. The bill's legitimate. Expenses are standard operating procedure. And go away. All I get from you is piles."

"Jim, I'm sorry about yesterday. I offered to get you a copy of Barry's report."

"Yeah."

He finally left and I went back to my ad.

We've taken some of the togetherness out of coach.

Now what?

Lucky Pierre, we've got him out of the middle.

I typed this and thought it looked silly. Then I put parentheses around it.

We've taken some of the togetherness out of coach.
(Lucky Pierre, we've got him out of the middle.)
In fact the 3-and-2 seating on our new Altojet not only
gives you more elbow room—it also means your dinner will
be along a little faster.
All those Pierres ahead of you are not even aboard.

Percy Holland came in. "See you a sec?"
"Sure."
You always had time to see Percy. Percy Holland was
fifty, stocky, bald and comfortable. You never heard his
name in the Gold Key awards. He just went on doing swell
ads in whatever time you gave him.
Percy said, "We got us a new account man upstairs."
He handed me an ad typed on yellow paper. Most of it
had been crossed out and rewritten.
The client was Miniflex cameras. Percy's headline had been

10 Easy Ways to Ruin a Swell Picture.

This had been changed to

A New Standard of Excellence.

I said, "This guy's pretty classy."
"Moves you, doesn't it? The traffic boy brought it back to
me. This new guy told him to have it retyped so he could
take it to the client."
I said, "What's this new guy's name?"
"Charles Leader. I hear he's real serious about that Charles,
too. Not Chuck or Charley. Charles."
"Okay, I'll drop around and thank him for helping us out.
A new standard of excellence. Why can't you write like that?"
"I came from an underprivileged neighborhood. We
couldn't afford big words."
Lydia came in. Black hair that looked like an explosion in
a bedspring factory. Glasses in big black frames. Fat legs
and an electric-pink miniskirt.
"Jim, what do you tell clients who say you can't end a
sentence with a preposition?"
"Send them a copy of Fowler's."
"We did that. They said you still can't do it."
"You can split infinitives and you can end sentences with
prepositions. Tell them God told you."

"The account man says he thinks they're right."

I said, "What other proof do you need?"

Lydia left and Percy said, "I hear her psychiatrist is going to a psychiatrist."

I said, "Perce, the only thing worse than a girl who's wrong is a girl who's right. They can't handle it."

As Percy left, in came our treasurer, Marion Simons. Marion was fifty-seven. He wore a dark gray worsted suit and a dark red necktie and a starched Arrow white shirt. Marion had a prosperous little belly and a lot of vertical lines in his face, like a coconut.

"Jim?"

"Hi, Marion."

"I came bearing arithmetic."

"Arithmetic doesn't sound like glad tidings."

"I just work here, Jim." That, in itself, had a bad sound to it. "Jim, Alec Mayberry. Nineteen thousand dollars a year. Have you seen his time sheets?"

Marion Simons had some time sheets and some sort of chart in his hand. He didn't look at them. He had probably committed them to memory.

I said, "Nope."

"You don't look at your writers' time sheets?"

I said, "No. I look at what they write."

"Then how can you tell whether they're working on billing that's in some proportion to their salaries?"

I said, "Well, I can't always. Alec Mayberry's on Mountainaire, though. That's three and a half million. I know that."

"Mountainaire International, Jim. Five hundred thousand in billing. Nineteen thousand dollars seems to be a lot of money to spend on half a million."

This was not Marion Simons' alley, treasurer or not. I lit a cigarette and said. "It isn't that simple, Marion. It's keeping Mountainaire happy on international that helps keep their three and a half million in the agency."

Marion Simons said, "Perhaps a less expensive writer and a little supervision might achieve the same thing and save us nine or ten thousand dollars, too, Jim. This is a public corporation. You don't tell stockholders how much business you're doing if you don't make any money out of it."

I said, "Yes, and you don't do the business at all if the client gets mad and pulls out. Sure I could put a kid on it. And in six months we'd start having those little client meetings to 'iron out our differences' and then where are you?"

Marion Simons crossed his legs and inspected one of his trouser cuffs for lint. "Jim, other agencies have trade and industrial departments. They keep their salaries on a level with their billing and, I might add, they seem to keep their billing too. We're simply too fat in creative, Jim. I know that's the way Max Gibbs liked it, but this throwing money around is no way to run a railroad."

I said, "Marion, other agencies are other agencies. Clients go to other agencies for their research or marketing or overseas connections or what-have-you. What they come to us for is the ads they get. That's all we have to offer, Marion. What you're saying is the goose could lay a few more golden eggs if we'd just fire the goose."

Marion Simons cleared his throat and seemed a little uncomfortable. He said, "Jim, do you mind if I say something for your own good?"

I said, "Of course not."

"Just a word of advice from a friend, Jim. Max Gibbs is dead. I don't think it would hurt you around here to keep that in mind."

I said, "I'm not sure I know what that's supposed to mean, Marion."

Marion Simons said, "Oh, you know what I mean, Jim. Don't think I don't know how you fellows in creative figure it. You're the fair-haired boys. Nobody can touch you. Well, it's tightening-up time, my friend. George Brice, chapter two, verse one. You think about it, Jim."

Marion Simons got up with his time sheets and charts and gave me what seemed to be a curt little nod and left.

Next, the traffic boy came in with some type proofs. He did not think humor was the way to sell an airline. Flying was a serious business.

I said, "Some days everybody in the world wants to help you."

He left with an unhappy look.

I went upstairs to see our new account executive, Charles Leader. Not Chuck or Charley. Charles.

His office had one of those phones with four buttons on it. He glanced up as I went in. He looked like a boiled egg, steaming in its shell. Bald, rimless glasses. It was August and he had a vest on.

"Yes?"

"Jim Bower. How are you?"

"Charles Leader." His voice was brusque. He had better things to do than make conversation.

I said, "I thought I'd drop by and pass on whatever pearls of wisdom will make you feel at home."

"Thank you, but could we make it some other time? I'm afraid I'm busy at the moment."

I said, "Well, no, I think we'd better make it now. I have the improvements you suggested for the Miniflex ad."

"They weren't suggestions. That's the way I want the copy to read."

I said, "Then let's put it this way. They just became suggestions and I just turned them down."

"I see. May I ask what your function here is?"

"Copy chief."

"Well, my function happens to be account executive and nothing goes over to my client without my approval."

I said, "Then I guess nothing's going over at all."

"You think that exercise in funsmanship was good copy?"

"Just about the best copy you're ever likely to see."

"I don't agree."

I said, "I'm sure you don't, if your idea of a good headline is *Miniflex, A New Standard of Excellence.*"

"And what's the matter with that?"

I said, "What could possibly be the matter with it? It's been used a thousand times."

"It also happens to be positive and it promises a benefit. I don't know if you're aware of the rules of good copy—"

I said, "Don't exceed the speed limit, friend."

His face took on a set look, his lips pursed like a Long Island Sound blackfish's. "Sit down, Bower. There's no point in our both getting off on the wrong foot."

I said, "Thanks. I really just dropped around to give you some of the ground rules around here. I know most agencies give account men a blue pencil along with the desk and telephone, and somebody ought to have taken the time to tell you how we do it."

"I was given to understand that I had complete freedom to handle my account in my own way."

I said, "That's all right. I was given to understand that I'd be president here someday. It's what they put in writing, you know?"

He thought this over and said, "And if I think a piece of copy is all wrong?"

"Talk to the writer or me. The guy in charge is Brook

Parker, and the guy in charge of Brook Parker is George Brice. You'd better ask around about Brook before you go see him, though. Brook is a kind of surprise for account men who don't know him."

"I've heard all about Brook Parker," Charles Leader said. "I'll deal with him when the time comes."

"Percy Holland is the guy who wrote this copy," I said, "and for what it's worth, he's one of the best copywriters in town. There isn't an account man in the shop who doesn't want Perce on his account."

"I can't say I'm comfortable with smart-aleck copy."

"Neither am I," I said. "But that copy isn't smart-aleck. Perce was just looking for some way to bring the subject up that would get people into the story. He's an old mail order man, Perce. Mail order guys don't waste much time being cute."

"He didn't even ask for the order at the end."

I said, "Neither do Volkswagen ads."

"They're different."

"Only because they've been done," I said.

I went on to Bob Coleman's office. Brook Parker was already there.

Bob Coleman was on the phone. With that white hair and those black eyebrows, he looked like somebody in a whiskey ad. He said into the phone, "I'm with you, Mark. I agree. Absolutely." Bob Coleman's voice had a low, confident sound. He sounded a little like a priest, I thought.

Brook Parker was out of sorts. His eyes seemed to be paler than usual. When he saw me, he said, "What's this all about?"

I said, "Den-Test."

Brook Parker said, "I have more important things to think about than Den-Test."

I said, "Talk to Bob Coleman about it. He's very inspirational."

Brook Parker gave me a dry, humorless look. "That's right, Jim. Laugh and the world laughs with you. Cry and you might be right." He picked up a magazine and turned the pages idly.

On the phone, Bob Coleman said, "Mark, I appreciate that but I have to be honest with you. The chances are you're absolutely right. Den-Test is a dead duck. But there's also a chance that we just didn't do the right job on it."

Brook Parker looked up from his magazine. "Brother," he said.

Bob Coleman said, "Mark, I have Brook Parker and Jim Bower in my office right now. Give me a chance to talk to them and get back to you, okay?"

Brook Parker said, "Bob, you kill me."

Bob Coleman was saying, "Pouring good money after bad isn't what I'm talking about, Mark. We just don't want to see the equity you have go down the drain. Mark, let me get back to you after lunch, all right? Well, about three-thirty. Of course, Mark. Sure. I understand, Mark. Mark, I'll call you then."

He hung up, and Brook Parker said, "Honest Bob Coleman. We might have been wrong, Mark. Spend some more money with us, Mark. Maybe we'll be right next time."

Bob Coleman gave him an annoyed glance and said, "You found something wrong with that?"

Brook Parker said, "The world doesn't need Den-Test. It's yesterday's news."

Bob Coleman said, "We never know what the world wants until we try, Brook."

Brook Parker said, "So we tried and it didn't need it, right?"

Bob Coleman said, "We don't know that at all, Brook. All we know is that what we did didn't work."

Brook Parker said, "That's the stuff, Bob. There's a silver lining in there somewhere."

Bob Coleman seemed to me to be sitting just a bit too erectly behind his desk and his face had taken on a set look. You could almost feel the grip he was trying to keep on himself. He said, "If I didn't think that, Brook, I wouldn't be in this business."

Brook Parker said, "So there you are with a Mark Cross attaché case full of Nielsen reports and a little crap about equity and you can go home and tell your wife what a day you had at the office. The world doesn't need it, Bob, and you don't even know it."

Bob Coleman's chin seemed pale and his eyes were blazing but somehow he kept his voice quiet. "That's right, Brook. Nielsen reports and equity. And cost per thousand and shelf space and everything else Landum understands so I'd better understand."

Brook Parker put the magazine down and said, "All right. Let's hear it. I'll ruin my lunch, but let's hear it."

Bob Coleman said, "Okay. Den-Test came out in 1927. It

was one of Landum's off-brands. Nobody expected it to go anywhere, but it did, so they put a little money behind it. *Liberty, Collier's,* the *Post,* outdoor. But they never went into radio. That's probably what killed them. 'The Landum Hour' was strictly for Landum brands. That was 1933."

Brook Parker said, "Bob, who cares? Nothing in the world happened in 1933."

Bob Coleman took a deep breath and went on. "That's exactly right, Brook. Nothing happened in 1933. That was the year Den-Test stopped advertising. There was some sort of fight inside the company. The Den-Test product group wanted a budget and the Landum crowd wouldn't give it to them. The idea was to put any profit on Den-Test behind Landum name brands. 'The Landum Hour,' Landum print in *Life* and *Look*—they shot the whole works on Landum and not a cent for Den-Test."

Brook Parker said, "It's been selling all this time without any money?"

"That's right."

"Maybe we're obsolete after all."

Bob Coleman said, "Anyway, a year ago they figured anything that survived this long might be worth a little budget. So they gave us the account and we laid an egg."

Brook Parker opened the magazine again and stopped to stare at a spread. "Look at that. I did that seven years ago. That son of a bitch stole it."

Bob Coleman said, "Well, I think I know where we went wrong. In fact, it's been right there in front of us. We ignored what we know."

Brook Parker said, "What does that mean?"

Bob Coleman said, "Consumer studies. What people want in a toothpaste. We had the answer all along and we ignored it."

"Consumer studies."

"Here. Reasons for buying in order of preference. One, prevents cavities. Two, brighter teeth. Three, taste. Four, sweetens breath. Five, all other."

Brook Parker closed the magazine and said, "That's what it says, eh?"

Bob Coleman said, "That's what people want."

"So if we just come up with a campaign with all those nice things, Den-Test will rise again."

"Well, it gives us something to check concepts against."

"I don't know, Bob. I used to think you knew what it was all about."

"Brook, we just did a campaign ignoring this sort of thing. It was all very nice. Nice concepts, nice photography, nice copy, and they lost a million and a half dollars."

"It couldn't possibly be the product."

"Of course it could, Brook, but that's the product we have to work with. Not getting everything on our side that we can is just ridiculous."

"Bob, that's where the Edsel came from."

"Brook, I'm not talking about making commercials from a grocery list and you know it."

"You just want us to go make commercials and take the list with us."

"I just want you to know what's selling toothpaste these days."

Brook Parker sighed. "Let's see the package."

Bob Coleman said, "I have one right here." He opened a drawer of his desk and took out a tube of Den-Test.

Brook Parker said, "This has to go."

"It can't."

"What do you mean, it can't? You people always say can't. Of course it can. They should have all-black tubes. Jet black."

Bob Coleman said, "Brook, they have to move the stock that's on the shelves right now."

Brook Parker said, "I guess I didn't understand you, I thought you wanted a way to sell this stuff."

"We won't even get it on the shelf if we don't sell the stock that's in stores now."

Brook Parker sighed. "Come on, Jim. I need a drink."

He walked out of the room without another word. I got up to follow him.

Bob Coleman said, "Jim?"

I stopped and looked at him.

Bob Coleman said, "I don't want him sitting down there designing packages for the next two months."

Brook Parker and I went over to the Algonquin, where you could sit around in the lobby and have drinks brought to you by ringing a little bell. The lobby was small and crowded and made me think of an overstuffed parlor during a wedding.

I had expected Brook to launch into one of his attacks on the Establishment, but he didn't. He said, "Do you know what they ought to do? They ought to put Central Park on stilts and run it all the way down to the Battery."

I said, "I kind of like Central Park where it is."

"I don't mean move it. I mean stretch it."

"What, and tear down all the buildings? No more Empire State?"

"That's a dumb thing to say. Sometimes I wonder about you, Jim. Of course you'd still have the buildings. They'd stick up through. What you'd do is put the park about forty feet up."

I said, "It wouldn't work. For one thing, there wouldn't be anyplace for all the automobile exhausts to exhaust to. You'd get in your car and die. And for another, what if there was a fire somewhere? You'd go tearing down to Bank Street and go to put up a ladder and there'd be a park where the ladder had to go."

Brook Parker said, "You know where the real trouble will be, don't you? Getting people to keep it up. You can't even get somebody to paint an apartment these days. Try getting somebody to come down to Fourteenth Street and cut the grass."

I said, "I thought you didn't like trees and grass."

"They serve a purpose. Jim, you could put the whole thing on hinges."

"What? Central Park?"

"Why not? You could raise and lower whole sections of it, like cellar doors. Air out the streets, let your stupid fire engine ladders through—they must make motors big enough for a thing like that."

It occurred to me that the lobby of the Algonquin looked a little like a used-sofa shop. There seemed to be too much furniture crammed into it, and hitting that stupid bell to get a waiter for another martini seemed quainter than a place with the Algonquin's reputation ought to get. Besides, I had hit the bell three times already and the waiter was still talking to a woman whose hat seemed to have been made from the hind end of a large bird.

I said, "I wonder if God's trying to tell us not to have another drink."

Brook Parker said, "God and I don't speak. God speaks to George Brice and George sends us a memo."

"What makes you think God would talk to George?"

"Because He knows George wants His job. What time is that dumb meeting with Powell Power?"

"Four o'clock."

"Do we have to go?"

"Be a little sticky if we don't. You're the guy the Powell people want to meet."

Brook Parker shook his head. "Power tools. I don't know if I want to work on an account like that."

I said, "Powell Power? What's the matter with it? That's a good account."

"Did you read their literature? A million people are home right now making ugly little tables with Powell power saws. Do you want to be a party to a thing like that?" Brook Parker put out his cigarette and said, "I don't know, Jim. Nothing's right any more. Nothing's been right since Max died."

I said, "What's bugging you? That Max is dead or that George Brice is running things?"

"Take away Max and there's nothing to keep the George Brices away. They take baths and use deodorants and go to church and they're the world's worst people. And I'll tell you why, too. Because they won't put Central Park on stilts. The George Brices think the world's a goddamned museum they're supposed to dust once a week. The idea of doing anything with it is subversive or something."

We had sausage sandwiches and German beer in a small new bright restaurant with wursts hanging on the wall and got back to Brook's office at about two-thirty.

Brook took his jacket off and tossed it on the floor. "Den-Test," he said. "It sounds like something they do to you with an X-ray machine or something."

I sat down in one of his director's chairs and lit a cigarette. The trouble with chairs like that is that you have to lean so far forward to reach an ashtray. I said, "One, prevents cavities. Two, brighter teeth. Three, taste—"

"Why don't we just run the list?"

"The list is longer than the commercials."

"What did you do, thirties?"

"Those are the Landum time buys."

Brook Parker said, "That's the first thing we're going to change." He opened his phone directory, looked for Bob Coleman's number and then picked up his phone and dialed.

Then he said, "Brook Parker. Is he there?"

Then he said, "Bob? What's this thirty-second business?"

Then he said, "I don't care what Landum time buys are. We want minutes."

Then he said, "Bob, don't talk to me about efficiency, okay? Just don't do it. Efficiency is what sells the product. Efficiency is not a time buy."

Then he said, "We won't discuss it later. Bob, the discussion is over."

Then he hung up. He said, "Efficiency. Where does he get that crap?"

I said, "I think Landum sponsors a lot of prime time. They piggy-back thirties to get the best time slots for them."

Brook Parker said, "Jim, let's don't start understanding their problems. There's only one problem they have and that's that nobody wants this gook."

"Well, what we have here, folks, is a tube of good old-fashioned toothpaste, just like mother used to use."

"Do you know what? I don't like this. I don't like being told if I don't do something, a product will go out of business. Why don't they do something? Why does it have to be us?"

"Well, let's go over the list and see if there's anything in it."

"Can we say Den-Test prevents cavities?"

"Regular brushing with Den-Test and a program of oral hygiene or something can help reduce cavities."

"Well, what's all that jazz?"

"That's the fine print. You've got the FTC, the NAB and the networks to get through."

Brook Parker closed his eyes. He said, with his eyes closed, "Do we have to say all that?"

I said, "It depends on what we say. If you don't say anything, you don't have to qualify it, you know?"

"And if we do, we do, eh?"

"Yep."

"This the oldest toothpaste in the world?"

I said, "I think sand or salt is."

"Sand?"

I said, "I'm not sure about it, but I seem to remember hearing some people use sand. I guess it's abrasive or something."

Brook Parker said, "How many toothbrushings to a tube?"

"I don't know."

"*Fifty smiles, fifty cents.*" Brook Parker sighed. "What do they want from us? They won't change the package. They won't change the product. But you boys will come up with something, won't you?"

I said, "How about what your teeth are all about, brought to you by Den-Test?"

"What do you mean?"

"Well, you have molars, bicuspids, front teeth, nerves, roots, enamel."

Brook Parker said, *"The Den-Test Tooth. It's all there."*

I said, "That's kind of interesting."

"What's a tooth look like?"

"Well, it looks like a tooth with roots."

Brook Parker picked up a layout pad and drew a tooth on it and wrote,

The Den-Test Tooth. It's All There.

I said, "That looks good."

Brook Parker said, "Ah, it's just advertising."

"What do you mean?"

"Nobody believes advertising. Jim, advertising is the great American lie. Everybody's on to it."

"Well, what does that leave, an inspirational little message on the Fourth of July?"

Brook Parker said, "We need something that hurts. Something people don't want to hear."

I said, "What do you mean?"

"When it hurts, people believe you. That's what we did with Willow. *If it tastes good, see your doctor.*"

"I don't know. Crest's doing all right."

"Crest has something to say. How was Rudy d'Franco to work with?"

"Once was enough."

Brook Parker nodded as if at some inner thought. He sighed and said, "What time is that Powell meeting?"

I looked at my watch. "In about fifteen minutes."

Brook Parker wrote on his pad.

Don't expect Den-Test to save your teeth.

I said, "Well, as claims go, I don't think we'll have to qualify it."

Brook Parker said, "How about *Landum's secret brand?*"

"Landum has their own toothpaste. They don't want anything infringing on it."

"You know, every twenty minutes you come up with a new rule for this game."

"Oh, hell, let's go up to Brice's office."

Brook Parker picked up his coat and put it on. He took the sheet he had written *Don't expect Den-Test to save your teeth* on, and stuck it on his wall with two strips of masking tape. He said, "That's to scare Bob Coleman when he comes down to see how we're doing."

We went up to George Brice's office.

Inside, with George, were two men.

George Brice said, "Gentlemen, our creative director, Brook Parker, and our copy chief, Jim Bower. Jim, Brook, this is Zeke Hall, vice-president in charge of sales for Powell Power, and Bob Bohn, advertising director."

We all shook hands and said hello and how do you do.

Bob Bohn, the ad manager, was a fatty little man with thinning black hair, a small mouth, white hands and brown eyes. He said, "I know the work you've done on Willow and Paragon. I just hope you didn't use up all your ideas before you got to us." He added, to me, "I used to be a copywriter myself once. I'm looking forward to getting in on the creative end with you fellows."

The world was filled with clients who used to be copywriters themselves once. I said, "Fine. I like working with somebody who knows copy."

Zeke Hall, the sales manager, was a tall, rumpled-looking man with heavy shoulders, wide, callused hands and an odd-looking haircut that looked as if his mother had given it to him. He had a flat, midwestern voice that was both rough and suave at the same time. I had the feeling that that voice had lived in Chicago. He said, "Well, fellows, I guess we're here just to listen today. I don't suppose it's any secret that we've been talking to several agencies. What I guess we're interested in is what you fellows call philosophy."

George Brice said, "Brook, I guess that means you."

Brook Parker said, "Well, I guess what I'm supposed to do is tell you what our philosophy is, and if I knew, I would." He lit a cigarette and said, "Hey, can we sit down? I hate talking on my feet. I always feel everybody's heading for the door."

Zeke Hall said, "Brook, sitting down is one of the things I do best." We all sat down and Zeke Hall said, "I take it you don't believe in a fixed philosophy?"

Brook Parker said, "I guess I'm dumb or something. I don't even know what it means. I hear people talk about the Ted Bates school and the Ogilvy school and the Doyle Dane school. I don't have any school. I guess I have an attitude, but you probably wouldn't like it."

"Fine," Zeke Hall said.

Brook Parker leaned forward with his elbows on his knees, his cigarette between his thumb and his index finger. He did not look at Hall or Bohn or anyone else. He seemed to be looking at the floor.

He said, "I think advertising's had it. I don't think people believe it any more. I think it's a waste of money. I'm not even sure it's moral. Anyway, we don't have any formulas here. There's no book we go by. I don't even know what to tell you. Half the time, I don't even know what I'm doing."

Zeke Hall said, "Well, I guess that's part of the creative process, isn't it?"

Brook Parker said, "I guess so. I think what you have to do is get under people's skin and that's getting harder and harder these days. What I think is that people are fed up. Not just with advertising. With everything. The Establishment. Phony morality that everybody talks about and nobody practices. Look, the white colonial in Connecticut used to be the thing to want. I don't think it is any more. If you want to know what's happening, spend a couple of evenings in Ann's Bar & Grille on the upper East Side, you know? I don't know what all this has to do with power tools, but your customers are people and people are what I'm talking about."

Zeke Hall said, "Brook, we're a couple of hicks and we're sure willing to learn. Just what do you mean, people are fed up?"

Brook Parker looked at Zeke Hall with a little smile. "Yeah, well, hicks never say they're hicks. Well, I don't know what I mean. I think everything's in for a change. I don't know whether it's the bomb or the war or the kids or the pill or what. Well, like once you could tell your daughter not to screw because she'd get knocked up and be ruined for life, right? Everybody liked to say nice girls didn't do it because it was a sin but that's a lot of shit. They didn't do it because they didn't want to get knocked up. Well, they have the pill now and and they're even changing the dormitory rules in college. Am I saying anything? I don't know."

Zeke Hall took out a pack of Camels and lit one and said, "Keep going."

Brook Parker said, "Everybody's had it. They go in hock to buy a Cadillac and what do they have? They don't have happiness. They just have a car. What I mean is, they've been lied to. How many times can you lie to people before they lynch you, you know?"

Bob Bohn said, "We don't lie to people, Brook. We don't even refer to horsepower in our ads because horsepower's a misleading term."

Zeke Hall said in that midwestern drawl, "I don't think that's exactly what Brook's getting at."

Brook Parker looked at me. "Jim, you're the copywriter. What the hell am I talking about, do you know?"

George Brice said, "Isn't it pretty much what Lincoln said, Brook? You can fool some of the people all the time and you can fool all the people some of the time, but you can't fool all of the people all of the time?"

Brook Parker said, "I knew I heard it somewhere."

Bob Bohn said, "I'd like to ask a few questions, if I may?"

George Brice said, "I wish you would. That's what we're here for."

Bob Bohn said, "Well, Ogilvy believes in long copy—I guess you'd call it the mail order approach—and Bates believes in the unique selling proposition. Do you have any convictions along those lines?"

It occurred to me that agencies get labels pinned on them and that the labels seemed to grow, like legends, until it reached the point where you were surprised to see an ad from an Ogilvy or a Bates that didn't go with their image. I wondered if my little talk with George Brice that morning was going to leave us with the label and not much underneath it.

To Bob Bohn, Brook Parker said, "Everybody believes in the unique selling proposition. Bates is supposed to trim it down to that, and Doyle Dane takes it and adds something to it. It isn't whether you believe in it. It's knowing what the hell it is."

Bob Bohn, the fatty little ad manager, said, "Well, that's one problem you won't have with us. Brook, we have the USP number one, two, three and four on every product we make. If there's one thing we spend on, it's research."

Brook Parker looked at him for a moment. He lit a new cigarette from the butt of his old one. Then he said, "Maybe that's your trouble."

I caught a quick, startled expression cross George Brice's face. Brook was going to boot it.

Zeke Hall said, "What trouble would that be, Brook?"

"Numbers. Everybody thinks they have the combination to the safe. You get all these questionnaires back and do ads from them and nobody ever got a good idea from a questionnaire yet."

George Brice said, "I think it might help if we distinguish between information and direction. Naturally, we want to know, and have to know, everything you know. What Brook is saying is that sometimes there's a synergistic action that takes place that you'd never get if we stuck to the numbers alone."

For Christ's sake, I thought, there's George dragging out synergistic. The son of a bitch didn't even believe in it, but when you're running an agency that does, that's the banner you pick up and march with.

Zeke Hall said, "Fellows, you're coming in loud and clear. One thing I think we ought to tell you is we're thinking of going into television. We're kind of babes in the woods here, but the way I get it, the cost of making commercials these days is getting a little silly."

George Brice said, "It is if you don't watch it. There are steps that can be taken to keep your costs in line. We have a cost analyst who goes over every spot creative comes up with—as a matter of fact we just shot a commercial in Italy because it was cheaper than doing it here."

Zeke Hall said, "Going to Italy was cheaper?"

George Brice said, "Residuals. There must be thirty recognizable faces in that spot. If we'd shot it in this country, the residuals would have run into a small fortune. And then, we get in estimates from at least three studios before we shoot. Incidentally, one of the areas where your costs get out of hand is where you depart from the story board, as it were. The studio gives you an estimate for exactly what's on the board. When you change your mind on the set, well, it's a little like changing your mind when you're having a house built."

Zeke Hall said, "George, you're a scary man to talk to. Let me ask you something. Isn't it possible to set a production figure and say we don't want any commercials that run more than that?"

Brook Parker said, "I don't know. That's like going to the hospital and asking what kind of an operation you can get for a hundred dollars. You don't do commercials by the pound. You get an idea and see what it costs and take it from there."

Bob Bohn had the soft white look of men I had known to be nice until they got something on you. "But there could be some norm, or cut-off point, we could establish. I have to present a pretty tight budget to management. Commercials that run thirty or forty thousand more than we figured on could put us in quite a bind."

Zeke Hall said, "Fellows, I guess what we're saying is we just don't want to run into some artsy-craftsy character who has to fly a cast of fifty fags down to Rio or he can't do it."

Brook Parker said, "I don't know fifty fags."

There was an edge to Brook's voice and George Brice said smoothly, "Brook, I know you and Jim have a campaign to work on. Unless Zeke and Bob have some other questions, I don't think we have to hold you up here any longer."

Zeke Hall stood up. "Brook, Jim, thanks for your time. Real interesting talking to you, Brook."

Brook Parker said, "Well, I'd rather talk than work anyway. It's easier."

We shook hands all around and when Brook and I were out in the hall, Brook said, "The son of a bitch. Anybody who starts talking about a cast of fifty fags has a problem he isn't even talking about."

I said, "Just the Midwest's view of New York. What did you expect?"

Brook Parker said, "Hobby tools. Do you know what they make? Toys for grownups. I hope we don't get it."

I said, "I don't know. This could be your big chance. Now you can saw a copywriter in half."

It was five o'clock and Brook Parker left. I went back to my office to go over the type proof for a Federal Airlines' ad. It had some bad word breaks in it, one being Fed-eral. I was trying to reword it to fix this when George Brice walked in.

I said, "How do they feel about us?"

George Brice said, "Why, Jim, how would you feel about an agency that told you advertising didn't work any more?"

I lit a cigarette and said, "Well, you have to say one thing. Brook doesn't con anybody."

"Why, no, Jim, Brook doesn't con anybody. He may talk about their daughters screwing their way through college, but you're right, he doesn't con them. I suppose I could ask you what the two of you were doing out guzzling martinis for lunch when you knew we had a new business presentation."

I said, "Guzzling's a little strong for it, George. We had a couple, but then we usually do when we have lunch together. A couple is a couple, incidentally. Two."

George Brice sat down in one of my chairs and said, "Jim,

I don't really see much point in discussing Powell Power at the moment. Let's talk about you."

He was looking at me with what almost seemed to be a fixed stare. It was a little like the look I imagined you might get in a court-martial.

I said, "All right, George."

"Jim, it occurs to me that there are certain things in creative that are not the way they might be."

"Such as what, George?"

"Jim, did you ever see this?"

George Brice took from his pocket a folded photostat of a story board and handed it to me.

I opened it up and looked at it.

On top, it read, "Den-Test Kissing Clinic. 30. A.D. R. d'Franco."

It was Rudy d'Franco's surrealistic dentist's office. He had described it to me but this was the first time that I had seen a board on it. I wondered when he had done this.

In this commercial, a pretty girl was standing in a room full of weird dials and lights and whatnot. A mechanical voice said, "May I help you?"

The girl said, "Is this the kissing clinic?"

"Do you have a problem?"

"No kisses."

"Smile, please."

The girl smiled.

"Thank you," said the mechanical voice. The floor now rose and the girl was brought to the second level. Here a dentist was putting Den-Test on a toothbrush.

The girl said, "Is that all?"

The dentist said, "Beautiful smile, beautiful breath. We call it the Den-Test smile."

The commercial then cut to a boy kissing the girl. The boy said, "How do you feel about spring weddings?"

An announcer said, "Beautiful smile, beautiful breath. The Den-Test smile."

I put the photostat down on my desk. I said, "This is something Rudy wanted to do six months ago. How did you come to get it?"

George Brice said, "Rudy showed it to me this morning, Jim. He wanted to know how I thought it would test."

I said, "I'll bet he did."

"Jim, would you like to know what I told him?"

"What?"

"I told him it would do better in Schwerin than anything we have on the air for Den-Test."

"Well, George, would you like to know what I think?"

"I certainly would, Jim."

I said, "I think you can run that spot for any toothpaste in the world. Brush your teeth with Den-Test and find happiness."

"That's right, Jim. Do you have any idea how many brands are doing very nicely with just that proposition?"

"George, as far as I'm concerned, all you have here is a twenty-five-thousand-dollar set and no idea."

"Jim, don't you mean no Max Gibbs idea? No Brook Parker or Jim Bower idea?" George Brice took out his cigarettes and lit one. "I understand, Jim, that the moment Rudy even suggested this, you had Brook Parker give him a talking to about who was in charge."

I said, "It wasn't exactly that way, but that's close enough."

"Jim, do you know what I think? I think you're trying to fill Max Gibbs' shoes around here."

"George, that's kind of your job, not mine."

"Oh? Why, that's very nice to know, Jim. I was under the impression when we were talking to Powell this afternoon that possibly I wasn't. Telling clients we do not believe in research here is hardly the way I'd run an agency."

Brook Parker had said this, not me. Still, I did not say anything.

George Brice said, "I might add, Jim, that if we had gone to Landum with this kissing clinic—if we had at least tested it against what we have on the air—Landum would be somewhat more inclined to listen to us in the future. I think, Jim, that I will put this plainly, so that we need not have this conversation at regular intervals like a dinner bell. I want things like this kissing clinic, Jim. I want people like d'Franco interested in testing. And, Jim, I do not want these things done grudgingly. I do not want a dog in the manger down here, sending out little vibrations to the rest of the department."

"All right, George."

"Please do not say all right that quickly. I want you to think about this, Jim. I don't want you saying okay, if you do not believe in your heart of hearts that you can work this way."

I just sat there, looking at him looking at me.

Then he simply said, "Good night, Jim," and walked out.

I caught the six-five and sat in the bar car with two paper cups of Scotch and soda. We stopped at 125th Street. Down there was Harlem. Poor whitey worried about his fifty thousand dollars. Whitey, you poor bastard, you.

We went over the black river and into the Bronx past the lofts and warehouses and lumberyards. Here and there, beside the tracks, was a car with no wheels, sitting on its belly like a big dead bug. What if there was a God and you asked Him to help you keep your job and He said, "Why?"

I did not think that this was the time to have a talk with God about things. It was not even the time to have a talk with Melinda.

We got to Westport at about seven-fifteen. What I ought to do, I thought, was drop over to the hospital and see Slim. I walked down to the Triumph and drove to Norwalk.

I found Slim Hawes on the second floor. He was not the same Slim I had seen a few days ago. He looked haunted. Bony face. Eyes staring out of dark sockets. I said, "I'm looking for a party pooper. Are you a party pooper?"

"What kind of party pooper are you looking for? Us party poopers all specialize these days."

I said, "Can I smoke in here?"

"Not with that oxygen dingus over there. There won't be any more Norwalk."

I said, "I'll bet you don't have any booze in here, either."

Slim Hawes said, "I asked Jean to see if I could keep a bottle around for spongers, but she didn't bring it in yet."

I said, "Yes, well, that's the kind of party pooping I expected. How are you?"

"Oh, just fine, Jim. It wasn't all that bad."

I said, "Got any idea how long you're going to be here?"

"Nope. I guess Jean told you this wasn't the first time."

I said, "Yes, and I think I've got it figured out. You put that dam up all wrong and you pulled this to get out of there before it fell down." I pulled over a straight-backed chair and sat down and said, "Why isn't it as hot in here as it is outside?"

Slim Hawes said, "I don't really know, Jim. It sure ought to be."

I said, "With all those flowers you've got there, the least you could do is have a wedding."

Slim Hawes said, "The azaleas are yours. Melinda brought

them over herself. Real pretty, azaleas. They make you think of Easter."

I said, "What have they been doing, giving you a lot of tests and all?"

Slim Hawes said, "Oh sure. 'Now just relax, Mr. Hawes. Just breathe normally.' These doctors have a great way of not telling you anything. You ask them a question and they just laugh and ask you if you want the Latin word for it and then they don't even give you that. Jim, if you want to smoke, there's a little reception room down the hall. . . ."

I said, "I'll wait until I get jittery. You owe me a quarter, incidentally. You guys who get sick when a toll booth comes up."

Slim Hawes sighed and looked out the window. "Funny, the things you think about when you're laid up like this."

I said, "What kind of things?"

"Oh, my daddy, for one thing, Jim. Daddy was quite a fellow. He taught me how to read. We didn't have a car and the school was near fifteen miles away."

"Was that on a ranch, Slim?"

"Yep. We had a little place way off from nowhere. I remember my mother was sick—she never did get well. So nights when he was finished with the cattle and I had my chores done, we'd sit down and go over my lessons. I must have been eight, nine years old before Daddy let me take one of the horses to that school. I remember they tried me out in the third grade and I did all right so they let me stay in it."

"Your dad must have been a good teacher."

"He was good at most things. By the time I was eleven or twelve, I was helping him with the cattle, those that we had. Yep. Daddy showed me how to ride and rope and shoot and he showed me how to read and do some arithmetic. We didn't have any money, but I didn't know it."

"Sounds like a good life for a kid, Slim."

"He died when I was about fifteen and my uncle took me in. He was a little better fixed than Daddy. He saw to it I went to college."

"What sort of fellow is he, Slim?"

"First you take care of your stock because that's your livelihood, then you take care of your house. My Daddy didn't do that, exactly. He borrowed some money from the bank to fix up our house for my mother, and my uncle said that's what he did wrong."

I said, "Slim, I always heard you cowboys have this thing about your horse. Is that just movie stuff?"

Slim Hawes said, "Oh, you find a horse you like and that's the one you favor, I guess. A horse is a means of transportation, Jim. He isn't a buddy."

"And now you're going back to Montana, eh?"

"Jim, just at the moment that's something we don't know."

"Well, Slim, we're playing bridge with the Reynoldses tonight, so if I want any dinner first, I'd better be on my way."

Slim Hawes said, "Real nice of you to look in, Jim."

I drove over the Post Road to Westport. It occurred to me that when they had you in a room in Norwalk Hospital and you just lay there remembering your father and looking at the oxygen apparatus, it did not very much matter what George Brice was thinking.

We got to Tom and Betty Reynolds' house at quarter to nine. Tom Reynolds said, "How do you feel about drinks that are not straight gin?"

"What kind of drinks?" I said.

"Pimm's Cups."

I said, "That's about what I expected from you."

The way Tom saw it, what got Slim was the same thing that got the dinosaur. "Inability to adjust to a changing situation."

I said, "Nope. What got Slim was trusting his fellow man. It's all those nice things they tell you in Sunday school—they kind of don't tell you about the guys waiting to screw you if you believe it."

It was not often that I had drinks with cucumbers in them. It was one of the little ways that Tom showed you he was a superior being. "You do play Stayman?" Tom said.

Melinda said, "He does not. He also does not play the diamond response or the club convention."

Tom and I bid six clubs and made seven. Melinda said, "Grossly underbid."

Tom said, "If I'd known about Jim's diamonds, I might have tried it."

I said, "What do you think I went to six on, an inner voice?"

Melinda said, "Do you know Jack and Peg Thompson?"

Tom said, "Fortunately, no."

Melinda said, "We seem to be going to their house for dinner tomorrow."

Tom said, "Couldn't you just make it cocktails? Cocktails only entitles him to use your name as a reference. Dinner and he'll have you cosigning a note."

Melinda said, "This is Jim's week for befriending the down-trodden."

Tom said, "In moderation, I understand that that is not a bad thing, but do you have to go overboard? Why don't you try the shallow end first? Have dinner with the Slatterys."

On the way home, Melinda said, "I hope you can go down early tomorrow and make sure the boat's gassed up."

"The boat."

"We're taking the Matthewses out."

"Where did that come from?"

"I was talking to Kate on the phone. Since our pool doesn't work, I thought we'd take them out for a ride."

I did not say anything. It occurred to me, not for the first time, that we were seeing a lot of the Matthewses lately. At least, one of us was seeing a lot of one of the Matthewses.

saturday

At nine on Saturday morning, I drove down to the Longshore Club.

It had an eighteen-hole golf course, red clay tennis courts, swimming pool, a strip of sand beach on the river, boat marina, summer cottages and a clubhouse that looked like a mansion.

I parked on the marina's black asphalt lot and walked down the green wooden ramp to the Texaco fuel dock and out the floating dock to the Bertram.

The air had come out of a teakettle. The water did not

look like water. It looked like fog and the boats seemed suspended in it.

I climbed over the stainless steel railing and lifted the hatch over the engines. Two little black 120-horsepower MerCruisers, two Exide batteries. I turned the batteries on and then went into the cabin.

Green V bunks. Stainless steel sink. Fiberglass icebox. Private toilet with mirror, light, sink and vanity. Holiday Inn goes to sea. I took the ignition keys from under one of the bunk cushions and went up and turned on the engines.

I let the engines run and opened the hatch over the gas tank. The gauge said one-quarter full. Twenty gallons. Everything seemed to be okay. I turned off the engines and went home. Melinda was putting things into plastic bags and putting them into a hamper. "Thanks for leaving the water on for the coffee."

I said, "Did I?"

"No. No, as a matter of fact, you didn't." Potato chips, hard-boiled eggs, roast beef sandwiches. You would think we were moving. "Did you wash the boat down?"

"In this heat?"

"Sometimes, Jim, the interest you take in things gives me a little tug."

We picked the Matthewses up in the Lincoln. Barlow, slim and tanned, in gray slacks and a white polo shirt, looked as if he were going to give you a golf lesson. Kate wore white slacks and a white shell and looked like his mother.

Barlow said, "Jim, we'll be back by four, won't we? I have a call coming in from Japan."

"No problem unless we sink." I tried to think of anybody else I knew who would have to get back for a call from Japan. Nobody. Barlow was my only natural resource in this category.

At the marina, I said, "You all go ahead. I'm going to get some ice."

Barlow said, "I'll go with you, Jim."

The ice was sixty cents. I had just paid for it when Ina Cross and Nora Slattery came up. "Hi. We came down to get in eighteen holes before it got too hot, but it got too hot."

I said, "Where are Helmut and Joe?"

Nora said, "Joe's home working on his roses. Did he tell you he's taking me to Ireland?"

I said, "No kidding."

Barlow said, "When are you going, Nora?"

"Next month. We're going to spend two weeks talking to all the Reillys in County Mayo. Reilly is my maiden name, Barlow."

Barlow said, "Nora Reilly. Now, what is that, German?"

"German!" Nora said. "You're all coming to our cookout tomorrow, now."

Barlow said, "We'll be tied up tomorrow, Nora. Didn't Kate tell you?"

"Oh, I was counting on your being there. You'll be there, Jim?"

I said, "Wherever Melinda says I'll be, I'll be. Look, it's over ninety out and these are ice cubes."

Barlow and I walked down the ramp to the dock and Barlow said, "Funny time for Joe to take Nora on a trip."

"Why?"

"Joe's in trouble, Jim."

"What, with his job?"

"They're thinking of letting him go."

"I thought Joe was supposed to be pretty good."

"He doesn't spend his time right. He doesn't call on the right people and he doesn't ask the right questions. I'm afraid Joe still thinks selling is supposed to be selling."

The bag of ice cubes was losing its firm, crunchy feeling. I said, "I don't follow you."

"Well, let's say Mobil wants a storage tank and they ask for bids on stainless for the corrosion. Jim, that's as far as Joe goes."

"What's he supposed to do?"

"Find out what they want it for. How long they're going to use it. Suppose they only want it for six months? Use plain steel plate and let it corrode and you save them the cost of stainless. Joe doesn't ask questions like that, Jim. He thinks it's none of his business."

I said, "How did you find out about it?"

"I'm on their board of directors."

I stopped and looked at him. This was getting to be like knowing a Rockefeller. "What's going to happen to him?"

"There might be a spot for him in Seattle."

We got to the boat and I started the engines. Barlow threw off the lines and we headed out the little channel.

Kate said, "I love your boat."

"It's Melinda's boat. Only the payments are mine."

"You're funny."

"I don't feel funny. Barlow just told me about Joe Slattery."

The channel was littered with tiny catamarans, Lightnings, Blue Jays and Comets. Most of their sails were limp. A little red Donzi shot by us like a stone skipping across the water.

We got all the way out to the black can buoy in the sound when white smoke came up from the engine hatch. I looked at the temperature needles. "Christ." The right one was over as far as it could go.

I stopped the engines. Barlow opened the hatch and Barlow found the trouble. "Jim, do you have any pliers?"

Melinda said, "You do know what pliers are, darling?"

I got the pliers from the cabin and said, "What is it?"

"Water hose came loose. I can put it back on but you'd better not use this engine for a while. You'll crack the block."

So Barlow fixed it and we chugged around the Norwalk islands at about nine miles an hour on the engine that was left and Barlow and Melinda sat up on the bow and when we came back I hit the side of a fiberglass sloop that we shared our slip with.

Melinda said, "Beautiful. Just beautiful."

We drove over to the Thompsons' at five. By now, although the air still felt like laundry fresh from a hot washing machine, the sky had begun to look a little dark and there was just enough of a breeze to tug at the tips of the leaves.

The Thompsons lived off Bayberry, a long, twisting, hilly and densely wooded road. Berrybush was the name of Jack Thompson's road, and when we got to it we found that it was just long enough to serve two houses. Jack's was the farther in, a colonial set on the side of a steep wooded hill as if it had slid down from the top and got hung up on a rock.

"Is that wash hanging out?" Melinda said.

"That's what it is."

"Don't they even have a dryer?"

"I wouldn't know," I said. The road was not paved but covered with gravel, and in case we might have a few too many, I turned around so that the car was heading out.

"Well," Melinda said, "they have a bicycle."

Next to the garage, a red and white bike was leaning against one of those kick-down stands. Something about it seemed peculiar and then I realized that it had no seat.

We got out of the car and walked along some slates laid in the grass in front of the house. The grass had a weedy look and seemed to grow in patches, and was probably the token seeding that the builder had put in several years before. Rhododendron huddled along the front of the house, and a red plastic toy automobile went crunch under my feet in the grass between the slates.

The front steps were concrete and the bottom one was twice as high as the others, probably because the earth had washed away at its base or because some more earth should have been brought in. Melinda had, by bending forward to keep her balance, just got up onto this step when the door opened above us and there stood Jack Thompson in lime-colored slacks and polo shirt. Weight lifting had given him quite a chest, shoulders and arms, and the Jolly Green Giant crossed my mind.

"Welcome to our home and hearth," he said.

I said, "If your hearth's turned on, we're going home."

"Too late now. I have machine guns trained on the road."

We got up to the door and he stood aside as we went into a cool narrow center hall, where we had to step carefully over a pile of what seemed to be undershirts. Jack said, "I'm going to kill that kid. That stuff was supposed to be taken upstairs. And on your right, ladies and gentlemen, can be seen the famous Thompson breakfast room, beyond which, at this moment, Mrs. Thompson is waiting on deck with libations."

The breakfast room was tidy, just possibly because there was no room for it not to be. A maple table with fold-down sides and four straight maple chairs barely left you room to get around to the door leading outside.

The deck Peg Thompson was waiting on was outdoors and ran from the front of the house to the rear. In the front it was almost ten feet above the ground, but the hill was so steep that in the rear you could step right off into the grass. A little grass, in fact, seemed to be growing up through the gray-painted deck boards at that end.

"Hello," Peg Thompson said. She was wearing something that wrapped around. It was loose-fitting and seemed cool enough and was a kind of florid Hawaiian print. She had sandals on and, without heels, seemed surprisingly short. I suppose Peg was about forty, but age was not what you thought of when you first saw her. Peg Thompson looked as if she had run full-tilt into a board that had caught her just under her upper lip, so that from the nose up she had kept on going while the bottom of her mouth and her chin had been stopped dead. She had surprisingly pretty brown eyes

and a beautiful complexion, and she wore her brown hair in
a short, mannish cut that was attractive. She said, "We have
already begun to drink. We were going to have daiquiris but
Jack couldn't find the book that tells you how to make them,
so we have gin and tonic or gin and bitter lemon or just gin.
We also have Scotch and bourbon. We had an ice bucket but
they repossessed it, so Jack will have to get you cubes from
the refrigerator, which they have not repossessed because
my father gave it to us. Isn't this weather glorious? Couldn't
you just die?"

Peg Thompson was loaded.

Jack said, "Well, Jim, boy, Melinda; what'll it be?"

Melinda said, "Gin and tonic."

I said, "Same here."

"Two gin and tonics, coming right up. Peg, do you want
to put some records on?"

Peg Thompson said, "I might, and then again I might not."
She held out her glass and said, "Bribe me."

"Two gin and tonics and one bribe coming up. Just talk
among yourselves, folks. I'll only be long enough to make
you miss me."

I said, "Can I help you?"

"No no no, Jim. You're a guest. You sit right down and
take it easy."

Peg Thompson said, "Sit down over here by me, Jim. I
want to hear all about your success in the world of business.
I know you're a success because we only know successful
people. Melinda, you don't mind if your husband sits over
here, do you? I'd sit over there, but it's such a long trip."

"Be my guest," Melinda said.

Peg Thompson was sitting in an upholstered cane chair and
next to it was a folding captain's chair with a blue canvas
back and seat and wooden arms. I went over and sat down
and said, "What do you have here, Peg? A couple of acres?"

"I do not. I am exactly one hundred and ten pounds."

Melinda said, "Your trees are beautiful."

"Trees are trees."

Melinda looked at me with her tongue poking into her
cheek but I simply looked away. For some time, I just looked
out at the yard. Then I realized that I had been looking at a
tire. I wondered how it had got there. It was clear around
the house from the garage. It was not the sort of place you
would leave a tire. But there it was.

"And here we are," Jack Thompson said. "Gin and tonic,

and gin and tonic, and gin and tonic. And now that I've bribed you, dear, how about putting on some records?"

"All right I will." Peg Thompson said this as a solemn pronouncement and got up and marched into the house.

Jack Thompson said, "I hope you people like steaks because steaks are what we're having."

"Sounds delicious," Melinda said.

"Peg will have to broil them in the kitchen. We had a grill but something happened to it." Jack sat down on a wooden bench. His biceps looked like bowling balls. "Jim, do you know what I've been thinking of doing? Starting a club. The Westport New Yorkers. Did you ever stop to think how many advertising men there are who live here that you don't even know?"

I said, "I see advertising men all day, Jack. I don't want to come home and see more."

"The way I see this, it would be a kind of fraternity of guys who have the same things in common. Same business, same home town, same trip on the New Haven—think of all the guys you'll meet."

I said, "I'm afraid I'm not much of a joiner, Jack."

"I thought we'd have meetings once a month, a spring and fall dance, family barbecues on Compo Beach. You'd like it, Jim. You really would."

The "Pilgrims' Chorus" suddenly burst from the house. Turned all the way up on a hi-fi, it came like a bombing. Jack Thompson stared, his neck got red and he went into the house. Over the music I could make out the words, "What the hell is the matter with you?"

The music stopped.

Peg Thompson came back out and sat down in the cane chair and drank a little of her gin and tonic. "What is it gin's supposed to be good for? Scurvy?"

I said, "I think that's what limes are for."

Peg Thompson said, "Oh."

Jack came out and said, "Stylus or something is stuck. Oh, the dip. I'll get it, Peg."

Peg said, "There's music on the radio. I love music. Don't you love music?"

Melinda said, "That's all right."

Peg said, "No. No, it isn't all right. If there's music on the radio, we ought to be listening to it. It's a waste if there's music and nobody's listening to it."

Jack Thompson said, "Did you get batteries for the radio?"

"Trees are trees. Do you know, I hate trees? I hate trees and birds and the oil company. They cut off our oil last year, did you know that? Just like that. No more oil."

Jack Thompson said, "Why don't you go in and take a little nap, honey."

"I can't go in and take a nap because we have guests. When you have guests, you have to be a hostess. I will get the dip. I made the dip and I will get the dip."

Melinda said, "I can get it, Peg."

"No! You sit there and be a guest." Peg got up again and went into the house.

Jack Thompson said, "I'd better go in for a moment. The heat gets Peg, you know?"

I said, "Sure."

He went in the house and Melinda said, "God."

I lit a cigarette and did not say anything. I looked at the tire in the yard and wondered how it had got where it was.

"Take your hands off me."

Silence.

"Let go of me. You son of a bitch, I'll kill you."

More silence.

Melinda drank some of her gin and tonic.

Jack Thompson came out with a big glass bowl. "You may think you've had clam dip before, but you never had a dip like this. Oh. Crackers. How are your drinks? Here, Melinda, let me freshen that up for you. You, too, Jim, boy."

"Thank you, Jack," I said.

He went back into the house.

Melinda said, "Dear Abby."

I said, "Do me a favor and don't be clever."

Melinda smiled and said nothing.

A bird with a blue back came down from a tree and walked around in the grass and flew away again.

Jack Thompson came out. "Here we are. Kids left these crackers open so they may be a little soggy—in fact, why don't I run out to the store and get some fresh ones? Just be a minute."

I said, "Sit down and relax, Jack. You haven't even touched your drink."

"No, sir. Only take me a minute. I'll be back before you're ready for a refill."

I said, "Jack, for Christ's sake."

"No. No arguments, Jim. A man's home is his castle, right?"

He went back through the house and presently we heard a car start up.

Melinda said, "Now why do I have the feeling we've rented this place for two weeks?"

I said, "She must have started drinking yesterday."

"I'll bet she started the day she got married."

After a while, Jack Thompson came back with a bag of potato chips. "Here we go, one and all. And just in time to get you more drinks, right?"

I said, "Jack, will you sit down? I'll get the drinks."

"Not while you're in my house." He was trying to open the cellophane bag of potato chips. "Tough stuff, this stuff." He grinned, as perspiration came out on his face, the cellophane crackling but holding out. He took a breath and tried harder and a vein stood out on his neck. Then he held the bag by its neck and swung it like a blackjack at the railing on the deck. The bag burst in the middle. Pale chips popped out in every direction, some falling on the deck, some going down to the lawn. Jack Thompson's jaw was rigid as he stood there, staring at the broken bag in his hand. I started to pick up some of the chips. He said, "Jim, sit down."

I sat down.

He said, "I'll just get a dish for these and put a little more nectar in those glasses of yours and we'll be all set, right?"

"Take your time," I said.

He took our glasses and went into the house and came out with fresh drinks and a dish filled with potato chips. "There we are. Jim, would you like one of my cigarettes? Here, try one. They're French."

"Thank you," I said. I did not want one of his cigarettes but I took one anyway and he lit it with that Dumont lighter.

Melinda said, "Don't you wish it would rain and break this heat?"

Jack Thompson said, "I'd put some music on the radio but the batteries are dead. I could turn the radio on in the car, though. I should have thought of that before."

I said, "Jack, sit down and have a drink. We couldn't hear the car anyway."

"It's no trouble," he said.

Melinda said, "Why don't we just talk?"

Jack Thompson sat down and said, "Well. Here we all are, eh? One of the things I like about it out here in the country, you get away from that rush rush rush of the city, you know? A man needs a place where he can stand back and think."

"That's right," I said.

"Some nights I just sit out here and look at the trees. I do most of my real thinking right out here, Jim. You look at those trees and think how long they've been here, it gives you a perspective." Jack drank a little of a drink that he had made for himself. "A lot of people think I'm strictly a hustle, get-on-the-ball type, but they don't know about old Jack Thompson's porch. I think about some pretty deep things out here, Jim. The state of the world, God, what it all means. How do you like that dip, eh? Isn't that something?"

Melinda said, "It's very good."

"Oh, say, I'll bet you're getting hungry."

"No hurry," I said. "Relax."

"Now, what we have are steaks for both of you, so sing out if you want them rare, medium or well-done. That'll give you time for another half a drink if you like your meat rare, a full one if you're the well-done type. Melinda, you look like a rare gal, right?"

"Well, medium rare," Melinda said.

"Good enough. Jim?"

"Same thing, I guess."

Melinda said, "Why don't I put them on, Jack? You can sit out here and talk to Jim."

"No! Absolutely not-o. You didn't come here to cook, right? Well, let's see. Medium rare, that's time for a three-quarter drink. Mind like a steel trap. Glasses, ladies and gentlemen?"

We handed our glasses to him and he went inside again. I looked at the tire and Melinda looked at the trees.

"Your drinks," Jack Thompson said, handing us back our glasses.

"Thank you," Melinda said. "Really, Jack, I'd be happy to put those steaks on for you."

"Wouldn't think of it. Out of the question and all that. Well, by the time you're through with those, it'll be chow time. Oh, hello there, Penny. How did the horse go today?"

Melinda and I turned to look at the little girl of about ten, who looked as if she had crawled through a field of dirt to get home. She wore jodhpurs and a blouse and had a hard riding hat in her hand and black riding boots on her feet. She was very thin and had long black hair and an open mouth and staring black eyes. She said, "Mr. Muller wants you to call him."

"I'll call him in the morning, honey. Why don't you go

inside and clean up so I can introduce you to Mr. and Mrs. Bower?"

The little girl said, "Mr. Muller says I can't ride any more until you call him."

"All right, dear. I'll give him a ring in the morning."

"He won't be there in the morning. They're all going to Darien for the show. He wants you to call him tonight."

"Then I'll call him a little later, dear. You run upstairs and take a shower, all right?"

"He said to tell you it's been three months now."

"Get upstairs, dear."

"You'd better call him now, Daddy. I think they're going to the movies tonight."

"Daddy will take care of it, dear. You take care of the shower and Daddy will take care of Mr. Muller. Go on, now."

The little girl stood there with her mouth still open and then went back into the house.

Jack Thompson said, "The steaks await me. Just relax, everybody. This is only the intermission."

He did not do a bad job with the steaks, but he had only broiled steaks for Melinda and me. I said, "Aren't you eating, Jack?"

"I'll have mine later," he said. "Oh, I'll bet you'd like some beer, right? Right."

Once again Jack Thompson was gone.

I said, "Pretty good steak."

Melinda said, "I want to go home."

"After a while, darling."

"I think," Melinda said in a very even voice, "it would be humane to go home now."

"Humane for whom?" I said.

Then we had beer. Jack Thompson said, "Nice here at this time of day. This is my favorite time, just before it gets dark."

I said, "Your daughter rides, eh?"

"Penny? Oh, sure. I'd like to see her in the Garden someday," Jack Thompson said. "To me there's nothing better for a kid than to grow up with horses. We were thinking of buying a bigger place, Ridgefield or someplace, where we could keep horses on our own property. Do you ride, Jim?"

"Only the New Haven, and it keeps trying to throw me off."

Melinda said, "This was really very nice of you, Jack. The steak was delicious."

"Well, you aren't going yet?"

I said, "Have to make this one an early evening, Jack."

"Oh, not this early. Relax and enjoy, Jim, boy." Jack Thompson sat down with a beer. "You know, when you work in the city, you get a pretty distorted view of this country. Everybody with their hand out, everybody in a hurry—it's out here in the woods where you really feel what it's all about. Like this company I work for—oh, the pay's good and there's a stock deal, but sometimes I wonder if it's all worth it. You know what I mean, Jim? Life is something you're supposed to live, right?"

I said, "I know what you mean, Jack."

"Now, me, I like to work with my hands. You know what I think sometimes? I think I'd like to just chuck the big money and be a carpenter. Honest money for honest work, you know? When a man builds something, something you can see and feel, well, that's something. That's what it's supposed to be all about, man's going through life paying his way by what he can do."

I said, "That's a nice way to look at it, Jack."

Melinda did not say anything.

Peg Thompson appeared in the doorway. "Where are the steaks? I can't find the steaks."

Jack said, "Why, I put them on for you, honey. Everybody's pretty well stoked up."

Peg Thompson came out and leaned against the side of the house. "Penny home?"

"Upstairs taking a shower," Jack said.

"Muller say anything?"

"I'm going to call him later, honey. Why don't you sit down? I'll put some coffee on for you."

"I don't want to sit down. I want to go up the hill."

Jack Thompson said, "Wouldn't you like some coffee?"

"Going to go up the hill and tell those snots with the house up there to keep their dog out of our yard."

"That can wait until tomorrow, dear."

Peg Thompson gave a kind of heave with her shoulders and straightened up and started down the deck toward the rear.

Jack Thompson said, "Honey? Where are you going?"

"Going to tell those snots what they can do with their dog."

Jack Thompson gave us a kind of frantic smile. "Sure a hot day, wasn't it? Excuse me. Just relax, one and all. You all take it easy like good guests should."

Peg Thompson had got to the end of the deck and had started up the hill. It was very steep and she fell down but got up again. Jack Thompson went after her, walking swiftly but trying to look as unconcerned as he could. "Honey? Come on down and have some coffee."

Peg Thompson got to a tree and put her arms around it and went down to her knees, hugging the tree.

Melinda said, "That's it."

We both stood up.

Jack Thompson was trying to get his wife to her feet. Peg said, "Take your hands off me. Just take your hands off me."

"Honey, we have guests. Now come on."

"You have guests. I don't have any guests." She said something else but she had started to cry and I could not make it out.

Melinda walked to the rear of the deck. "Jack?"

"Be right with you, Melinda. You ready for another drink? I have some B & B coming up. Come on, Peg. Maybe you'd like a brandy. Would you like a brandy, Peg?"

Melinda said, "The heat's got her, Jack. I think it would be better if we finished this some other time."

Jack Thompson came back down the hill. "Hey, you can't leave yet. I have the coffee on and the brandy just waiting to be opened. Peg will be all right. Sit down and relax. Matter of fact, I'll go in and get the coffee right now."

He started for the door and Melinda said, "I think you should take care of Peg, Jack."

"She's all right. I'll just get the coffee."

I said, "Jack, some other time."

"It's all made. Come on, people. It's still early."

I stood there, looking at his wife partway up the hill, on her knees, holding on to the tree. I said, "Let's have lunch next week. Right now I think the thing to do is get Peg into bed."

"Stay for a brandy, at least."

"Some other time, Jack," I said.

Melinda picked up her purse and her cigarettes and the sunglasses she had worn on the way over. "Thanks again, Jack. The steaks were marvelous."

He stood there, trying to smile, his big chest heaving. "Well, I'm sure glad you could make it. And you're on for next week, Jim."

I said, "Fine. You call me."

"Monday morning, first thing," he said.

He came out to the car with us and Melinda told him again how good the steaks were. He stood there, trying to make conversation, as I turned on the ignition.

He was saying, "Jim, if you like Italian food, I know this sensational place on Third, way up near the Fifties. You never had meat sauce like it; it's a secret recipe."

I said, "Let's look into it. Good night, Jack. Thanks again."

"Sure glad you could make it, people."

I put the car in gear and we left.

Melinda said, "Would you like to talk about social acumen now or in the morning?"

sunday

On Sunday, the Indians staked me out on an anthill.

Melinda said, "Much as I'd like to make our grand entrance together, I have to stop off at Marge Hill's and check our telephone list."

Our grand entrance was supposed to be at Nora Slattery's barbecue. I said, "What telephone list?"

"For the women's club, dear. I'm on the telephone committee."

I said, "Suppose I wait here. This is no day to stand around on somebody's lawn."

Melinda said, "Suppose you don't, dear. Since I don't

intend to stay at Nora's any longer than I have to, you can put in a respectable appearance for the two of us. Just think of all that time you can spend with Harriet Van."

It was now two-thirty. I said, "How long do you plan on taking with this telephone list?"

"Just as long as I can, darling. Marge's house is air conditioned and Nora's lawn isn't."

I got the Triumph out and drove over to North Avenue.

Joe Slattery's house was a yellow split-level that had been built on an acre of open field. You couldn't even stand under the trees. The only trees they had were specimen trees that Joe had put in. They weren't as tall as we were.

In the back yard a table with an umbrella had been set up, and from the crowd gathered around it this had to be where the drinks were.

Nearby stood a long redwood table with two redwood benches. The table was piled with picnic things and off a way stood a black grill.

Tom Reynolds said, "Welcome to the cremation party. We're all going together."

Helmut Cross said, "How about it, Jim? Do you know the steps to the rain dance?"

I said, "Yeah. You walk around as if you're killing ants. Some Indians did it for us for a Federal commercial."

Ina Cross said, "How long before you got the rain?"

I said, "Four years. Who's giving this cookout, Nora or God?"

Joe Slattery said, "Scotch and soda, Jim? After everybody has a couple, I'll tell you about the nudist camp we're starting."

Tom Reynolds said, "I don't believe in nudity for groups larger than three."

Nora said, "Where's Melinda?"

I said, "Checking some kind of telephone list. She'll be along. What we ought to do is sink some big ice buckets in the ground and just stand in them."

Joe Slattery said, "Jim, that's thinking. We connect these buckets with tunnels, right?"

Neil Van said, "If you think this is something, wait until I get you in hell."

I said, "You've already got me in hell." Everybody seemed to be either pulling their collars away from their necks or their shirts away from their stomachs.

Betty Reynolds said, "Why can't we go skinny dipping? So we do without the water."

Nora Slattery said, "Not in my yard, you don't."

Joe said, "That's right, Betty. Come into the house."

Tom Reynolds said, "Helmut, doesn't your company make any chemicals for this?"

Helmut said, "We specialize in dyes, Tom. I can give you a purple day but I can't make it cool."

I said, "Joe, how's it going?"

Joe Slattery said, "Jim, they've got this kid over me, one of those Harvard Business School types, you know?"

"Well, that seems to be the thing these days."

"I just wish I knew what to do. Kid's never been on the road. He doesn't know selling from the hind end of a horse. I don't want to go over his head, but he's screwing up the works, you know?"

Joe Slattery. Hawaiian sports shirt, red slacks, big chest, big middle. The U.S. Marine in his fifties, about to get canned.

I said, "Well, Joe, if that's the guy they put there, that's the guy they want there. What you do is roll with the punches and play ball."

And there was Harriet Van. "Don't you want to go skinny dipping?"

She was practically skinny dipping already. If her shorts were any shorter, they'd arrest you for sending her through the mails. I said, "Not on the lawn."

"Do you like my shorts?"

I said, "Sure."

"They're so tight I didn't put anything on under them. The seam feels funny."

Right out here in broad daylight. What could you say? I said, "Lucky seam."

"It moves around when I walk, if you know what I mean."

"Then maybe you'd better not walk around."

"But I like the feeling." She went on smiling and sort of staring at me.

I said, "Well, Harriet, just think what jogging would do."

I walked over to Tom Reynolds. "Okay, tell me all about the oil depletion allowance."

Tom Reynolds said, "Jim, I think that you, Harriet and I should get into an ice bucket."

I said, "What the hell do I want to get into a bucket with you for?"

"There isn't even room in those shorts for pubic hair."

I said, "You don't want to talk about the oil depletion allowance."

Nora Slattery came over and said, "Has anyone seen Slim?"

I said, "I saw him Friday night. I think Melinda dropped in on him, too."

Helmut Cross said, "I saw him this morning after church."

I said, "How is he?"

Helmut said, "I wouldn't take any children over to see him."

Ina Cross said, "Well, I haven't been to see him. The Slim Hawes I want to remember isn't lying in some hospital bed."

Joe Slattery said, "He isn't dead yet, Ina."

Ina Cross said, "I don't want people to get old and sick. I don't want to look at people like that."

No one said anything. At the silence, Ina suddenly looked wounded.

Helmut Cross said, "Nobody else does, either, Ina. You're just honest about it."

Betty Reynolds said, "Tom says visiting the sick is just showing off to them how well you are."

Nora said, "We went over, Joe and I. The flowers are beautiful. Everybody sent flowers. It was like a wedding."

Neil Van said, "It does not lift the spirits to realize you have to get married or die to get flowers."

Ina Cross could not leave it alone. She said, "All I know is I'm not going near that hospital. I'm forty-three years old and the big tits aren't where they used to be and I don't want any previews of what happens next."

Nora Slattery was just standing there, twisting her hands. This was a party. Everybody was supposed to be happy. "Joe, you aren't even watching the drinks."

I went over to the Styrofoam ice chest and took out some cubes and made Ina a drink.

Neil Van said, "I wonder what happened to the brimstone. I told them I wanted it here by three."

I ignored him and brought the drink over to Ina. "I leaned a little on the Scotch. We're expecting a mass attack of tsetse flies."

"Thanks, lover. I talk too much, don't I?"

"Don't worry about it, Ina. You just said what everybody else is thinking anyway."

Joe Slattery came over. "Hey, old buddy, how'd you like to be an old buddy?"

"What's up?"

"Too many Scotch and sodas and not enough gin and tonics. You don't have any extra soda home, do you?"

"Sure."

"That's good. You're the last car in the driveway. Thanks, Jim."

I put my drink on the table and walked around the house, looking at the ramblers on Joe's split rail fence. You had to be a rose to take this weather.

I backed the Triumph out onto North Avenue, drove up to Cross Highway and turned down to Post Hole Road. Our house was set back from the road about one hundred yards, and I went up the driveway and stopped in the turnaround.

I did not get out of the car. I just sat there.

In Melinda's side of the garage was Melinda's white Lincoln.

In my side was a white Ford LTD.

I did not know how many white LTDs there were in the world. All I knew was that Barlow Matthews had one.

I got the soda at the Country Store just before it closed, and went back to the party. Well, there it was. Melinda had a boyfriend.

Joe Slattery said, "Jim, thanks a million. Just for that, you get the pick of the girls."

I said, "We'll discuss girls later. I think what I'd like now is a drink."

monday

On Monday morning, my secretary, Edna, had a little announcement. "Mr. Breeze is here."

I said, "Who is Mr. Breeze?"

"Thirty years in the trenches."

"Oh." It was the guy looking for a job. I wondered if he
had put in for his unemployment and whether he had put
down "vice-president" under Occupation.

I wondered who his wife was sleeping with.

I said to Edna, "Get some coffee for both of us, will you?"

"That will make him feel wanted."

"Boys never make passes at girls with smart asses."

I could not imagine Melinda in bed with Barlow. There was something too self-contained about her. It would muss her hair.

No, that was just the Melinda that I knew. There was another one that I did not seem to know at all.

Melinda and the White Knight.

Presently a slight, gray, neat, exotic-smelling man walked in with a black leather portfolio.

He looked as if he were about fifty-five. His face had a dark healthy tan but his hands were white. His hair was slicked back and was black and thin except at the edges, where it was white. He had a pinched look, as if his mother had just given his mouth and chin an angry little squeeze. His eyes were a pale, watery blue. His shirt collar was just a little too large—you could have stuck two fingers in the gap. He was dressed like a man on his way to church.

"Mr. Bower?"

I was startled at the heartiness of his voice. It came out like a boom. Well, what the hell, he was looking for a job. You're supposed to look confident.

I said, "Mr. Breeze? Sit down. The coffee's on its way."

"Thank you." He sat down and crossed his legs and leaned back in the chair like one businessman talking to another. "Been following your Federal campaign, Mr. Bower. Damned good ads. Had one up on my wall to show some of the kids in our place what good copy was all about."

I said, "Do you have a copy of your résumé with you? My secretary filed the one you sent us."

"Certainly do. Toughest piece of copy there is to write, a résumé."

He had opened his portfolio with his white hands and took out a sheet of bond paper. It quivered a little in his hand as he passed it across the desk to me. "I tried to follow the same rules I use in copy there, Mr. Bower. Cut it to the bone, let the facts speak for themselves."

I looked at it. Albert Breeze, Dartmouth, World War II major, hard goods, soft goods, packaged goods and automotive.

He had started at Thompson in 1938. Young & Rubicam in 1940. Young & Rubicam again after the war. Mehean-Root as copy chief, 1949. Jensen, Todd & Harper, copy supervisor (a step down?), 1953. James Nicely as a special copy supervisor in 1961.

I said, "What's a special copy supervisor?"

Albert Breeze recrossed his legs. He wore black shoes that looked as if they had just been shined and black silk socks. "That was an idea Nicely had. Our accounts were getting good work on print and TV and lousy work on collateral. You know, booklets and brochures?"

I nodded.

Albert Breeze took out a pack of Camels. "Oh, do you mind?"

"Go ahead."

He lit up. "Well, Nicely figured that that's where you start losing an account, not on the big stuff but on the sales promotion. Some assistant ad manager figures he's getting the short end of the stick and there's a little voice in the client's ear. That's what Nicely asked me to take over. He figured a consumer copy chief on sales pro would give us a leg up where most agencies are weak."

"Good idea," I said. "Is that what you had in mind here?"

Albert Breeze recrossed his legs again. The crease in his gray trousers was as sharp as a knife. "No, Mr. Bower, it isn't. I'm a packaged goods man, print and TV. That's what I'd like to get back to."

I said, "Well, let's take a look."

Albert Breeze put his cigarette carefully in the ashtray and lifted the portfolio from his lap and set it on my desk.

The first ad was for a 1947 Heuger. The Heuger had gone out of business in 1950. There was a red convertible flying through the sky at night.

Paradise with the top down.

Albert Breeze lit another cigarette. The first one was still burning in my ashtray. "Incidentally, that's not the headline I wanted to use. The original headline was *Take off in a Heuger*. We had a real knock-down drag-out battle about that one."

I began to read the copy.

"You have to remember, that was written over twenty years ago. I wouldn't okay a piece of copy like that today if you held a gun to my head."

The thrill ride was Heuger. You knew it the instant you turned on the zesty Heuger V-8.

Albert Breeze said, "Funny thing about that ad. That wasn't the way I wanted to write it at all. You wouldn't believe it, but the first piece I wrote read just like a Volks-

wagen ad. But that was twenty years ago and they thought
I was crazy."

The next ad had a refrigerator with a bow tied around it.

There's more Christmas in an Elco.

Albert Breeze gave what I think was supposed to be the
comfortable chuckle of an old pro. "Did they ever fritz that
one up. What happened was, we were up against Westing-
house and their frost-free and the client wanted something
competitive. 'More' makes it competitive." A little more
chuckle. "The client mind at work, eh?"

The Elco, I learned, had nineteen cubic feet of kisses from
Santa Claus and would keep your holidays freezer fresh.

Albert Breeze settled back comfortably in his chair. "Headline I wanted for that was *A Little North Pole from Santa
Claus*. But they had a new sales manager in and the old man
said we had to tread water until we could read him."

Edna came in with the coffee. "They're both regular. If
you'd rather black, the coffee wagon is still here."

"No, no, no," Albert Breeze said. "This is fine. Thank
you."

I turned to the next ad.

For Disten air conditioning, Albert Breeze had a family
sitting on a big ice cube.

Will your family melt this summer?

The copy told me that I could keep spring breezes in my
home all summer long with Disten air conditioning. My home
would be cooled, ventilated, dehumidified and free of pollen.
I would be surprised at the low cost.

I looked at this and thought of our Mountainaire ad.

For 9 months a year, you'll wonder why you spent the money.

This was what George Brice would have called positive.

Albert Breeze said, "What I wanted to do was a campaign
on surgically conditioned air, but you know how engineers
are. You can't say anything in an air conditioning ad. They
keep saying it depends on the climate, the insulation, window
exposure—God, the engineers, eh?"

I said, "Yeah, they're out to kill us all."

I began to wonder whether I was supposed to go on work-

ing with Brook Parker on Den-Test or not. George Brice
had told me to think things over. What was I supposed to do?
Tell him I'd thought things over?

As I went through the rest of Albert Breeze's book, he lit
another cigarette and said, "Look, I know how it is, Mr.
Bower. I'm not the sort who says I'm a copy chief or nothing.
I mean, if you even wanted to put me on doing trade ads
until something turned up, well, I'd understand that and I'd
certainly consider it."

He now had two cigarettes burning in my ashtray and one
in his hand.

I said, "I wouldn't hire you for that."

I did not know what else to say. The best of Albert Breeze
was ordinary. Still, I was looking at his golden days. Why
knock them?

I took out some of his brochures and began to look at them.

> Economy, dependability, long life—
> get all three with Allied Air
> Conditioning Copper-Finned Coils.

The brochures were complete, professional and dull. But
they had the specifications for finned coils. hermetically
sealed compressors, paper dryer rolls and what-have-you and
that was what sales brochures were supposed to have.

"It kills me sometimes," Albert Breeze said, "the ads I
could have done if I'd been in a place like this. But they put
you in the trenches and give you the orders, eh?"

I found myself wondering whether George Brice had been
talking to anyone about my job. George had come from a
packaged-goods outfit. The city must be full of writers who
did just what George wanted. I wondered if he had their
names and addresses up there in that drawer with his miniature pistol and miniature grandfather clock.

I said, "Look, Mr. Breeze, I don't have an opening here
even for trade. And if I did, it would only be twelve or
fourteen, tops. What I can do, if you like, is have copies of
your résumé sent over to some of our clients. I can send a
little note along saying I've seen your work, if you'd be
interested in the client side of things."

Albert Breeze sighed and seemed to be giving this some
deep thought. "Well, Mr. Bower, that wasn't exactly what
I had in mind, but what the devil, I'm basically a doer,

not a talker—if you have some clients who need a little help, why, I'd certainly consider a thing like that."

I stood up. "I'll get some letters off this morning. Mr. Breeze, it's been very nice talking to you. That's quite a book you have there."

"Thirty years." A little of the heartiness seemed to have slipped now, but he took a deep breath and gave me a smile. "Mr. Bower, thank you very much. Nice to talk to an old pro now and then, what with all the kids they have running things these days. Appreciate it."

He gave me a hearty handshake, remembered to put out the cigarettes and then knelt down to pick up one of the brochures that had fallen out of his portfolio when he picked it up without zipping it closed first.

I said, "The elevator's just down the hall, just turn left at the end."

"I'll find it. Thanks again for your time, Mr. Bower."

"Sure thing," I said.

I sat down. For a few moments, I just smoked and drank some of my coffee.

Then I put a piece of paper in my typewriter and wrote:

Dear—
This is a résumé for a guy called Breeze. I've been over his work and if you're in the market for somebody who knows how to dig out facts and knows what to do with them, you might want to talk to him.

I took this out to Edna and said, "Did they teach you to type at the snotty college you went to?"

"To type, to spell and not to use words like snotty."

"Fine. Dig up the names of the ad managers on our client list and send this out to all of them. Get this guy's résumé Xeroxed."

Edna said, "You want to call him a 'guy' in your letter?"

I said, "That's what I wrote. What do you deduce from that?"

I went into Brook Parker's office.

Brook was on the phone. He said, "I don't believe that." Then he said, "I don't believe that, either."

Then he looked surprised and said, "He hung up."

"Who was it?"

"Garage I brought my car to. Do you know what they're asking for parts for a 1930 Cadillac?"

"I didn't even know you still had that thing."

It was a kind of convertible limousine, pin seal leather, wheel wells in the fenders. It was about one inch shorter than a hearse.

"Of course I still have it. It's the only honest car in the world. I bought some Den-Test last night."

"Did you use it?"

"Yes. It stings."

I said, "Oil of wintergreen. Can we do anything with that? *You can feel the difference. . . .*"

"Jim, do you mind? Let's don't get the answer so fast." Brook lit a cigarette and said, "What time is it?"

"Quarter to eleven."

"I have the screening room for eleven. They're running kines of what's on the air these days."

"Fluorides and whiteners are what's on the air." I picked up a lined yellow pad and wrote,

The Stinger.

I showed it to Brook. He shrugged. "Fine, if it came in a jet black tube."

"Yes, but it doesn't come in a jet black tube. Why can't we call it the Stinger anyway?"

"It doesn't go with the tube they have. With the tube they have, they ought to call it Mother's."

Charles (not Chuck or Charley) Leader came in. He reminded me of something but I was not sure what. "Brook Parker?"

Brook said, "Yes?"

"Charles Leader. Account man on Miniflex."

I knew what it was. He reminded me of a bee. Short, busy and buzzing around.

Brook Parker just looked at him. "So?"

"Bower here and I disagree on how copy should be written."

"I'm sure you do," Brook Parker said.

Charles Leader handed him the ad that he had written in pencil. "You'll see the copy that was turned in to me and the way I want it changed."

Brook Parker said, "What do you think Bower and I were doing when you came in?"

"I wouldn't know."

"Of course you wouldn't. You're an account man and we were working."

"I came in here to have an intelligent discussion with you about a piece of copy."

"I don't discuss copy with account men. I also don't discuss copy with my doorman or my cat."

"You'd rather I went to George Brice with this?"

Brook Parker shrugged and looked at the copy. "This dumb stuff written in pencil—that's what you wrote?"

"That dumb stuff happens to be consumer oriented."

"Who hired you?"

"George Brice."

"I'll have to talk to him."

"You think Percy Holland's copy is all right?"

"Percy Holland is one of the best writers in the business. You're one of the worst. What else do you want to discuss?"

"Well, we seem to have different philosophies."

Brook Parker said, "Come on, Jim. The screening room's ready."

Brook put on his jacket and walked out. I put out my cigarette and started to follow him. Charles Leader said, "He's difficult to talk to."

I said, "You wanted to talk to him."

We had two screening rooms. One was on this floor and was primitive. The other was in our TV complex and looked like a theater. In the TV complex you could run sixteen millimeter or thirty-five millimeter and you could also run tape. On our own floor, we could just run sixteen millimeter. The kines would have been transferred to film.

Mel King, our TV producer for Den-Test, said with a sour look, "Rudy d'Franco wants to be here. How about it?"

I said, "What for?"

Mel said, "I think he thinks we're going to talk about him."

Bob Coleman said, "I don't think we need d'Franco. We're just looking over the kines on the toothpaste business."

Brook Parker said, "Tell d'Franco to come in."

Bob Coleman sighed and said nothing. Mel King gave me a look and went over to the phone and dialed d'Franco's extension.

By now we were all sitting in the little plastic chairs in various stages of discomfort.

Bob Coleman said, "What you're going to see are the commercials that represent the biggest share of market in the industry. And I might add that they're right in line with that list we were talking about."

Brook Parker said, "Crest cuts cavities because it has stannous fluoride and Den-Test cuts cavities because we say so."

"Brushing your teeth helps cut cavities, Brook. I don't see anything wrong with telling people that Den-Test does it."

Mel King said, "Do we start or wait for d'Franco?"

Bob Coleman said, "Let's start. I have a lunch date with Landum."

Brook Parker said, "Wait for d'Franco."

Coleman said nothing.

The door opened and Rudy d'Franco came in. "Well, do we have the big campaign yet?"

Brook Parker said, "Roll it."

The lights went down. We saw commercials for Crest, Vote, Macleans, and Landum.

In the dark, Rudy said, "What bad cuts. Whoever cut that one ought to be shot."

Then we watched Den-Test, Colgate and Close-up.

The lights came up. Brook Parker said, "Well, that was a waste of time."

Rudy d'Franco said, "If you didn't like the commercials, why didn't you call me?"

He was talking to Coleman. Coleman said, "We didn't say we didn't like them, Rudy. They just didn't sell toothpaste."

"And I'm off the account and Bower isn't."

Brook Parker said, "Do you want to stay on the account? I don't want it."

Bob Coleman said, "I've already told Landum you're on it, Brook."

Rudy d'Franco said, "Okay. I get the message." He started for the door.

Coleman said, "There isn't any message, Rudy. We're in trouble. When you're in trouble you bring in the names they know."

Rudy said, "Sure." He walked out.

This was followed by silence. Then Mel King said, "Do you want to see them again?"

"No," Brook Parker said.

Bob Coleman said, "The brand manager from Landum will be in this afternoon. Do you want to talk to him?"

Brook Parker shrugged. "Why not? Maybe he knows something we don't know."

Bob Coleman said, "Three o'clock in my office?"

"All right."

Mel King said to me, "Rudy's been running off at the mouth about you."

"Running off at the mouth how?" I said.

"How as soon as the account started bitching, you told everybody it was his fault."

I said, "I didn't tell anybody anything."

Mel King said, "The idea is that you're over the hill and you're afraid to let anybody look good. I hear he even went to George Brice about it."

I said, "Well, Mel, it's a free country, right?"

Bob Coleman said, "What's the matter?"

I said, "Nothing. D'Franco's been in talking to George, that's all."

Bob Coleman said, "I can look in on George, if you like, Jim."

I said, "What is this, save Jim Bower week? Screw it. Screw the whole goddamned business."

Bob Coleman looked as if he did not know what to say. Then he said, "Well, Landum will be in about three."

Brook Parker and I walked back to his office. "What was that all about?" Brook said.

"D'Franco thinks I sold him down the river. I guess he's going around bending ears about it."

"Rudy d'Franco has bad manners."

I looked at Brook. I laughed in spite of everything.

Brook Parker said, "What's the matter?"

"Nothing."

Brook Parker's secretary had taken a telephone message for me. Jack Thompson had called. He would meet me for lunch at the Leaning Tower, on Third between Forty-eighth and Forty-ninth.

"That," I said, "is just what I need today. Jack Thompson."

"May I come in?"

It was George Brice.

Brook Parker said, "Hi."

George Brice said, "Brook, you ought to have a sofa put in here. Why don't you pick out something you like and tell office services to order it."

Brook Parker said, "Yeah, well, you put in a sofa and people sit on it. I mean, they don't go away."

I did not say anything to George. George did not say anything to me.

He said, "As a matter of fact, what you ought to do is have that wall knocked out. I'd put in a bar, if it was my place, Brook. I think the agency can afford that."

Brook Parker said, "I know what you're trying to do. You're trying to get me to work nights."

George Brice laughed. "Brook, your hours are your own and your assignments are your own. You know that."

"Then what am I doing on Den-Test? The world needs Den-Test like it needs acne."

"You don't have to work on Den-Test, Brook. Say the word and I'll put somebody else on it."

"Well, I told Coleman I would."

"Are you getting anywhere?"

"I don't know. Jim? Are we getting anywhere?"

I said, "Not yet."

"Fellows, if you go by the book, and that's what I happen to do, Den-Test is due to be taken off the market."

Brook Parker said, "Then what did they give it to us for?"

"A brand manager gave it to us, Brook. That's how companies like Landum operate. They'll turn a terminal case like Den-Test over to one of the young Turks to see what he does with it. First he'll try a place like this and see if we can make a hero out of him. If we can't, he'd better have sense enough to drop the line."

Brook Parker said, "That's nice. No matter what we do, it's a flop?"

"Of course not. There are no absolutes, just probabilities. But then probabilities are one of the things we deal in. I turned down the Crash account this morning, Brook, just because of the probabilities."

Brook Parker said, "What, the detergent?"

You could not turn on a TV set without seeing a Crash commercial.

George Brice did not look at me at all. "Brook, at the moment, it's worth just about five million dollars. But it's seven years old and that's where the probabilities come in. That's what the marketing manager wanted to talk to me about. What to do with his P & A."

Brook Parker said, "P & A . . ."

"Profit and advertising. At the end of the year you divide the money you've made into two piles, as it were. He wanted a little advice and I had to tell him to keep the money."

If George was not going to talk to me, I was not going to talk to him. What the hell.

Brook Parker said, "So what's seven years got to do with it?"

"Life cycle for detergents. That's one of the things a packaged-goods agency is supposed to know. And just at the moment, it's more important to me to establish us as a packaged-goods agency than to pick up five million dollars we wouldn't have more than a year anyway."

George Brice turned back to the door and then looked back again.

"Brook? Call office services any time you're ready."

When he was gone, Brook Parker said, "What was all that about?"

I said, "That was today's sermon. You got a brand-new office just for listening." I called my secretary and told her to phone the printing outfit that Jack Thompson worked for and tell him I couldn't make lunch.

Brook Parker said, "Do you know what George is? He's an actuary, like in insurance companies."

"George is the head actuary," I said.

"You know what it is? It's like he found God and he's letting us in on it."

"It's worse than that. If we don't believe it, we go to hell."

Brook Parker's phone rang. It was my secretary. She couldn't reach Jack Thompson. He had left for lunch.

I said a dirty word.

Brook Parker said, "Where are you going?"

"If I'm lucky, I'm going to eat and run."

It was dark in the Leaning Tower. I went to the bar and asked for a dry martini on the rocks.

What do you do when you find your wife with somebody else? I was not even sure how I felt about it. Obviously, it had not driven me berserk. I had not done them in with a butcher knife. I had gone back to the party.

I was not even sure that *sad* was the word for it. I felt strange. What had happened yesterday might just stand my life on its head.

And yet I found myself wondering whether yesterday had any real significance at all. For all I knew, it had been happening right along. Yesterday had just been when I found out about it. So far, the only thing that had changed was that I knew.

"Jim, boy."

"Hello, Jack."

Jack Thompson said, "I wasn't sure you'd make it. Oh, Eddie? Put that on my tab."

I said, "I have to make this one a quickie, Jack. We're up to here in a campaign."

"Got to eat, boy. Hey, is that drink all right? If it isn't dry enough, we'll get you another one."

God in heaven, I thought. "It's fine. Listen, this is Dutch, Jack. Two tabs, okay?"

Jack Thompson punched me on the arm. "You son of a gun. I told Peg you guys weren't phonies. We were talking about you yesterday, Jim. I don't know whether you know it or not, but there aren't many people Peg likes."

I said, "I really mean it, Jack. This is one day when I don't have any time at all."

Jack Thompson said, "Eddie? Send another round over to our table and don't listen to anything this man says about the tab."

"Jack, let's just make it this one drink."

"Order's already in, Jim, boy." He had already started through the dining room.

The Leaning Tower had just enough tables so that there was no way to get to any of them without bumping into people who were already sitting down. Ours was the size of a bridge table with the corners rounded off. I sat down and somebody said, "Would you mind taking another chair? You're backed right up against me."

I took another chair and backed up against somebody else. I had brought my drink and now I drank some of it and found myself looking at a girl with a mile of black hair. She was just sitting there by herself, peering at what seemed like a Tom Collins. She looked as if she was about twenty-two and she did not seem to believe in bras.

Jack Thompson said something to the waiter, but I did not hear it. She wore a tan stretch-knit top. You could not have seen more of her breasts if she took it off. You could even see her nipples, sticking out like little exclamation marks. She glanced up, saw me watching her, looked down, glanced up again and then looked down again.

Jack Thompson said, "Do you know what I was saying to Peg, Jim? You're a listener. You knew what I was talking about. Most people don't listen, but you do. There aren't many people like that, Jim, boy."

She turned in her chair to look back at the door and her

breasts bumped into each other. It was something to see, but she caught me at it.

She looked down immediately.

I said, "Well, it was an interesting talk we had, Jack."

"Jim, remember what I was talking about? A commuters' club? What if we met once a month at Mario's, down by the station?"

"A lot of commuters meet at Mario's now."

"But this would be a formal thing, a kind of alumni association."

"I thought alumni was after you graduated."

She was turning her glass around and around, as if it gave her something to look at. The bones of her face were something. She looked like an artist's sketch of somebody just out of a snooty college. Smallish mouth, lips a little parted, eyes as dark as black piano keys.

The waiter put another martini in front of me. Jack Thompson said, "What we need is a catalyst. Somebody who'll pull people in."

"Why don't you ask Mario?"

She lifted her eyes again and for a moment she looked right at me, and then back to that glass, turning it around and around. Her arms were slim and her throat was slim. Except for that small crowd in her sweater, everything about her was slim. You wanted to put her in your pocket.

Jack Thompson said, "I was thinking of Barlow Matthews."

Barlow Matthews? What was this? I said, "I don't think Barlow's much of a joiner, Jack."

"Well, what I had in mind was, I'd do all the work. There wouldn't be a thing for Barlow to do but be a kind of chairman of the board. Jim, he'd love it. I met him once."

"I don't think he'd be interested, Jack."

"Sure he would. Jim, the way I see this, we're all like ships that pass in the night. We all go through the same thing, the grind in the city, the grind on the New Haven, and we don't even know each other. That's what this would be."

She did not have a wedding ring.

I said, "Jack, that's just a club to remind us what a pain in the ass all this is. Who wants to get together to celebrate a thing like that?"

"Jim, what we're celebrating is getting to know each other. It's just like a lot of marines in the same outfit. They go through hell and don't even know each other."

Marines didn't get fifty thousand a year. What marines

did was get their heads shot off. "Jack, I just don't think it's anything anybody wants."

She glanced at me again. Her hair curved around her face and streamed down past her throat, as black as two o'clock in the morning, the ends curling out next to her breasts. Then she went back to turning her glass around and looking at it.

Jack Thompson said, "Another round here, Tony. Jim, that, old buddy, is where you're wrong. This is the age of belonging. Everybody wants to belong. We're all out in the cold and it's getting dark."

I lit a cigarette just to stop looking at her. Stare at a girl long enough and she'll think you're a nut. "Now, let me get this straight. Barlow Matthews is out in the cold and it's getting dark?"

"Not Barlow, but Barlow has instinct, Jim. He knows that that's how it is with people and that's what Barlow understands. It's empathy, Jim. Barlow would back a club like this because people need it."

A commuters' club. Christ, that was what the bar car was. "Well, you can always call him and put it to him, Jack. I don't think he'd touch it with a ten-foot pole, but it's a free country. You can always try, right?"

I looked over again. She glanced away quickly. What the hell do you know; this time she had been looking at me.

"Jim, I only met him once. You know how people are. Somebody they don't know calls up on the phone and they're afraid they're getting into something. What I was thinking was that maybe you could arrange lunch or something. I'd pay for it. You and Barlow would be my guests. Just so it wouldn't be as if he were talking to a total stranger."

"Jack, I'd rather not."

"It would just be lunch, Jim. You have to have lunch anyway. Barlow and I are both friends of yours. What's wrong with having lunch with a couple of friends?"

"Jack, it comes under the heading of presuming on a friendship." What was I doing here, anyway? Two martinis and you thought you had something going with some secretary who'd have you arrested if you said hello. There wasn't anything going but Jack Thompson's mouth. "Look, I've got to get out of here. I've got a campaign I'm nowhere on and the client's coming in this afternoon."

Jack Thompson said, "Tony? My friend's in a hurry. One more here and we want to put our order in at the same time. We'll get you back for your meeting, Jim."

I heard all this without really hearing it at all. She was looking at me now. Not glancing. Looking. And as I sat there looking back at her, she lifted her hand to her cheek and ran her fingers down along her hair until she caught the end of it between her thumb and forefinger. Her hand swung in and out absently, like a pendulum, brushing against her breast. She went on doing this and looking at me.

"Do you know why I like this place, Jim?"

"You said you liked the sauce they had."

"Their sauce has to be good to get these people in. That's what I like here. They run this place for the guys who are making it. That's the thing about New York. Anyplace else in the world, you can get by. In New York, you have to be good."

The son of a bitch couldn't even pay his kid's stable bill. "That's right, Jack."

"Do you want to know something, Jim? I have a feeling I know you very well. Isn't that funny? I'll bet I can tell you just what you're like."

"What am I like, Jack?"

I had never seen eyes that black before. Now she began to wind the end of her hair around her finger. It was so casual you would never notice what she was doing. She was looking at me and slowly pushing her nipple back and forth. And then, for about two seconds, she just held it between her thumb and her finger. And then she quit and just went on looking at me.

"You're an observer, Jim. You see what's wrong with the world, everybody making a mess out of things, everybody afraid to communicate or identify—you see it all and you shrug it off. You're just passing through town, right?"

"Could be."

"Could be isn't the half of it. Jim, I'm going to get you out of that shell if it's the last thing I do. I'm not kidding, Jim. If there's one thing I know, it's what makes people tick."

I did not see the man come in, but there he was. Tall, slim, silver hair. He kissed her and I wondered if he was her father, but somehow I knew that he wasn't. Well, what did you expect? Expecting things was stupid.

I said, "Jack, what time is it?"

"Two o'clock. It's early yet."

"*Early* is a relative term. Jack, I hate to eat and run without the eating, but I have a meeting."

"You just got here."

"No, I got here quite a while ago. Jack, look, if you're paying for this, the next one's on me."

"Jim, you will have lunch, if Barlow can make it? I mean, if he's free and you're free?"

I did not remember agreeing to anything like this. I said, "Jack, if Barlow wants to have lunch, I guess I can come along for the drinks. Just don't tell him it was my idea. I mean that, Jack. I'm not interested in any commuters' club and I'm not about to go through the motions, okay?"

"Well, of course, Jim. You know I'd never go around using your name or anything."

She looked up as I passed her table. "Excuse me. I think you dropped this."

She handed me a folded piece of white paper and just looked at me with those dark eyes.

I said, "Oh. Thanks."

I went out into the hot bright street and opened the paper up.

Essex Manor. Room 321. Edith. $100.

Christ.
I went back to the office. I had had three martinis and nothing to eat.

It was twenty to three when I got to Brook Parker's office. He was sitting at his desk looking at a set of toy false teeth, the kind that you buy in a novelty store.

I said, "That's a nice smile you have there."

Brook Parker said, "What makes cavities?"

I said, "Acid."

"What do you mean, acid?"

I said, "Acid dissolves the calcium."

"What kind of acid?"

I said, "Well, when you eat something, these little microorganisms stick to your teeth. Your saliva has something in it that turns them into acid and it's like that."

Brook Parker picked up the toy teeth and put his finger on the biting edge of one of them and said, "This is the calcium?"

I said, "That's the enamel. The calcium's inside. It's called dentine. The enamel's mostly inorganic and the dentine's sort of half and half."

"I don't have any idea what you're talking about. Now that's enamel, right?"

"Right."

"But these acids dissolve the calcium inside the enamel?" I said, "That's the way I get it."

Brook Parker said, "Well, how does the acid get through the enamel to get at the calcium?"

"I guess it eats its way through. I mean, it's acid."

"Then what good is the enamel?"

"Well, it's hard, you know?"

"Well, what's Crest got in it that stops this?"

I said, "Some kind of fluoride. What it's supposed to do is louse up the formation of the acid. Now wait a minute. I'm not sure whether that's what it does or whether it makes the teeth less soluble. We had a meeting at Landum and this guy told us about it but I'm not sure which is which."

Brook Parker said, "We don't have this fluoride, eh?"

"Nope."

"Is that what fluoridation of water's all about?"

"Yes."

"So what does Den-Test do?"

"Well, it's a paste with a kind of abrasive in it, little grits, you know? You can't even see them. Anyway, that's for brushing, and then there's an alkali that neutralizes these acids, but they kind of come back again. I think the fluoride keeps them from working on your teeth later on."

Brook Parker said, "All toothpastes have this alkali business?"

I said, "By and large."

"How did Crest get this official dentist endorsement?"

"I guess they went to them and said they had this stuff."

Brook Parker picked up the toy teeth and began putting marks on them with a Flair pen. Then he picked up a toothbrush and brushed the marks off, dipping the toothbrush in a paper cup full of water. It made quite a mess and he wiped it off the teeth with one of the paper napkins that you get from the Schrafft's coffee wagon. He said, "Why can't you Simonize teeth?"

I just looked at him. I said, "God Simonizes teeth. That's what the enamel is."

"You'd think it would burn your tongue. Jim, we have to do something everybody else is too smart to do." He got up and began to walk around the room. "People expect commercials to go a certain way. What we have to do is not be so smart. Look, there's a professional way to do this and what the world's looking for is a nice dumb amateur. That's right, isn't it?"

I said, "How would you feel about putting a kid in a glass jar?"

"Why?"

I said, "Well, he's doing just what the commercials tell you. No between-meal treats. No chewing gum while he's playing ball. No candy after school."

Brook Parker sat down at his drawing table and drew a crude jar with a boy inside. He said, "Look, Mom, no cavities."

I said, "What do you think?"

He shrugged. He wrote,

Look, Mom, no cavities.

under the picture and tore the sheet off the pad and pasted it on his wall with masking tape.

We both looked at this for a while.

My back had now begun to feel sweaty. Two martinis were all that any sane man should have for lunch. Anybody who had three ought not be let back into an office until the next day.

Brook Parker had sat down at his drawing table again. He now drew a large picture of a row of teeth. Next, he drew an American flag on one of them.

Under this he wrote,

The American Tooth.

I said, "That's kind of nice."

"We'll play 'America the Beautiful' and pour chocolate syrup over it."

I said, "I don't think you can do that."

"Why not?"

"It's like the national anthem."

"It's a comment on things. They have to let us do it."

I said, "So you get it through one network and two others won't take it. Where are you?"

Brook Parker said, "There's something here somewhere."

I said, "Where does Den-Test come in?"

"It stings. You have to pay for the soft life somehow."

I said, "I like that."

"You sure you're all right?"

I looked at him. "Sure. Why not?"

Brook Parker said, "Okay. You just looked a little funny."

I said, "Three martinis and nothing to eat. The guy I was with began to bug me."

"I don't have drinks with guys who bug me."

"Yes, well, this is a guy nobody on earth will have a drink with, you know? I figured somebody ought to."

Brook Parker nodded as if to himself. Then he said, "You want to write something for this?"

"I think we'd better get to that meeting."

"What meeting?"

"Landum. You told Bob Coleman you wanted to have a meeting with the guy from Landum."

"When did I say that?"

"This morning in the screening room."

Brook Parker said, "What are we seeing this guy for?"

I said, "He's the brand manager. He'll have the poop on what we can and can't say. One thing Landum knows is what the lawyers think."

"Lawyers think you shouldn't do it. That's how they get to be lawyers."

In Bob Coleman's office, a tall, lean man in his early thirties stood up to meet us. Outdoorsy look, weathery sun lines, short scruff of windblown black hair, a long irregular nose that wandered a little as if he'd been a fighter and had got it bopped.

Bob Coleman, every white hair in place, said, "Jim, Brook, this is Mark Penman, brand manager for Den-Test. Mark, Jim Bower, our copy chief, and Brook Parker, our creative director."

Mark Penman had a nice easy grin. "Well, fellows, I guess there are guys you'd rather see than me, eh?"

Brook Parker said, "I don't know. There can't be any bad news we don't have already."

Mark Penman laughed. "I hate throwing guys a curve like this. In fact, I've been wondering if we shouldn't just pack Den-Test in and forget it."

I said, "I don't know. It could be the commercials we did just didn't get through, you know? I can say that. I did them."

Bob Coleman said in his low priest's voice, "Jim, we've been over our Burke reports. The problem wasn't communication. Everybody got the message."

The Burke report was a survey of what people thought

the commercial was all about. The research people phoned homes in a given area and asked you if you saw it and what it meant to you. It was all supposed to be pretty reliable.

Brook Parker said, "They were just commercials."

Mark Penman, our affable client, said, "They did very well, Brook. They got the story across."

Brook Parker said, "Yeah, but nobody said Wow."

Bob Coleman said, "That's why we wanted you on it, Brook." Bob Coleman had a smile that turned on and off like a light. "In fact, Mark came over to see if a look at the product from the plant's point of view would tell you anything."

Brook Parker said, "Why not?"

Mark Penman said, "Brook, all I do is add up the numbers and see if they come out even. Let's see now. Chapter One. Den-Test. Ten million dollars, fourteen million retail. Gross is about six million five before advertising. Normally, that would be worth two million for you fellows to work with, but we went for three to see what would happen."

Brook said, "The big tube costs about a buck?"

"That's right."

"So how does that break down?"

Mark Penman slung a long leg over the arm of his chair. "About forty percent mark-up for retail. Our fixed cost is thirty-five percent, about three million. Add on twenty-five cents a tube for advertising—that's not counting promotion."

Brook said, "Twenty-five cents a tube!"

Bob Coleman said in a quick low voice, "That's the only selling Den-Test gets, Brook. There aren't any salesmen in a supermarket."

Mark Penman said, "Brook, up to 1950 Den-Test wasn't even in supermarkets. Landum didn't believe in grocery store distribution."

I said, "Neilsen says you're off a million and a half. How do you know Neilsen's any good?"

Bob Coleman said, "Okay. The Neilsen Food Index is a bimonthly thing. Every two months they check sixteen hundred stores to see how much they sold."

Brook Parker said, "How many stores are there?"

Mark Penman said, "In the country? About three hundred thousand. At least, that carry groceries."

Bob Coleman said, "Thirty-eight thousand of these do sixty-eight percent of the business, Brook. Neilsen mixes their checks up between the big ones and the small ones."

I said, "How many homes are we selling into? Does anybody know?"

Mark Penman said, "Well, there are sixty million households in the country. We reach about five percent of them. Say three million."

Bob Coleman said, "The key to this is distribution. We have forty percent. Get that up just ten percent and it will pay for the advertising by itself."

Brook Parker said, "Distribution to who?"

"Stores. Sell-in." Bob Coleman lit a cigarette. "A & P won't handle Den-Test. Get A & P and you'll be a hero."

I said, "What's the matter? Quality?"

Mark Penman gave me his easy grin. "No. It just isn't a seller, Jim."

Brook Parker said, "What about putting this stuff out in jet black tubes?"

Bob Coleman looked at the ceiling.

Mark Penman said, "It's possible for the future." He had answered instantly. He had not even had to think it over.

Brook Parker said, "I know. You have to sell what's on the shelves now."

Mark Penman said, "The average supermarket has a thirty-day supply and there's another thirty-day supply in the warehouses."

Bob Coleman said dryly, "Please tell Brook how long it takes to change the package."

Mark Penman blew air through his pursed lips as he toted it up in his mind. "Thirteen weeks from design to cylinders."

I said, "What's that mean?"

Mark Penman said, "Cylinders for printing. Thirteen weeks to cylinders. Another two to four months for distribution."

Bob Coleman said, "Six or seven months, in other words, Brook. And Den-Test has to pay its own way in the meantime."

Mark Penman said, "And that, fellows, brings me right back to the big question. Fellows, I'm going to level with you. Landum wants to kill it off. If I go into test market, it's going to amount to a commitment on my part in the eyes of management."

At that moment, George Brice walked in.

Mark Penman got up and shook hands with him. "Hello, George. I was going to drop in and say hello before I left."

George Brice smiled his enameled smile. "Mark, how are you?"

"Up a tree. I guess you know the story."

"Neilsen? I saw it." George sat down. Scrubbed-looking, smiling, inscrutable George. "What part of the conversation did I walk in on?"

Bob Coleman said, "Mark has to make a recommendation to management, George."

Mark Penman grinned. "I'm a coward, George. I'm asking Brook and Jim here to make my decision for me."

George Brice looked at me without any particular expression at all. "What do they say?"

I looked at Brook. Brook did not say a word. He was looking at the floor.

Bob Coleman said, "Brook? Jim?"

According to George Brice's school, you just added up the numbers. There were not any other ingredients to be considered.

I said, "If there were any guarantees, I'd go into the toothpaste business."

Mark Penman took out a little thin green cigar and unwrapped it. "I know that, Jim. What I want is your educated guess."

I said, "Yeah, well, you've got two ways you can look at this. The smart thing to do is dump it, so what you're really asking is whether Brook and I can beat the odds, right?"

"That's the question."

"Well, I have to think we can. I don't know. The odds were against Willow. The odds were against Paragon. What can I say?"

"You think you can do it?" Mark Penman said.

"Yes."

Mark Penman said, "George? What would you do?"

George Brice said, "Mark, you asked Jim the question and Jim answered you. If you're trying to beat the odds, you couldn't do better than Brook and Jim."

Mark Penman grinned. "I can't get the ball out of my court, can I?"

George Brice said, "You're asking us to make a decision that isn't an agency decision to make."

Mark Penman said, "Okay. It is my decision, and I guess I've made it."

Bob Coleman said, "Go?"

"Go."

George Brice said, "Call me the next time you're in town, Mark. We'll have lunch."

Brook and I ran into George Brice again at the elevator. George said, "Brook, I'm on my way up to the Gaslight Club to have a drink with Ed Farrel. Can I drop you off?"

Brook said, "Yeah. I have to go up to the Oak Room and tell a girl I don't want to get married."

George said, "I noticed you didn't say anything when Mark popped the question, Brook."

Brook said, "Den-Test is a dog."

George said, "Mark Penman is putting his job on the line. If we didn't think we could do it, it seems to me we had a moral obligation to say so."

I said, "George, if I didn't think we could do it, I would have said so."

The elevator arrived and we all got in. I stepped off at my floor and said, "Good night."

Brook Parker said, "Good night, Jim."

George Brice looked at me with what could or could not have been a smile.

When I turned the Triumph into the driveway that night I saw that our mailbox and its stand were no longer standing there. It had been pulled out of the ground, concrete ball and all, and was lying in the forsythia.

I drove on up to the garage and went in through the kitchen and out to the porch, where Melinda, in tan shorts and a pale green blouse, was having a gin and tonic.

I said, "What happened to the mailbox?"

"Kids. It was worse up the street. They broke the Coughlins' carriage lamps and let the air out of Al Coughlin's tires. It must have happened sometime between nine and ten last night, because Al got in at nine and then went out at ten to get something at the store and his tires were flat."

I said, "Well, I suppose I'd better see if I can put it back up again." I took off my jacket and my tie and rolled up my sleeves.

Melinda said, "Don't you need cement to hold it in?"

I said, "I'm going to see if I can't just stand it on the ball."

I walked down to the mailbox and picked it up and tried to stand it in the hole. It stood there as if it were balancing itself on one foot like a long-legged bird. I scooped up some stones and dirt with my hand and packed it all in around the base and then stamped it down with my feet.

The box looked steadier but it did not appear as if it would take any punishment. I stood there, looking around. The neighborhood had a hot, still, lifeless look. Long lawns and trees heavy with motionless green leaves. It seemed as if everybody had moved out.

I walked back up the driveway to the house and wiped my neck with a wet washrag and made a martini and went out to the porch. "Well, it's standing up, but I don't know what it will do if anybody puts any mail in it."

"Oh, there's something wrong with the top of the Lincoln, too. I called Lincoln-Mercury about it and they said I'd have to leave it with them. They said there are a thousand little wires in those tops and they didn't know how long it would take to find out what's wrong."

I said, "That's our world, all right. The disposable Lincoln. Well, what the hell." I lit a cigarette. "Today I had lunch with Jack Thompson."

"You didn't."

"It was the price of getting out of there Saturday night, remember? He wants to start a commuters' club. The way I get it, all he needs is Barlow Matthews."

"Barlow?" It seemed to me that Melinda's face froze.

"Catalyst was the word Jack used. Barlow's supposed to be the catalyst."

"And how did Barlow's name happen to come up?"

"Don't ask me. Jack Thompson met him somewhere, I guess."

"I would just as soon not involve the Matthewses with the Thompsons, if you don't mind."

"Fine. Call Jack Thompson and tell him that."

"It seems to me you could have told him that."

"I did. Jack Thompson has this way of not hearing you."

I looked out at the back yard. We had our own hill in the back and a pretty good woods. Some trees that I think were oaks stood up as straight and high as flagpoles and mixed in with them were some firs and some trees that I could not identify at all.

I drank some of my drink. Melinda did not seem to have a thing to say.

Sparrows swooped down from the trees and ganged up on a little spot on the lawn. They walked around in jerky little steps the way people used to walk in old movies. I wondered whether they had spotted a bug or a worm or whether one of them had just felt like looking things over and the others had followed him because they did not have anything better to do.

Melinda said, "I think you ought to call Barlow and tell him this wasn't your idea."

I said, "I don't see why. Barlow is perfectly capable of saying no without any help from me."

Melinda said, "Under the circumstances, he just might not say no."

"What circumstances?"

Melinda said, "All right. I'll call him myself."

She went into the house and I lit another cigarette and watched the sparrows. There seemed to be at least fifteen of them. I wondered how Melinda was doing, under the circumstances.

Presently she came back out to the porch. "That idiot must have called him the moment you left. Do you know what he told Barlow? He said it was your idea."

I said, "That's about the way he'd put it, yes."

"So now Barlow's having us all over Friday night."

I said, "Uh huh. Why didn't he just say no?"

"I told you if he thought it was something that you wanted, he would probably do it."

I said, "I don't understand that at all." I got up and went into the den and turned on the television set. We had a twenty-three-inch Sylvania ($456 plus nineteen dollars for the stand plus tax). In the little room, it was like being attacked by a giant watercolor set.

Melinda came in and said, "There's too much yellow, I think. It's making everything green."

I adjusted one of the knobs. "How's that?"

"It looks all right, but the man said you shouldn't set the color by the commercials. He said they're always different from the show."

I said, "I don't see why. We spend more on the color for a commercial than they do on the program."

"I didn't know that."

I said, "Figure it out. Twenty or thirty thousand dollars for thirty seconds? They can't put that kind of money into programs."

"Would a TV dinner suit you?"

"Why not?" I said.

Melinda went out to the kitchen and then came back after a while. "What are you watching?"

"The Yankees."

"Oh. Baseball."

I said, "Well, at least you don't know how it will come out before it starts."

The telephone rang.

I said, "Do you want to get it? It's probably for you."

For a moment, Melinda looked at me, as if she were wondering what to make of this remark. Then she went out to the kitchen, either to keep from having to turn down the TV set or to keep from being heard.

I lit a cigarette and put my feet up on the desk and drank some more of my martini and Melinda came back. "Jim?"

"Yeah?"

"That was Jean Hawes. Slim just died."

I took a deep breath and drank some more of the gin.

Melinda said, "They're going to have a little service Wednesday morning at the Congregational church. She's going to take the body back to Montana."

I said, "That's where he wanted to go."

"You liked Slim, didn't you. . . ."

"Yep."

"I guess everybody liked him."

"I guess so."

"Is there anything I can get you?"

"Nope. I think I'll just watch the Yankees for a while. Who knows? This may be the year they win a game."

tuesday

In the morning when I got to the office, Edna said, "Marion Simons was looking for you. He wants you to call him when you can."

I said, "Did he come down or phone?"

"He was down here."

I said, "Okay. Dig up some coffee and then get him on the phone."

I went into my office. At least, I thought, Marion was still coming around in person. I had not slept well and my face, around my eyes, felt a little like the skin of a prune. The papers on my desk looked as if they had been dumped there out of a wastebasket. I was depressed by the sight. Every piece of paper represented something that I was supposed to do. There were requisitions, memos, pieces of copy that had to be changed, type proofs that had to be checked, letters from people wanting jobs, a time sheet that I was supposed to fill out describing what accounts I had spent my time on for the past two weeks, an expense account form for a trip I had taken to California, and papers whose origins I had forgotten.

What a job like this needed was an orderly mind and I did not have one. George Brice's desk was always empty. Mine was always the same damned clutter. I just wasn't on top of my job.

"Coffee, and we're out of coffee money," Edna said.

I said, "I could keep a mistress for the money you run through on coffee. Are you sure you aren't putting half that dough in a Swiss bank?"

Edna said, "Ben Polo was looking for you, too."

"He didn't have a story board with him, did he?" Ben Polo was the art director who worked with Barney Marker. They did not want to do print. They wanted to do TV and be famous.

"I think he had a proof of an ad."

"Well, get Marion Simons on the phone. Maybe we're behind in the rent."

Presently my intercom buzzed. I picked up the phone and said, "Jim Bower."

It was Marion Simons. "Jim, could you come up here about ten-thirty?"

"Sure. What's up?"

"I'm in a meeting now. We'll go over it when you get here."

I said, "Okay."

An art director named Emil came in. Emil looked like a man emptying an attic. His hair went off in several directions. He wore a Buffalo Bill shirt, held up his pants with a rope and wore sandals. He said, "Hey there, Jim, you tell me this, eh? What's Lydia doing on the payroll?"

I said, "Why? Did you fire her?"

"I can't communicate with a person like that. She can't be communicated with, Jim."

"What's the problem?"

"She doesn't know where it is. I mean, she's like selling, you know?"

I said, "Emil, so far I don't know what it's all about."

Emil produced a folded-up piece of layout paper. He unfolded it and put it on my desk. It was an inkblot. A 2,700-line inkblot. Big enough to run full-page in *The New York Times*.

> 19th Century vodka.
> It is what it is and you are what you are.

I looked at this for some time.

Emil said, "Now, the problem with Lydia is, Lydia doesn't understand. Like if it doesn't say *Pure* or *Save 15%*, Lydia doesn't understand, Jim."

I lit a cigarette and looked at the ad awhile longer. There were no ground rules for ads like this. Somebody had to say yes or no and it was up to me to decide which.

I said, "I don't understand it either, Emil, but what the hell. I like it. Go ahead."

Brook Parker walked in just as Emil was leaving. Brook's shirt sleeves were rolled up. His collar was open. His chin was covered with stubble. He said, "You get in late enough."

I said, "What are you talking about? I was here at nine-thirty."

"I was here at four."

I said, "That isn't devotion. That's nuttiness."

"Well, I had a few drinks last night. Before the night was over, I guess I had a lot of drinks."

"Just what kind of night did you have?"

"I think I told a girl I'd marry her. Oh, boy. Jim, I didn't want to do it."

"What, get engaged or get drunk?"

"Marriage is on the way out, right? I mean, isn't it dumb?"

The only marriage that was on the way out that I knew of was my own. I said, "I think a lot of people still do it, Brook. You don't hear about many unemployed ministers, you know?"

"I don't know what she wants. Yes, I know what she wants. It's possessiveness, Jim. They have to own you." Brook rubbed his eyes. "Well, would you mind telling me why you told that guy we could do it?"

"What, Den-Test?"

"What made you say a thing like that?"

I sighed and said, "George, I guess. I guess I just didn't think the world ought to just be George's way."

Brook sat down and closed his eyes. "That's as good a reason as any."

"He say anything to you in the cab?"

"He talked about architecture. That's another thing I don't like. He knows all about architecture."

"What's the matter with that?"

"He has no business knowing all about architecture. I'll bet he even goes home and paints. Jim, I don't want George Brice knowing architecture." Brook leaned back and looked at the ceiling. "I ought not to be a husband, Jim. I'd make a rotten husband."

I said, "Well, anyway, congratulations."

"Okay. Now that we said we can do it, what do we do?"

"Damned if I know."

"What ideas have we had? We had some ideas, didn't we?"

"You still don't like *The Stinger*?"

"Nobody's going to say Wow."

"Well, you said they might as well call it Mother's. How about calling it Mother's?"

He just looked at me. "How about calling it Fred's? Sometimes I wonder about you, Jim. Is there any Bufferin around here? I think my head's growing in."

I went out and got two Bufferin from Edna and a paper cup of water and brought it back. I said, "Too bad *the shame of the nation* doesn't mean anything. Advertising's about ready for another shame of the nation."

Brook looked interested in this. "What was the first one?"

"Search me. I just have a feeling there was one."

"The shame of a nation. We have the best of everything and we even have toothpaste to keep it from giving us cavities." Brook lit a cigarette and began to walk around the room. "The Pilgrims wouldn't know the place, you know? We have gook for pimples, gook for your armpits, now there's even a vaginal gook. Will the real Miss America stand up?"

I said, "She can't."

"Remember what they used to have in bathrooms? Iodine. Soap. Shaving cream and toothpaste. That was back when women didn't tell dirty stories and the men didn't smell like women."

I said, "Yeah. It was called the Depression."

"Jim? Remember the woman in *American Gothic*?"

"Sure. She looked like my first girl friend's mother. She also looked like her father."

"All the old New England virtues. Jim, we get a woman

like that. Call her—what do we call her? Frances. Frances
Beaker Smith."

"Where did you get a name like that?"

Brook Parker said, "Write this down."

"My name is Frances Beaker Smith. I'm sixty-five years
old and all the teeth you see are mine. They tell me I'd sell
more Den-Test if it didn't burn your mouth."

I wrote this down and then added,

"That may be. But I was brought up to believe that if
something good for you smarts a bit, that's the price you
pay."

Brook Parker put out his cigarette and said, " '*I brought
my children up that way and I make Den-Test that way.*'
Jim, this is it."

I said, "How about, '*I'm too old to change Den-Test now
just to sell a few more tubes.*' "

Brook said, " ' *If it stings, just close your eyes.*' "

I had it all written down. I said, "You know what? You
have the soul of a quack."

"Quacks sell things that don't work. This stuff works and
we're just looking for something that goes with the image.
Jim, I'm going home and clean the place up. If the cleaning
woman sees my room, she'll spend a week in church praying
for me."

I said, "Was that where you proposed?"

"No. That's where I went for a drink after I proposed. I
think I finished half a fifth and I didn't even feel it. Then
I think I went out for a walk."

"Can the world expect to see you again?"

"I don't know. I'm going to try to die." He stopped at the
door and looked at me. His face was gray. "If you feel like
a quack, you're in the wrong business."

I just sat there, after he left. The son of a bitch came in
with a hangover and did it and went home.

Alec Mayberry came in. He was a tall, slim man of about
thirty with light skin and a young bright look. I had heard
that Alec was a playboy and that his family had money. He
was a good writer.

"Jim?"

"Come in," I said.

Alec wore a lime-colored jacket with wide lapels and a nipped-in waist and gray bell-bottom slacks with a wide black stripe in them. His shirt looked like silk and was open at the throat and he had tied a handkerchief around his neck like a cowboy.

He looked around with a little half smile. There was something about Alec that made you think he was laughing at either himself or you or the world in general. He plopped himself down on my sofa and crossed his long legs and said, "I have been confounded by procedure. I put in for supper money last night and accounting asked me for a written explanation of my time."

I said, "Just put down on your petty cash slip what you were working on. You know. Mountainaire International. Supper money. Nine P.M., or whatever."

Alec Mayberry said, "I did that. I gather that I do not get the money until I produce an explanation in writing of why I couldn't get my work done during the day."

I buzzed Edna. "Get me accounting."

Edna said, "Who in accounting?"

I said, "Mr. Accounting."

Presently a voice came on. "Joel Babcock."

I said, "Joel, this is Jim Bower. Alec Mayberry tells me you guys won't fork over his supper money until he brings you a note from his mother."

Joel Babcock said, "I expected a call from you about this, Jim. The fact is, supper money in creative seems to be turning into quite an industry, and I don't see why we're paying people to do things at night that we're already paying them to do during the day."

I said, "You don't have to see why. All you have to do is take care of it."

Joel Babcock said, "Jim, I have no intention of withholding supper money on any legitimate night work, but I also do not intend to be the pigeon for every kid who figures he'll hang around a couple of hours and pick up three dollars and a half."

I said, "Just who in the hell do you think you are? Nobody in my department answers to you for anything. They don't answer to you and they don't explain to you."

Joel Babcock said, "Apparently they don't answer to anybody, Jim. You're aware, I suppose, that Alec Mayberry didn't get to work until eleven o'clock twice this week? In fact, if you want to look at it that way, all he did was put in a full day even with his overtime."

I said, "When Alec or any other writer turns up is my business, Joel. Please don't start minding my business for me."

Joel Babcock said, "Very well, Jim. For the time being, I'll honor any vouchers with your initials on them. But I must tell you, Jim, that this is just a temporary courtesy until we have a discussion with Marion Simons or George Brice about it."

I said, "Thank you," and hung up.

Alec Mayberry said, "I gather Big Brother is now counting the minutes of the working day."

"Well, Alec, I'll tell you something. We do seem to unlock the doors around here a long time before some people show up."

"That is true and I have sinned, although in my own defense I must say it's an easy habit to get into. We have art directors here who don't work weekdays."

"Well, we'll talk to them, too. I guess you can pick up your supper money, anyway."

"I thank you, sir."

I just looked at him. This time I had the feeling that Alec Mayberry was laughing at me.

It was time to go up to Marion Simons' office.

In the hall, I ran into Charles Leader. He said, "Well, I took that smart-assed ad over to Miniflex and they threw it out. And, I might add, *A new standard of excellence* is perfectly acceptable to them."

His glasses seemed to have an annoyed look, and he was carrying his little pot like a badge of office.

I said, "And how did *A new standard of excellence* happen to come up?"

"I asked them if that was the sort of thing they were looking for, and it certainly was."

I said, "That's nice. Now just what in the hell did you ask them a thing like that for?"

"I was under the impression they were clients of ours."

I said, "We aren't exactly house painters, friend. We aren't here to ask them what color they want the living room in."

"If that's supposed to mean something, it escapes me."

I said, "It means we're supposed to tell them what they ought to do. We don't pull samples out of the drawer and ask them to take their pick."

"Well, that's the ad they're expecting."

"Well, they aren't getting it. Now you figure out how to tell them that."

"The only opinion that counts is your opinion?"

"You're goddamned right."

"We'll see about that."

I said, "Excuse me. I have to go to a meeting."

I went on to Marion Simons' office.

Waiting inside were Curt Johns, our production manager, Ben Polo, Jeff Sermon, the account executive on Federal, and Marion Simons.

Curt Johns was a chunky, red-faced man with a British guardsman's mustache. His job was to get type set for ads, have engravings made for printing and proofs corrected for submission to magazines and newspapers. He was our quality-control man. He was in the office until ten or eleven every night and had a staff of five production men under him.

Marion Simons said, "Sit down, Jim."

Marion had a black desk, and on it were several tear sheets of newspaper ads. They were upside down to me but I could already see something strange.

The ads had a headline and body copy and space for a big picture, but there was no picture in the space for it. The top half of the ad was simply blank. Then the headline and the copy.

I said, "What's up?"

Jeff Sermon usually came on like a bull. Today the big fat man was quiet. "It's a boo-boo, Jim, and a pretty bad one." He handed me one of the tear sheets. It was a Federal ad. There was a big *Federal Airlines* signature at the bottom.

The headline read,

> When it goes down in the West,
> you ought to be in the West to see it.

I said, "Jesus Christ."

Jeff Sermon said, "That's the way it ran. I'm supposed to be over at Federal this morning with the reason why."

I said, "What is the reason why? When Barney Marker told me about this ad, he said there was going to be a big sunset in it."

Curt Johns said, "The sunset dropped out. I said it would drop out, and all the experts around here said it wouldn't."

Jeff Sermon said, "Nobody's pointing any fingers, Curt."

Curt Johns said, "I am. I told you this was trouble and you said go ahead."

Jeff Sermon said, "Curt, what you said was that we might lose some of the detail. You didn't say there wouldn't be a dot left."

Photographs prepared for printing were rephotographed through a screen. What you printed were thousands of tiny dots. Where shadows were supposed to be dark, the dots got very dense. Where shadows were light, the dots thinned out.

Marion Simons said, "Jim, the question is whether the agency should pick up the cost on this."

I said, "How much was it?"

Jeff Sermon said, "Fifty thousand dollars."

I said, "How did it happen that I didn't see this?"

Ben Polo, the art director, was a slight, gentle Italian youth. "Jim, it's what happens when they want something at the last minute. You were at the studio shooting Den-Test and they had to have plates that night."

Jeff Sermon said, "Well, it wasn't a last-minute job, Ben. Let's get that straight right now. You had six weeks for that job and you know it."

Ben Polo said, "They kept turning ads down until we didn't have any time left to do it right. We gave you six different concepts on this job, Jeff. You came in and said we'd be in trouble if Federal didn't have an ad in the papers in forty-eight hours. That's one day for concept, typesetting and engravings. We didn't even have time to see proofs."

Jeff Sermon said, "Then why did you give me a picture that wouldn't reproduce?"

"That picture was to show the client what we wanted to do. I told you I wanted to have it retouched and you said there wasn't time."

Curt Johns said, "Ben, didn't I call you and tell you you'd lose it? You know the screen you get with newspapers."

Ben said, "You called me and I told you to call Jeff."

Jeff Sermon said, "And I repeat, all you told me was that we wouldn't get it all."

Marion Simons said, "From all I've heard, the client took this risk when he didn't give us time to do it right."

Jeff Sermon said, "Marion, as far as they're concerned, they gave us six weeks."

I said, "Did they know there was a risk, Jeff?"

"Jim, they'd turned down six ads already. They were on

my neck about whether we could deliver. My job was to show them we could, not tell them we couldn't."

I said, "Looks like this is a question for George Brice, Marion."

Marion Simons said, "I'll get him." He pressed his intercom button and asked his secretary to get George Brice on the phone. Then he said, "George? Could you come over to my office? We're having a little trouble and I think you're going to have to make the decision on it."

Presently the door opened and George Brice walked in. We all said good morning and George Brice said in his soft voice, "Marion, you said we were having trouble?"

Marion Simons showed him one of the tear sheets. "This seems to be one of those things, George. If anybody was at fault, everybody was or nobody was. At any rate, this ran in every paper from Chicago east and Federal's raising the roof about it."

George Brice said, "I don't blame them. Jeff, what's our position?"

Jeff Sermon shrugged his huge shoulders. "George, we kept bringing over ads they wouldn't buy until there just wasn't any time left. That's supposed to be a sunset on the ocean, incidentally. Family fare to California? Anyway, we only had forty-eight hours to plate and ship and this happened."

George Brice said, "Yes, but what's our position?"

Marion Simons said, "Can we ask the papers for a make-good?"

"Not with the plates we sent them," Curt Johns said.

I said, "I hate to say it, George, but this is one we'd better take a bath on."

George Brice said, "How much money are we talking about?"

Marion Simons said, "Fifty thousand dollars."

"That's the commission for over three hundred thousand dollars' worth of billing," George Brice said. I wondered how he had been able to figure this out so quickly. He said, "Marion, how often do we run into something like this?"

Marion Simons said, "Practically never."

George Brice said, "All right. We'll pay it. Jim, walk back to my office with me, will you?"

I said, "All right."

We left Marion Simons' office and walked down the hall. George Brice did not speak and so neither did I.

When we got to his office, he seated himself behind his desk nd said, "Sit down, Jim."

I sat down.

George Brice said, "How did it happen?"

"Human error, I guess, George."

"You saw that ad?"

"I was over shooting Den-Test. I okayed the idea over the phone but I didn't see it."

"Who looks at ads when you aren't here?"

"Well, Feldman's the art director but he's on vacation. Brook would have stopped it but they probably didn't even hink to show it to him."

"But you'd have stopped it?"

"If the photo was that light, I'd probably have been able o tell. I'd probably have changed the ad to something that wasn't so chancy. All type or artwork from an ad we'd already run. Hell, we have enough palm trees in the art files o start a forest."

George Brice said, "Then it was really a matter of supervision."

I said, "Well, Ben should have known better."

George Brice said, "Jim, I had a few drinks with Ed Farrel last night. He asked me a question I didn't know how to answer."

I said, "What was it?"

"He wanted to know if we really wanted the Federal account."

"Because of one goof on one ad?"

"No, Jim. Because nobody seems to be minding the store here. Jim, we've had this discussion before and you didn't seem to be listening. I hope you are listening now, Jim. I hope that very much."

I said, "I'm listening."

"Ed Farrel wanted to know why they haven't seen a single ad they asked for in the last month. I gather their ad manager calls Jeff Sermon and Jeff tells them he'll get right on it and that, Jim, seems to be as far as anything gets."

"George, I don't even know what he's talking about. What ads?"

"The Buffalo ad, for one, Jim. I believe that's the ad that Barney Marker is going to come up with any day now?"

"I'm on top of the Buffalo ad, George. If Barney doesn't have one this afternoon, I'll do it myself. Did anybody happen to tell Ed Farrel their flight scheduling department kind of forgot to tell advertising about that flight until the last minute?"

"I'll get to Barney Marker presently, Jim. This agency is not going to get into any blaming matches with clients. They asked us for an ad late and you turned it over to a beginner. I'm sure I also do not have to tell you that the California ad came up in our little talk?"

I said, "They got six different concepts on that damned ad."

"And the only one acceptable seems to have turned into a small disaster. A disaster I gather you could have prevented if you'd been here."

I said, "Well, they got six ads on California, just the same, so when Farrel says they haven't seen anything he's kind of leaving a little gap."

George Brice said, "Ed also mentioned a travel agent ad they asked for two months ago and an ad for Houston that their Houston city manager finally had to write himself."

I said, "What ads are those? I've never heard of them."

"May I ask why you've never heard of them?"

"How do I know? George, requisitions don't come to me in a dream. Somebody's supposed to come in and give me a piece of paper."

"Jim, I'm afraid I've been forced to make something of an experiment."

"What kind of experiment?"

"I now have thirty-two depth interviews from Barry Gorner. I have Senser Research's breakdown of these as well as Barry's own preliminary reports. I take it, Jim, that you haven't been to one of these sessions, nor have you read one word in the report."

I said, "I've been up to here in Den-Test."

"Jim, I know what you've been doing. We are now talking about what I've been doing. I promised Federal a business commercial based on Barry's work with Senser and I've brought a writer in to do it. He'll be working with Rudy d'Franco."

I stared at him. "What do you mean, a guy from the outside?"

"To save you any embarrassment, he'll report directly to me."

I just sat there. "Well, that's a new ball game."

"I've also been forced to do a few other things in creative, Jim, since you haven't bothered to do them yourself."

"Do I get to hear about them?"

"First, Jim, neither you nor Barney Marker will do the Buffalo ad. You will sit down with traffic this afternoon and go over every job and every due date in this agency. Percy Holland will do the Buffalo ad. Alec Mayberry will do the travel agent ad. And you will give Barney Marker his notice."

I just sat there. I found that I was breathing a little heavily. I wondered if my face was red.

I heard myself saying, "Alec Mayberry is on Mountainaire International."

"Alec Mayberry is now on Federal. We are not paying nineteen thousand dollars a year for international ads. Mayberry will also find it in his heart to get in here when the office opens. In the future, Jim, everybody will get in here when the office opens or they won't be here when it closes."

I said, "Well, aside from going over all the requisitions in traffic, just what am I supposed to do around here now?"

"What do you think you should do, Jim?"

"If I remember the script, I think I've just had my cue to quit."

"Jim, if you feel in your heart of hearts that the situation has become intolerable for you, I'll respect any decision you make. I hope you understand that no one has asked you to resign and that, for the time being at least, you are still copy chief. Please try to understand that none of these decisions has been pleasant for me, either."

"What am I copy chief of?"

"Everything but this one commercial."

"Well, do I go on writing Federal or what?"

"I think what we should do for the moment, Jim, is just take one step at a time. Finish anything on Federal that you've started, of course."

I got up. "Well, George, all in all, it's been quite a morning."

George Brice smiled away. "Please do not make any hasty decisions, Jim."

I went back to my office.

When they bring somebody in from the outside to do your work for you, what you are supposed to do is go back and clean out your desk.

I was not quite sure what had happened. Was it because some ads were late, or was it the kind of ads that we did?

I rubbed my face. I thought that I knew what George Brice was doing. He had found a way to get his kind of guy into the place "just to do one commercial." Of course, he did not want me to resign. Let's not have any rumors about shake-ups getting out the door. We'll just put old Jim down in traffic checking requisitions for a while.

How long was it going to take to work a few more of George's kind of people in? How long was it going to take before the only thing left of Gibbs & Wilson was the name out front?

What's the matter with you? I thought. The guy just kicked you in the teeth. You ought to be on your way out the door by now.

No. That was not how you did it. You do not quit and get another job. You get another job first, and then quit.

I wondered if I would need any samples of my work. If you were copy chief of Gibbs & Wilson, what did you have to bring samples around for?

My stomach began to hurt. I got up from my desk and went down the hall to the elevator. I passed Ben Polo, Rudy d'Franco and Barney Marker. They had been standing next to the supplies cabinet talking. They stopped talking as I walked by.

I went over to a Third Avenue bar and had a seventy-cent martini. It was the sort of bar that had a big piece of roast beef turning on a spit. You could get a hot corned beef sandwich for ninety cents. Half the people in there were construction workers. The other half looked like kids from advertising agencies.

I looked at myself in the mirror behind the bar. I could not tell whether I looked old or not. Age was supposed to be very important in this business. I wondered if I was too old to get another job.

A stab of fear went through me. Ads were not good or bad in this business until somebody like George Brice said they were. Even if I got a job somewhere else, how long would I last before somebody said, "Bower, this may be your idea of an ad, but it isn't ours."

There was nothing you could say to this. If you did it one way and they did it another, they were not going to keep you around.

This was worse than when I had started at Mercer in 1950. When they hire you for fifty thousand dollars they expect ads that look like fifty thousand dollars. There was no way of telling what looked like fifty thousand dollars to a new agency and what did not. You go in and do some things and they look at them and look at each other and look embarrassed. This wasn't what they had in mind.

I had another drink.

Back at the agency, I found Brook Parker in my office.

I said, "I have news for you."

"What's the matter?" he asked.

"George Brice is bringing in some guy from the outside to write a Federal commercial."

Brook Parker sat down on my couch. "You fired?"

"No. Not yet, at least. This afternoon I'm supposed to go through every requisition in traffic and see what's late."

Brook Parker said, "Why doesn't traffic go through every requisition in traffic?"

I said, "I think this is George Brice's way of making me wash behind my ears."

Brook Parker said, "Are you still copy chief?"

"For the moment. I don't know how long that'll go on. I have an idea all I'm supposed to do is not let any headlines out with *fuck* or *shit* in them."

Brook Parker said, "George Brice grinds exceedingly small."

I said, "He's also reassigned a lot of stuff, and my next official act is to fire Barney Marker." I lit a cigarette. "This new guy's supposed to work with Rudy d'Franco."

"What are you supposed to do, show an airplane getting a headache?"

"Search me. Something nice and positive and fun-loving, as far as I can tell."

Brook Parker said, "Rudy d'Franco's an imitation art director." He looked at me. "You talk with Bob Coleman about all this?"

"What would I talk with Coleman about it for?"

Brook Parker shrugged. "He's on the board of directors, isn't he?"

I said, "The board of directors hired George Brice, and the board of directors will back George Brice up. He's supposed to lead us all across the Red Sea, remember?"

"Well, I called casting. They'll have our Frances Beaker Smith in at four. Let me have your phone. I'm going to put this on the Sony."

I pushed the phone across the desk and he dialed the Sony recording room in our TV complex. "This is Brook Parker. I want to tape something about four this afternoon."

Then he said, "What appointment? No, I don't have any appointment."

Then he said, "Yes, well, that's very nice but I want that room at four o'clock."

Then he said, "I don't think you understand this conversation. I want that room at four. I want a mile of white noseam paper. And I want every light we have, in that room and working."

Then he said, "I don't check things with your superior. I'm your superior's superior."

Then he hung up and said, "You'll be there, right?"

I said, "Nope. I'll be in traffic, checking requisitions."

The head of traffic was a tall, thin, hawk-faced man named Joe. Joe was in his fifties and had a gravelly voice and a very clear mind. "What I have here is a crisis chart. Things that are late, you know?"

I said, "What do you have down under Houston and travel agents?"

Joe smoked nonfilter Chesterfields out of the corner of his mouth. "They're both in hot water."

"Why didn't I hear about it?"

"Jim, I told Jeff Sermon about them and Jeff said the ads on Buffalo and California came first."

I said, "Why did anything have to come second? If we were in trouble, we could have put people on them."

Joe said, "That's what I told Jeff, but he said all the flak was about Buffalo and California."

"Give me your phone."

I called Jeff Sermon. I said, "Explain life to me. George Brice just stood on my face and told me about two ads on Houston and travel agents. Joe says you told him to hold up on them."

Jeff Sermon said, "Now, Jim, I did not tell Joe anything like that. I just told Joe where the pressure was, but I certainly never told him to hold up on anything. Jim, if Joe said I did, I'm afraid I'm going to have to call him a liar."

I said, "Joe, just what did Jeff tell you?"

Joe said, "I told him both those ads were late and he said never mind that until we get the Buffalo and California ads out."

I said, "Jeff? Joe said you told him Buffalo and California came first. He said you said never mind about Houston and the travel agents until we finished those."

Jeff Sermon said, "Well now, Jim, Buffalo and California were hotter than anything else. I called you myself about Buffalo. You know that, Jim. You know I called you."

I said, "We're not talking about Buffalo. We're talking about two ads I never heard of. I just got reamed about this, old buddy."

Jeff Sermon said, "Jim, I never told Joe to hold up on anything. He had the requisitions. He knew about those ads."

I said, "Sure, Jeff."

I hung up. I should have guessed what had happened, anyway. The client yelled at Jeff about Buffalo and California. Jeff only heard yells. Good old Jeff.

It did not really matter. That was not what George Brice was giving me the business for. That was just a little more that George had been able to pile on while he was at it.

I went over tissue-thin yellow requisitions until my eyes began to water. I said to Joe, "You know, we aren't in such bad shape? Just Miniflex, Den-Test and Federal, and Miniflex and Den-Test I know about."

Joe said, "Who's supposed to send George Brice the report, you or me?"

"What report?"

"He wants a daily report on everything that's late. Didn't he tell you about it?"

"Nope. No, Joe, he didn't."

"What's going on around here, Jim?"

"What do you mean?"

"The word's out George Brice is bringing somebody in to do one of your commercials."

I said, "That's right. What did he do, send out an office memo?"

"Rudy d'Franco was telling everybody about it."

I said, "Well, Joe, I guess if you want to know what's going on, you'll have to ask d'Franco, right?"

Back in my office, I buzzed Edna. "Ask Barney Marker to come around, will you?"

Edna said, "I've been hearing things. Is there anything I ought to know?"

I said, "I don't know. What did your mother tell you?"

Barney Marker turned up some ten minutes later. Hair, checkered wool tie, tight pants. "Jim, have we got an idea. You know those family fares Federal has? What do you think of the Federal Stowaway Plan? We could call it the new escape for wives."

I said, "Sit down. I want to talk to you about something."

"Jim? Don't tell anybody about it until we do a story board. Wait'll you see what we're working on."

I said, "Barney, you've kind of had your nose against the grindstone around here—I guess you're wondering when you're going to get a raise, right?"

"Well, I didn't want to say anything. . . ."

I said, "Well, Barney, I figured it would only be a favor to you to tell you we don't have you in for one."

Barney Marker blinked and opened his mouth but did not seem to know quite what to say. It occurred to me that he had popeyes. Not markedly so, but that was what they were, just the same. I had not noticed it before. I said, "So since you'll probably be leaving us for somebody who isn't so cheap about it, I thought I'd call you in and tell you we'll give you a month instead of the customary two weeks to look around."

Barney Marker said, "What do you mean? You mean if I quit? . . ."

I said, "I also thought you ought to know that you can use me for reference anywhere. Incidentally, in case you don't know how it works in this business, any ads you started and I helped you on are considered your ads. You ought to have a fairly decent book by now."

Barney Marker said, "Well, look, I didn't ask for a raise, Jim. I mean, I never said I'd quit if I didn't get a raise."

I said, "Another thing you can use, for the next month, at least. You're still on the payroll here. It gives you a little better bargaining position if they think you still have a job. That's one of the dumb things that goes with the business, you know?"

"Jim, that's all if I quit, but I don't want to quit, Jim. I think we have another ad for Buffalo ready to show you."

"Barney, one of the reasons I called you in here is that it's tightening-up time. You know how agencies figure. Cut a few salaries off the top and cut a few salaries off the bottom. Hell, you've been here long enough to start talking about a raise and if you wait around we'll be by with your two weeks' notice. It's always kind of lucky to know what's in the wind, you know? It gives you a chance to make the first move while you still have the advantage."

Barney Marker seemed stunned. He said, "Jim, wait a minute. Am I giving you a month's notice or are you giving it to me?"

I said, "Barney, if I ever had a raise coming and I got this kind of treatment, I know what I'd do."

"Well," he said. "That's how it is, eh?"

I said, "This could be the smartest move you ever made. If you don't think of yourself first in this business, Barney, nobody's going to do it for you."

"Well, do you want to see that Buffalo ad? . . ."

I said, "That's already been reassigned."

"Oh."

I said, "Barney, good luck to you. Let's hear how you make out."

"Sure," he said. "Sure, why not?"

He left my office in a daze. He did not know what had hit him. Well, at least he wasn't married.

I got up from my desk and walked out into the hall. Barney Marker was talking to Rudy d'Franco and two of the other kids. They looked at me. D'Franco pursed his lips and turned around and walked into his office.

Melinda's car was not in the garage when I got home. I let myself into the kitchen and made a Scotch and soda and took it out to the porch.

We still owed twenty-two thousand on the mortgage. My pension plan and profit sharing ought to take care of this and tide me over until I had something. If the house was paid for, I could take a job for twenty-five.

The phone rang. I went into the kitchen and answered it.

"Mr. Bower?"

"Yes."

"This is Ben Alder, Bridgeport Irrigation?"

I said, "Who?"

"Ben Alder. Bridgeport Irrigation. Your wife asked me to come over this morning?"

I said, "I'm sorry. I just got in. My wife asked you over?"

"Yes, sir. For the sprinkler system?"

"We don't have a sprinkler system."

"We install sprinkler systems, Mr. Bower. Mrs. Bower wanted an estimate."

I said, "Oh. Well, all right. How much did it come out to?"

"Well, you have a half-inch line. Three-quarters of an acre. We checked with Bridgeport Hydraulic to be sure you have enough water pressure—there doesn't seem to be any trouble there."

I said, "Three-quarters of an acre?"

"That's about your lawn area. It doesn't include your house or the woods in back. Mr. Bower, we come out at about nineteen hundred dollars."

"Nineteen hundred dollars?"

"That's an automatic system, of course, underground; we cut away strips of turf and replace them. You won't even know where the lines are after a week or two."

I said, "Yes, well, this is something I want to think about, you know? I guess my wife has your number."

"You understand, Mr. Bower, we'd be in and out in four days. Everybody on the crew is a trained man. We don't believe in dragging jobs out—"

"Okay. Thank you."

"Mr. Bower? I think I mentioned this to Mrs. Bower—I think you have chinch bugs."

"Chinch bugs."

"Something you might want to check out. Chinch bugs and you won't have any lawn at all."

I went back to the porch. We really needed a nineteen-hundred-dollar sprinkler system. Everybody did.

Melinda drove in and I made her a martini. "Somebody from Bridgeport Irrigation called. It took me five minutes to realize it wasn't some kind of medical service."

Melinda said, "How much did they say?"

"Nineteen hundred dollars."

"Nineteen hundred? I thought more like five hundred."

"For five hundred, you can water the living room."

Melinda said, "Are you going to the funeral tomorrow?"

"Yes."

Melinda fell silent.

I said, "So, no more Slim."

Melinda said, "I suppose I should have gone over to see Jean."

I said, "I think her daughter's staying with her."

"It was all so sudden. Slim didn't even look sick to me."

"Yeah, well, when he keeled over, you kind of weren't around."

Melinda did not answer this directly. "Do you have any cigarettes?"

I gave her a Marlboro. "As a matter of fact, it seems to me you kind of head for Barlow Matthews every chance you get. I mention it because if I notice it, I'm sure other people do, too."

Now she drank some of her martini. "Is that what's

bothering you? That some other people might think they notice something?"

"I'll lay you odds Kate has."

"What nice little people we know. Everybody with their noses in somebody else's business."

"It is Kate's business."

"And yours, I suppose."

"There are those that would say so, yes."

"I see."

I said, "Melinda, you'll just wind up on the outside looking in. The guy's not only got kids but a job that won't bear any funny talk, you know?"

"Would potato salad and a sandwich be enough for you tonight?"

"Why not?"

"You don't mind if I finish my drink first?"

"Finish the bottle, if you want."

I had put my pack of cigarettes on the glass table and Melinda now took another. She had not quite smoked half of the first one. "So now everybody is talking about me, is that it?"

I said, "No. Not that I know of."

"Then why did you bring it up?"

I said, "Oh, I guess I thought I ought to."

"And you'd like to hear what I have to say."

I said, "Let's just say as the landlord here, I'd like to know if I still have a tenant."

"I'm forty-three years old, Jim. Forty-three."

"I know."

"There's got to be more to life than this."

"Than what? Busy old Jim and the sock drawer?"

"I don't know, Jim. All I know is that you can't really say our life together has been one big electric charge."

I said, "I guess not."

Melinda said, "I don't know what else to tell you."

I said, "Well, I'm sure when there's anything you do want to say, you'll get around to it."

Melinda said, "Now you're going to be understanding. God."

wednesday

The Congregational church was on the north side of the
Boston Post Road. It was one of those pretty white New
England churches, white steeple, white frame, as honest-
looking as the Pilgrims you read about in grade school.

The minister was a big guy with big hands and a tan and
a voice that had about the same pitch as a saxophone. He
said he had not known Edward Hawes well enough to call
him Slim. He said he wished he had known him. He talked
about the dams and bridges that Slim had built.

I had the feeling the minister wished that he was halfway
up part of Slim's Andes, building a bridge himself. I do not

know what this has to do with your soul. On the other hand, I had never seen a soul and I had seen a bridge. It was a nice service.

The minute everybody was outside, Helmut Cross had a story. Helmut had been waiting to nail a raccoon that had been at his garbage cans. This morning, Helmut had got him with a .22. "I tell you this, however, without pride. Or to put it another way, at five o'clock in the morning, the difference between a raccoon and a skunk is practically invisible."

Betty Reynolds said, "You shot a skunk?"

"Come closer and you can tell."

I lit a cigarette and thought, That's the way it will be. Five minutes after you're dead, they'll change the subject.

Everybody was going over to the Slatterys' for coffee. Kate Matthews said, "Jim? You aren't driving into the city, by any chance?"

I said, "Sure. Do you want a lift?"

"If you don't mind the company."

We walked over to the Triumph and I said, "Hope you don't mind the seats. They go with the mystique."

"I'm sure my seat will fit your seat."

I drove over the Wilton road to the Merritt. By this time, Kate had said that it had been a very nice service and I had said that funerals were just a way of pretending that somebody who died was still hanging around.

Kate said, "Please don't be grim. Every once in a while I can't take any more grim."

"Okay. How come Barlow didn't drive in?"

"Today is Barlow's day for his thinking man's course. He's writing it at home."

"He's writing it himself?"

"I think he's rewriting something somebody else wrote. I wouldn't be going in myself but a girl I knew in college is in town. We're supposed to have lunch or something."

The Merritt is a four-lane blacktop highway with an island in the center. Lots of trees and grass. No billboards. The speed limit was fifty. I was doing about fifty-five. A Volkswagen passed me as if we were parked.

I said, "I guess you heard about Jack Thompson."

Kate said, "Barlow said he was sorry about that, Jim. He thought it was your idea."

"Jack Thompson pulls that stuff," I said. "Melinda was pretty sore about it."

Kate Matthews said, "Is that a country club?"

"Westchester, I think."

"Where are we now?"

"Well, Rye's over that way. I don't know what town this is. Harrison, probably."

"Do you drive in often, Jim?"

"Practically never unless we're shooting a commercial. If I'm going to be late, I want a car there."

"Jim?"

"What?"

"Were you and Melinda at the Slattery cookout Sunday?"

I was reasonably certain that Kate could not have driven up our driveway and seen Barlow's car in our garage. I said, "Yep."

"We couldn't make it. Barlow had to see that fellow in Darien again."

I said, "A lawn party when it's a hundred in the shade is nothing to make, Kate."

A Mustang the color of a burning barn went by me on the right. I thought we were going to be pulled over into his lane from the suction. "I hope this is one of the days they have radar on the Hutchinson River Parkway."

Kate Matthews said, "What time was the party, anyway?"

I thought, Oh oh.

I said, "I don't know. I got there about quarter to three."

"Oh, then you went alone."

I said, "Melinda had to drop off a telephone list or something with somebody. She's on so many committees she could run for office."

We got onto the Cross County Parkway and I said, "Now, that is one hell of a thing to do to a Rolls-Royce."

The Rolls was ahead of us. It had been painted in what I suppose were psychedelic flowers.

Kate Matthews did not say anything.

I lit a cigarette and said, "Anyway, the West Side Highway should be clear now. Hit it at nine o'clock and it turns into a parking lot."

Kate Matthews said, "Where's your office, Jim?"

"Lexington Avenue. In fact, we keep a lot of trains in the basement. Where are you meeting your friend?"

"She's staying at the Gotham. I was just thinking that there's a little matter that you and I had better discuss."

I said, "Well, it's just about eleven. We could pretend it's Eastern Standard Time and have a drink."

Kate Matthews said, "Jim, no matter what, you're always in there thinking.".

I turned and grinned at her. There seemed to be an odd sparkle under one of Kate's eyes. Kate was crying.

I said, "Did you see that? That hearse was filled with kids. What the hell would kids buy a hearse for?"

The West Side Highway was three lanes in both directions, concrete, with the Hudson lying there on your right like a bathtub full of dirty water. A barge and three lighters were on their way upriver. They did not seem to be moving. There were some men in green fatigues cutting down the brush on the divider between the north and south lanes. A sign said that it was ninety-one degrees. The sky and the street and the river all seemed to be the same color. Slim could not have picked a better day to leave town.

I said, "Big liner pulling in down there. Remember when they had the tugboat strike or whatever it was? I think it was the *United States*—the captain docked that thing by himself. I think the bow smashed up part of the dock but he got it in. I think it was the *United States*."

Kate Matthews was now fighting the tears with a handkerchief. I said, "Any particular bar you like? I'll drop you off in front and find a garage."

Kate was trying to stop crying. "You just want me to go in alone so they won't think you were beating me."

"Well, let's don't pick a place with a bouncer."

I turned off the West Side Highway at Fifty-sixth Street. We ran into a red light and a Con Edison hole in the street at Eleventh Avenue. We ran into a red light at Tenth Avenue. We ran into red lights at Ninth and Eighth, and then we ran into a block where somebody seemed to be putting up a skyscraper on one side of the street and you had to get your nose in ahead of a big blue delivery van driven by a teen-ager with a vacant look before he crushed you. I made it and behind me he honked again and again because there was a truck in front of me and I did not drive through it.

I said, "Son of a bitch has a personality problem." I got out of the Triumph and walked back to the van and said to the youth, "What's the matter with you?"

A cop, not one of those nice understanding cops on television but a real goddamned cop, said, "Get that car out of there. What do you think this is, a garage?"

I got back into the Triumph, stalled it, started it again, and got as far as Sixth Avenue, where we now sat behind a

charter bus that solved its diesel emission problem by sending all the fumes into my front seat.

Kate said, "Jim, turn left here and let's go to the Cornwall."

"What's the Cornwall?"

"Our apartment. They'll park the car for you."

"All right. How do I get there?"

"Turn right on Central Park South. I'll tell you."

The Cornwall was a high narrow apartment building in
with all the other high narrow apartment buildings facing
Central Park. It seemed to be white brick and sure enough,
a man in an admiral's suit opened the door for Kate and
then came around to my side after she spoke to him. "Just
leave the key in the transmission, sir. We'll take care of it."

"Fine."

I got out and realized I was as wet as if I had got caught
in a shower. Kate was waiting for me in the doorway and I
went into the lobby with her and said, "Where's the bar?"

"The bar is in there. We also have liquor in the room. Jim,
I'd rather not sit in the bar with my face in a handkerchief."

"Well, okay."

She got off a grin and said, "If you'd rather not . . ."

I said, "What the hell."

The apartment was on the seventh floor, one long room
with a Pullman kitchen on the left and a bathroom on the
right and, on the other side of the floor-to-ceiling windows,
Central Park.

I said, "Where's the booze?"

"In the cabinet in the kitchen. Bourbon for me, with a little
water and no ice."

I went into the kitchen and found a bottle of just about
everything that you could think of and made a Scotch and
water for myself and a bourbon and water for Kate. Kate
had turned on the air conditioning. Even the slight feeling
that the air was moving made things seem a little cooler. I
said, "Mind if I take off my coat?"

"Take off your tie, too. Well, Jim, I can't say a funeral was
just what I needed today."

I said, "When do you need them?"

Kate said, "You know, of course, what's going on."

"Barlow and Melinda?"

Kate said, "Barlow and Melinda."

I said, "Well, Kate, I guess I've kind of known something

was going on but I'm not all that sure what and I sure don't know what to do about it."

"I don't know what to do about it, either."

I said, "Maybe that's what we're supposed to do about it. Nothing."

Kate said, "But you did know they've been seeing each other?"

"Not exactly, I didn't know it. No."

"Then you didn't know she was up here."

"Here?"

"Mm hmm." Kate drank some of her bourbon and water.

I said, "Kate, how do you know she was here?"

" I just know, Jim."

"Yes, well, knowing and thinking are two different things."

"Jim, the doorman asked me when we got the Lincoln."

I said, "There are a million Lincolns."

"Convertibles, with Connecticut plates and Barlow and my cousin in them?"

"Your cousin?"

"That's what the doorman said."

I said, "Well, there's still something of an outside chance it wasn't Melinda."

Kate smiled a little. "Yes."

"But you don't believe it."

"Do you?"

I said, "Kate, sometimes I think it's not so dumb to be a little dumb."

"How do you do it, Jim? How do you just watch and say nothing?"

At least she was talking about it instead of crying. I did not particularly want to talk about it or cry either. I said, "Well, Kate, I drink."

"Will you give Melinda a divorce if she asks for one?"

"Yes. I guess so. How about you?"

"I don't know. I just don't know. We sound like the walking wounded, don't we?"

I said, "Kate, this walking wounded had better get to the office. I think I have to go in so they can fire me."

"Fire you?"

"It's beginning to feel that way, yes."

"Oh, Jim, isn't there anything right in this world?"

I said, "I don't know. I have an idea for Slim everything ought to look sensational, just about now."

I got to the office at quarter after two. I said to Edna, "Anything cooking?"

"Brook Parker was looking for you. So were Alec Mayberry and Percy Holland. I think you ought to know something. . . ."

"What?"

"The grapevine around here has it that the agency got in a lot of trouble with Federal, and"—Edna took a breath here—"according to the grapevine, you fired Barney Marker to get out from under."

"That's what the grapevine says, eh?"

"You know grapevines." Edna handed me a green mimeographed office memo. "Here also are the new rules on the wearing of the hair and beard."

I looked at it. It was signed by Marion Simons. Everybody would be in the office in the morning. This was a place of business. If our clients could operate their businesses efficiently, there was no reason why this advertising agency could not. Attendance reports would be turned in monthly by department supervisors. I said, "The Third Reich will last a thousand years."

I went into my office and turned on the light and sat down and looked at all the papers on my desk. I picked up a yellow requisition and looked at it for a while without really seeing it. Then I realized that it was an old one for a job that was already done. I threw it in the wastebasket.

The phone rang. A woman with a sexy voice said that she was with Venier Productions. She wanted to know when it would be convenient for them to show me their reel of commercials. I said that it would be a waste of their time. I told her to call Brook Parker or Feldman, one of the art supervisors. I said that I did not select studios.

Charles Leader came in. It was the first time he had been in my office. He stopped and looked around. You could almost hear the whirring of little gears in his mind. My office was bigger than his. My furniture had not come out of the supply room.

"What are we supposed to do about Miniflex?"

I said, "Tell traffic to give the requisition to Alec Mayberry."

"Does he know cameras?"

"Alec knows ads. Knowing cameras is your job."

"Is this Mayberry a professional writer?"

I looked at him. I said, "What kind of a question is that?"

"I don't want a copy cub on this, Bower."

I said, "Why don't you just see what he comes up with?"

"And if we're late again?"

"If you'd sold the ad Percy Holland did, you wouldn't have been late the first time."

He did a little breathing but did not pop off this time. He said, "Mayberry. Very well. Tell him to come up to my office."

I said, "You tell traffic and traffic will tell Alec."

"I might add, Bower, that George Brice wanted to know why we missed the deadline that we did."

I said, "That's George's job. I'm glad to see he's keeping busy."

Charles Leader's mouth made a funny little quirk and he simply said, "Very well." He left.

I just sat there. Nothing in particular came to my mind. I did not feel like looking in on Brook Parker and I did not feel like talking to Alec Mayberry or Percy Holland.

What I felt like doing, I realized, was sitting in the park. Jeff Sermon filled my doorway with fat. "Jim?"

"Hi."

"Did you tell traffic to go to George Brice about those ads?"

"What ads?"

"Houston and the travel agent."

I said, "I didn't tell traffic anything."

The big fat man came in and sat down on my sofa. "I really got the business this morning, Jim."

I said, "From George?"

"What does he want from me anyway? You'd think that California mess was my fault."

I said, "Jeff, it's your turn. I got the business for ads you never even told me about, so what do you want?"

Jeff Sermon said, "Have you seen anything from Mayberry or Holland yet?"

"Nope."

"What about this guy George brought in to do a commercial?"

"I don't get to see that at all, Jeff."

"Who do they show it to?"

"George, I guess."

"I wish I knew what was going on around here."

I said, "You aren't even in the right room."

"I have kids in college."

"Jeff, tell them to write if they get work."

"You wouldn't know anything I ought to know . . .?"

I said, "I don't know a goddamned thing, Jeff. All I know is a lot of things got screwed up on Federal and we're all getting a little of the buckshot."

"It was just that they kept after me for California and Buffalo. . . ." The big man had a lost expression. He looked as if he were trying to tell Saint Peter that none of it had been his fault at all. He was against sin; ask anybody.

I said, "Don't worry about it. Everybody knows the real problem's in creative, right?"

"Jim, I didn't point any fingers your way."

"The hell you didn't."

"I didn't, Jim. I swear I didn't."

"Sure."

"Well, I didn't."

I said, "What are you worried about? George isn't going to ask me about you. He isn't going to ask me about anything."

The fat man sort of shuffled his feet and said, "Well, I just thought I'd look in and say hello."

"Yeah, well, take it easy."

When Jeff Sermon left, I told Edna I would be in Brook Parker's office. My office was getting visitors I did not need that day.

I walked down the hall to Brook's room. On a wide, low black steel cabinet he had a Sony videotape recorder and screen.

Brook was sitting on the floor in the corner, smoking, with his knees tucked up under his chin. He saw me and did not move. He said, "The guys from Den-Test will be in about three."

I said, "What for?"

"I put our commercial on tape yesterday."

"Let's see it."

He got up and walked over to the set and turned it on. There, in a high-backed wicker rocking chair, was a sixty-five-year-old woman, hair in a bun, bony and hawkfaced.

"My name is Frances Beaker Smith. I'm sixty-five years old and all the teeth you see are mine. Now they tell me we could sell more Den-Test if it didn't burn your mouth. Well, that may be. But I was brought up to believe that if something good for you smarts a bit, that's the price you pay. I brought my children up that way and I make Den-Test that way. I'm too old to change Den-Test now just to sell a few more tubes. If it stings, just close your eyes."

I said, "Anybody seen it?"

"Coleman, and then he brought George Brice down."

"What did George have to say?"

"He said it was very original. I couldn't tell whether that was good or bad."

I said, "You aren't supposed to. George wants you, but he doesn't want any of your commercials."

Brook Parker said, "Then what does he want me for?"

"I think he read somewhere that he was supposed to. George has great hopes for you. One of these days you're going to come up with some way to electrify the world without turning any brand managers gray."

Brook Parker said, "I tried to get you this morning but you weren't in."

"I went to a funeral."

"Oh. George thought you were out for other reasons."

"What, looking for a job?"

"That's what everybody's saying."

"Did that make George happy?"

"A happy George looks like all the other Georges. I think they carved him out of soap." Brook lit a cigarette and sat down in one of his director's chairs. "Are you looking for another job?"

"Not yet. I'm not that bright."

"He doesn't like you, you know."

"He's done everything but send me anonymous notes. I know he doesn't like me." I lit a cigarette of my own. "He going to try to sell this spot?"

Brook Parker said, "Who knows? Are you going to be here?"

"What for?"

"Well, we kind of did this together."

"The hell we did. All I did was copy down what you said."

"That isn't true. We pushed each other along. If I didn't think of it, you would have."

I said, "I don't even know whether I'm supposed to be at your meeting."

"It might even up the odds a little."

I said, "Well, why not? Look, Percy and Alec were looking for me. I'll see what they want and be back here by three."

The meeting would have to be in Brook's office. A Sony

machine was not exactly an attaché case you could carry all over town.

I walked around to Alec Mayberry's office. "I hear you were looking for me."

Our playboy copywriter said, "What with all the new rules around here, I wasn't sure what to do with this. Do I still show you ads?"

"What is it?"

"Travel agent ad."

"Let's see."

He showed me the layout. It was practically a full-page picture of a man's face. The headline was,

He thinks he's your mother.

I said, "Bet you could do better."

"Not funny?"

"Not funny enough to be funny."

Alec Mayberry said, "That is unfortunate. I understand we're supposed to have something today."

I said, "Got a pencil?"

"Be my guest." He handed me a soft-lead drafting pencil and a lined yellow pad.

I bent over the edge of his desk and wrote,

Do not leave town without calling one of these numbers.

Under this, I put in some little lines to indicate the names and numbers of travel agents.

Alec said, "I take it that is the reason you're the copy chief around here."

"Nope. You work on an account long enough and you get so things just kind of occur to you."

I went around to my office and a man I did not know came in. Balding, heavy-set, the grin of an Irish fat man. "Jim Bower?"

I said, "I think so."

"Tim Malloy. Okay if I come in for a sec?"

"Why not?"

He came in and shook hands with me. "I feel kind of funny about this, Jim. The way I got it from George, I was just coming in to do a commercial because everybody was busy."

I said, "Oh? How are you doing?"

"Oh, I don't know. We just got started. The thing is, I didn't know this was one of your commercials or I wouldn't have taken the job."

"Nothing sacred about my commercials," I said. "There's a cardinal rule in this business, friend. Take the money. How did you find out it was one of mine, anyway?"

"The kid I'm working with. Rudy something?"

"Rudy d'Franco. Yeah, Rudy would have been the first to tell you."

"He's sure something. All I want to do is a commercial and he's in there telling me all about what the French are doing on film these days."

"The French, eh? It used to be the Italians."

"Anyway, they want something on reservations. The account guy—Sermon?—he was giving me the poop on some kind of computer they have."

I said, "I have a couple of ads around here I did on it. Let's see if I can find them." I went over to the cabinet in the corner and began to look through an accumulation of junk. "It's quite an operation. They put ten million bucks in that thing."

Malloy said, "Hey, I don't want to put you out."

I said, "That's all right. One thing about getting your information from ads they've already run—you know what they'll let you say. Here. Here's the first one we did, if it's any help to you."

It was a long copy ad. The headline was,

Introducing Federal Airlines' new
$10,000,000 reservations computer.

Under this was a subhead.

It never forgets a customer.

Malloy looked at the ad for a while. "Well, it's got everything and the kitchen sink."

I said, "We must have changed that thing five or six times before everything was right."

Malloy said, "How does Federal feel about animation; do you know?"

I said, "I don't think they have any opinion about it one way or the other. I can tell you how I feel about it, if you want to know."

"Sure."

"I wouldn't touch it. For one thing, it will take too long—I'll bet it takes you ten days just to get a ten-second pencil test. The way I hear it, they're kind of in a hurry. But that's just one reason. The other is you can get halfway through it and Federal will turn up with some new twist they want to promote. You can cut up film to make it say something else, but that's one thing you practically can't do with animation."

Malloy nodded. "Well, I wasn't sure animation was the right thing for them, anyway."

I said, "George going to give this the full treatment?"

"What's that?"

"Test it against twenty or thirty other ideas?"

Malloy said, "I don't think he can, can he?"

I said, "No. An airline isn't a bottle of Relief. You can run one spot for a year if you're selling aspirin, maybe, but you sure can't run one spot for a year for an airline. Unless you're selling cross-country tickets for fifty bucks a throw."

Malloy said, "I told him it wasn't the same as Relief."

"You did the Relief commercial?"

Malloy laughed. "Somebody has to have done it."

I said, "I wasn't commenting. What the hell, the way I get it, it outsold everything on the market."

Malloy said, "Jim, if it means anything, Relief was Relief and Federal's Federal. I have an idea George knows it, too. You may not like his Relief commercial, but the guy knows what he's doing."

I said, "Well, keep your cool with Rudy. Resist all those little urges to bust him in the mouth and he may just come up with something."

"You want to see what we come up with before I show it to George?"

I said, "Nope. A good idea can't stand going through too many filters. Good luck."

Malloy said, "Anyway, I just thought I'd look in and tell you I didn't know what the score was when I took this job. Thanks for the ad. Sermon didn't even give us that."

I said, "Sermon's all right. He's just dumb."

Malloy left and I was about to go around to see Percy Holland, but before I could get out of the door, the crabgrass came in.

"Hello, Jim." Marion Simons. Treasurer. Member of the board of directors.

"Marion," I said.

"You weren't in this morning."

"I had to go to a funeral."

"Oh? Your secretary didn't seem to know that."

I said, "I forgot to tell her."

"Jim, that strikes me as a very strange coincidence. The day I put out a memo on getting in on time, you don't come in at all."

"Yes, well, my friend didn't know you were going to put a memo out or he wouldn't have died."

"I can do without any flip answers, Jim."

"All right, Marion. What can I do for you?"

"You gave Barney Marker a month's severance?"

"That's right."

"He wasn't even with us a year."

"He didn't do anything to get fired for, either."

"If that's going to be your attitude, Jim, perhaps there is no further need for conversation at all."

I said, "Marion, what in hell attitude do you want me to have? You walk in here and throw a couple of rocks and then you get sore because I didn't bleed enough."

Marion Simons crossed his legs. I had a mental picture of sharp, thin, white little chicken bones under that neatly pressed gray worsted. "Jim, I believe you were told yesterday that everyone in your department was to observe this company's office hours. If any of the secretaries on this floor is keeping a record, I'm afraid you'll have to point her out to me. I couldn't find her."

I said, "Marion, a record of what? When people get in?"

"When people get in and if people get in."

"Nobody's keeping a record. We don't pay writers by the hour—what do you want a record for?"

"I was not aware that I had to explain myself to you, Jim. I still am not aware of it."

I wondered what had got into him. I had known Marion Simons for eight years. He had groused from time to time about this guy's expense account or that guy's raise, but this was a different Marion altogether. This Marion was telling you to salute.

I said, "All right, Marion. We can keep a record. I don't think that's the best way in the world to boost the morale around here. . . ."

"I'm getting a little tired of worrying about creative's morale, Jim. In fact, I'm getting quite tired of it. Everyone in media seems to get in here on time. The account people come in on time, the traffic people and the people in production all come in on time—everyone in the agency, Jim, seems to believe in a day's work for a day's pay but creative. Creative? Heaven forbid. The muse won't speak to them. I think, Jim, that your people had better find some way to get in touch with the muse under the same working conditions the rest of us observe."

I said, "Well, Marion, it's your agency."

"That's right, Jim. It's my agency." Marion Simons walked to my door and stopped and turned to look at me again. "I would like the records brought to my office every Friday, Jim. If anyone gets in more than twenty minutes late, I would also like your explanation delivered along with the record."

I said, "I'll do what I can."

"Jim, I did not ask you to do what you could. I believe I just told you what I wanted done. It's not a question of doing what you can. That isn't the question at all."

It was just about three o'clock when he walked out the door. I got up from my desk and went down the hall to Brook Parker's office, wondering about this. That had not been the businesslike, we've-got-to-get-this-place-organized discussion that Marion Simons had pretended it was. That had been Marion versus us.

Could he possibly resent the idea that it was the creative department that made this place? Yes. That, I thought, was something that Marion Simons could very easily resent.

In Brook Parker's office, I found George Brice in his neat blue suit, scrubbed-looking, quiet and ordinary. Bob Coleman, white-haired, athletic, radiating that peculiar force of his. Mark Penman, the brand manager from Landum, lanky, outdoorsy, cheerful and unnecessary-looking. And a man I did not know at all.

Brook Parker was fiddling with the controls on the Sony.

Bob Coleman said, "Jim, how are you?"

"Fine," I said.

Mark Penman gave me his lopsided grin. "Bob tells me we're all going to say Wow. Jim, this is Tom Sloan, our director of marketing."

Tom Sloan was in his fifties, glasses, thinning gray hair, a rather slight man with a face that was all business. We shook hands and said hello to each other. Tom Sloan was short of effusive.

Brook Parker said, "Okay. If this thing will work, I guess we're ready."

Bob Coleman said, "I'll get the lights."

George Brice said, "I'll get them, Bob." George turned off the lights and Frances Beaker Smith appeared on the screen and scolded us all.

It is strange, but I had always noticed that the idea that looked swell when you first saw it finished always seemed a lot less than swell the moment that you showed it to a client.

Mark Penman was the first to speak. He said, "Tom, I think it's great."

I looked at him in some surprise. I was surprised that he liked it and I was surprised that he did not wait to see how his boss felt about it.

Tom Sloan said, "May we see it again?"

"Sure," Brook Parker said. He put the machine on rewind.

Bob Coleman said, "We went to this because—if I can remember Brook's words—the only way to shake Den-Test loose is with blasting powder." Bob lit a cigarette and added, "Brook's our resident magician, Tom. Brook, remember the Willow cough drop campaign?"

Brook Parker said, "Mmmm." He did not look up. He was getting the Sony ready to play again.

Bob Coleman said, "*If they taste good, see your doctor.* Nobody on earth would have thought of a line like that but Brook."

Tom Sloan did not say anything.

I thought, Shut up, Bob. The guy doesn't want you selling him.

"Okay," Brook said.

He played the spot again. This time I had the feeling that the actress's inflection was wrong on a couple of lines.

Mark Penman said, "Well, Tom?"

Tom Sloan said, "Interesting. I don't know what our legal problems with this might be."

Mark Penman said, "I think it's a pistol."

Tom Sloan said, "George, I think it's very interesting. I have a few little nits—"

George Brice said, "That's permitted, Tom."

Tom Sloan ignored whatever humor George had had in that and said, "I think we could go a little stronger on the end benefit. I know it's implied. I'm wondering if there isn't some way to strengthen it."

Bob Coleman said, "Jim? Can do?"

I said, "I don't know. This thing's kind of all of a piece. It isn't something you can just slip other things into, you know?"

Tom Sloan said, "Still, people don't buy toothpaste to get toothpaste. They buy fewer cavities or fresher breath. I've always found that spelling out the benefit gives people a little more assurance. Jack, I'm sure you can work it in. I seem to remember there was the perfect spot for it. I think she said, 'something that's good for you,' or something. I don't see why we couldn't be a little more specific."

It was not the time to tell him that my name was Jim, not Jack. I said, "Look, I can always try it and see. If it doesn't work, it doesn't work, but we already have this. Why don't I see what happens if I spell it out?"

George Brice lit a cigarette. He did not seem to have a lot to say. There was, I thought, a certain amount of strength in his silence.

Mark Penman said, "Jim, you understand we're not talking about the concept."

I said, "I understand."

Tom Sloan said, "Now, I'm wondering about the advisability of casting. I understand the value of a type like this. Still, I wonder if she has to be such a crone. I don't really think we're taking any of the integrity away if we went with a woman with more of a smile. Someone like Claudette Colbert, for instance. George, I'm talking about someone people could identify with. This old hag could just turn people off."

George Brice said, "We can look at some other women, Tom."

Tom Sloan said, "I'm not talking about a professional smiler. . . ."

Bob Coleman said, "As Jim said, let's give it a try."

Brook Parker had not had a thing to say. He was sitting on the floor, smoking a cigarette, watching all this with pale eyes.

Mark Penman said, "Would it hurt anything if she said the sting kept her breath fresh, Jim? It's certainly a believable claim, if we're making a thing out of the sting."

I said, "Gee, I wouldn't, Mark. That's kind of forcing her out of character, you know?"

Tom Sloan said, "I'm not so sure about that, Jim. Is it Jack or Jim?"

"Jim," I said.

"I think Mark is right. If we're making a point out of the sting, I don't see why we can't make a benefit out of it, too."

George Brice did not say anything at all, and neither did Brook Parker.

I said, "Look, this basket will only hold so many eggs, you know? What we have here is a kind of moral image for this stuff. You start futzing with that and you'll lose what we started out with and not get the impact or whatever word I want to make up for it. What I mean is, that's just something you ought not to do."

Tom Sloan said, "I don't understand that."

I said, "This commercial is a thing. Just the way it stands, it is a complete thing. It even has edges, you know? It's like taking a solid red square and saying, Couldn't we use a little green in it? It won't be a solid red square any more."

Tom Sloan said, "The commercial is not the end, Jim. The end is a sale, not a commercial."

I said, "Well, yeah, but you keep thinking about the end and you kind of don't use the means right. Forget the end and do this right—that's what I think I'm saying."

Tom Sloan said, "And still I have to ask myself if this concentration on execution is in the best interest of the product. Jim, there are certain things we know about brands like this. I find it a little hard to ignore them. Believe me, no one is trying to put a damper on your concept. We're really just talking about a few refinements to make this concept work as hard for us as possible."

George Brice said, "Tom, I see no reason why we can't explore the suggestions you've made. Brook, if you'll see about getting the dupe, I'd like to talk to Tom for a few minutes before he leaves."

Brook Parker still had nothing to say, but Mark Penman said, with his nice, boyish grin, "Fellows, the last thing we want to do is change the basics in this. We aren't talking about a new commercial, if you follow me."

I said, "Let's take a look at it the way you see it. What can it cost?"

Mark Penman said, "That's the idea, Jim."

Tom Sloan said, "Brook, Jack, thank you very much."

George Brice said, "Bob, if you're free to drop in for a minute in the morning, there's something I think we might discuss."

George Brice and Tom Sloan went off to George's office to talk over whatever you talk over in the president's office. Brook Parker took the tape off the Sony and said good night

o Mark Penman. Brook went downstairs to our TV complex to get the new dupe.

Mark Penman said, "Well, Jim, how does it feel to come
up with a winner?"

I said, "Winners beat losers."

Mark Penman said that he had to get his car from some
garage and I went back to my office.

Joe Slattery had called. Could I meet him for a drink? I
sat at my desk awhile. George Brice had not really spoken
to me once. I was not sure which was better, Marion Simons'
talking to me or George's not.

I met Joe Slattery at five in Michael's Pub on Forty-eighth
Street. There were very low round wooden tables in the front
of this place where you could have drinks. Joe's big body, in
one of the chairs next to one of these tables, looked weirdly
outsize. He saw me as I came in and waved and said, "You'd
better start with four if you want us to start off even."

I said, "I don't care if you're ahead of me, Joe. It will give
me something to look up to."

"What are you drinking?" Joe Slattery. Big chest. Seer-
sucker suit.

"Martini, I guess. What are you doing in this part of town?"

"Look at that. Jim, that has to be the cutest little ass I ever
saw."

The girl attached to this wonder had made her way by us.
A great deal of pale hair, long tanned arms, sensational legs.
I said, "I have an idea that could be very expensive."

"Jim, you're the only guy I know who daydreams about
the price. Hey, garson, waiter, George, you. Bring my friend
a nice dry martini. Jim, how's the ad game?"

I said, "Not so hot, Joe. How's the engineering business?"

"Beats the hell out of me, lieutenant. I'm not in it any
more."

I said, "What happened?"

"You know all these kids running around with the hair
and beards? Jim, they're just a front. The real kids are right
behind them with big glasses and slide rules, only they aren't
kids at all, Jim. They're germs. MIT makes them in test tubes
and packages them in glass jars."

I said, "They got to you, eh?"

"I think I was put out with the garbage. Hey, did you
know Barlow Matthews was on their board of directors?"

I said, "Yes."

"I'll bet that son of a bitch knew about it and didn't say a word."

I said, "Well, Joe, if he did know about it, what could he have said?"

"He could have told me what was up and given me a running start. Christ, now I got to look around on just a month's severance."

I said, "How do things look?"

"Oh, boy. Who knows?"

I said, "Guy with your experience ought to be able to call his own shots, Joe."

"Well, I don't know. I talked to an employment agency and all they said was it's cold out there." Joe Slattery lit a cigarette and said, "You know, all I know is fieldwork, calling on guys like Mobil or what-have-you. Well, guys like Helmut Cross, you know? Helmut needs a storage tank or some kind of processing vessel, Christ, give me the specs and I'll get you an estimate. Now they tell me they don't do it that way any more."

I said, "How do they do it?"

"Well, let's say Helmut needs some kind of reaction vessel, okay? You know what I'm supposed to do? I'm supposed to work all the way back from the finished product to this one lousy vessel and tell Helmut he's doing business all wrong."

I said, "Sounds like the way the banks are beginning to operate. They have banks now that can tell you how to start your own country."

Joe Slattery said, "You know what it is? It's guys like Barlow, Jim. They put the whole frigging world on a slide rule. There you are, out there in Stamford telling Helmut Cross you can save him thirteen percent if you use stainless clad, and there are these kids back in the office—your own office—telling Helmut he shouldn't be making this shit at all, the swing's to some other shit and they've already got some people interested in buying something Helmut isn't even making yet. Now you tell me, how does a guy beat that?"

I said, "I don't know."

Joe Slattery said, "They're setting up this superworld, Jim. Every goddamned thing in this superworld of theirs is going to be super, right? Jim, they're so efficient they're going to do away with people and get something better."

I said, "They're going to have a lot of parts left over."

Joe waved to the waiter. "George? Again." He said, "Guadalcanal, Tarawa, Iwo Jima. How the hell about that."

I said, "Joe, there ain't nothing more useless than a used calendar."

"I know. I know, old buddy. It's just that for the last twenty-five years, well, who cares? I guess the old sarge was just full of shit, that's all."

I said, "I thought you were the old sarge."

"I was talking about me." Joe looked around. He looked, for a moment, as if he was going to pick up a chair and throw it through the window just for openers.

I said, "Joe, I don't know the business, but there have to be places that still do it your way."

"Employment agency says there are more of me than there are of them. Hey. Let's get out of here. This place makes me nervous."

"Why? A martini's a martini."

"You hear these bastards at the next table? One of them just said they have a dichotomy and the other wants to discuss the parameters of the problem."

"Account executives. They talk like that so you'll know how important they are."

"You know what, Jim? You bust your ass and what you get for it is a busted ass."

"You've got Nora and some pretty nice kids."

"Kids will be married off soon. What I got is Nora and let me tell you, Nora doesn't understand."

The waiter put our drinks on the table and I drank some of mine and said, "Understand what?"

"Jim, the way it is in our house, I always came home with the money. I put the kids through school. I paid off the car. Every month the mortgage comes due and I write the check. Jim, to Nora I'm Tom Mix and they don't fire Tom Mix."

"That's the damnedest silliest thing I ever heard of."

"Hey. Now that bastard next to me is talking about demographic breakdowns. Let's blow this joint."

"Can I finish my drink?"

"Sure. You got twelve seconds."

We walked over Forty-eighth Street to Sixth Avenue. Sixth Avenue had once changed its name to the Avenue of the Americas and there were the new CBS Building and the Time-Life Building and the big new Hilton, but you can only fool all of the people some of the time. It was still Sixth Avenue.

We walked along Sixth for a while, past little luggage shops and pawnshops and Con Edison holes in the street, and Joe Slattery said, "What are we, on maneuvers? There has got to be another place in this great city of yours that sells people gin."

"We can try in here," I said. At this time of day in New York the heat is not replaced by any particular coolness. The city gets to its hottest at about three or four in the afternoon. If it gets up to ninety-two at four, it will still be about eighty-nine at six. We had walked several blocks and the two martinis that I had had were working their way out through the back of my shirt.

This was a reasonably neat-looking little bar with a number of reasonably neat-looking—in fact, very neat-looking—men having drinks. "Dry martini," Joe said to the bartender. "Two dry martinis. Jim, do you want anything?"

I said, "I'll drink one of yours."

Joe Slattery said, "Yes, sir. They don't have any jobs for any fifty-six-year-old marines. You know I was fifty-six, Jim?"

I said, "I thought your chest was fifty-six."

"Jim, old buddy, let's say you're in Easton, Pennsylvania. You want a good, clean weld. You know anybody on earth who can tell you where to go?"

I said, "You look for the red light over the door, don't you?"

"Three places I'd trust in Easton, Jim. I mean, if I wanted welding and didn't have any way of checking it, I got three places to go in Easton. Now, Jim, there has got to be a job for a man who knows where to go in Easton."

I said, "What do you do, look up Welding in the Yellow Pages?"

"Now, you want a hot wort tank, you only go to one of these places. Very important to know where to go when you want a hot wort tank in Easton."

I said, "I never wanted a hot wort tank all that much, Joe. I don't think I ever knew anybody who really did want a hot wort tank."

"You run a brewery, you want a hot wort tank."

I said, "That's a very good thing to know."

"Ceramic-lined, solid stainless or clad. Jim, I'll bet you nearly everybody in Easton wouldn't know where to go. Right in their own home town and they wouldn't know where to go for a hot wort tank."

I said, "I wouldn't even know where to get a hot wort tank in Manhattan."

"You wouldn't get one in Manhattan. You'd go to Brooklyn or over to Jersey."

I said, "What if after I get this hot wort tank I don't want it any more?"

"You got to want it. Nobody ever bought a hot wort tank who didn't want it, Jim."

I said, "Do you just go in and buy one off the shelf or is this something you have to have made?"

A man standing beside me suddenly walked around and said to Joe, "Howard, can that be you?"

Joe Slattery said, "Howard? Name's Joe, friend."

"Oh, I'm terribly sorry. You do look so much like a very dear friend of mine."

Joe said, "Nope. Sorry."

The man returned to his place at the bar beside me. He was slim and neatly dressed and had sleek gray hair. He said to a young man with curly black hair and a cleft chin next to him, "Stunning resemblance. I'd have sworn he was Howard, wouldn't you, Don?"

The young man with the curly black hair said, "Howard has green eyes."

"Not necessarily. Hazel eyes fool you that way. Sometimes they look green and sometimes they don't."

I said to Joe, "How about hitting the road?"

"Anything you say, old buddy. George, what's the tab?"

"Three dollars, sir," the bartender said.

Joe said, "Martinis are a buck and a half in here?"

"Yes, sir."

Joe said, "Okay. But for a buck and a half, you ought to have dancing girls."

The young man with the curly black hair said, "That certainly isn't Howard."

Joe and I walked over to Seventh Avenue. Joe said, "That place seem a little funny to you?"

I said, "The guy next to me was in love with you."

We went into a bar on Seventh and had two martinis. Joe said, "Jim, you ever get the feeling the world's turning goofy?"

"Many times."

"Kids today. What would they do if the Japs hit Pearl Harbor tomorrow?"

"I don't know. I guess a lot of them would enlist."

"Run off to Canada is more like it. They don't make any sense, Jim. Not to me, they don't."

A youth in a blue short-sleeved shirt looked up from his beer. "What does make sense? Killing everybody you can?"

Joe said, "How would you like to call it fighting for your country?"

"That's it, all right," this youth said. "Wrap it in the flag and don't ask any questions."

Joe said, "Sonny, have you ever heard a shot fired in anger?"

"Do I have to hear a shot to know it's making some bullet factory rich?" The youth leaned on one elbow on the bar and looked up at Joe and said, "You got any kids?"

"I have."

"I'll bet you haven't talked to them since they were five years old."

"Sonny, I don't know what that means at all."

"It means you're the type that doesn't listen. You can't breathe the air, you can't swim in the rivers, you can't even eat the fish from the rivers, and nobody's doing one damned thing about it. Ask your kids. They'll tell you what a sewer this is. But we can't do anything about it just now, right? That big shiny Pentagon of yours needs all the money. But don't ask any questions, mister. Just wrap it in the flag and it's all all right."

Joe turned his back on the youth and said to me, "Jim, from now on I pick the bars, okay?"

The youth said, "What's the matter, mister? Do the questions hurt?"

Joe said, "That kid's beginning to turn this gin."

I said, "So let's find someplace else."

The youth said, "What? No answers from the American Legion?"

Joe said, "You know, he sounds a little like a dog I used to have. Damned dog used to yap at everything. Flies, birds; Jim, that dog even barked at ants."

The youth said, "What's on for tonight, fellows? Get a little drunkie? Pick up a couple of girls? Go home and tell your wives you had to work late?"

Joe said to the bartender, "I hope you appreciate the mess I didn't make in here."

The bartender said, "I appreciate it, I appreciate it."

I paid for the drinks and left fifty cents. On our way out the door, the youth said, "God bless America."

Joe and I walked out onto Seventh Avenue. It was beginning to get dark. The sidewalk seemed to have got crowded. Joe said, "Wonder where that kid lost his straitjacket."

I said, "Same place he lost his muzzle."

Joe said, "Where to—uptown, downtown or across town?"

I said, "Let's head over toward Eighth. Times Square gets a little weird for me."

"What's on Eighth?"

"Not Eighth itself, but there are a couple of nice bars on the side streets."

A trio of youths with black beards and Chinese tunics began to bump into us on the sidewalk. "So solly, so solly."

Joe said, "Shove off."

One of them said, "Listen to the man."

Another one said, "Did the man say something?"

The first one said, "The man doesn't like us polite types."

Joe said, "I'd like you to bump into me again."

"Listen to the man."

Joe stood there looking at them and began to smack his fist into the palm of his other hand. "You punks just going to stand there talking?"

"Oh, the man's going to get tough."

A cop came over. He looked just exactly like a cop. "On your way."

One of the youths said, "Hot damn, if it isn't police brutality himself."

The cop said, "Okay. We'll do it another way."

Joe said to the cop, "Christ, there's only three of them. Why don't you go watch the banks and jewelry stores?"

The cop said, "Mister, go back to Ohio and tell them what a good time you had. You three. Over by the wall."

Joe said, "We can handle them."

The cop said, "Good-bye, mister."

I said, "Joe. He's working and we aren't, okay?"

Joe grunted and shrugged and one of the youths called, "Good-bye."

We walked south on Seventh and came to another bar. This one was filled with music and people and Joe said, "Martinis. Doubles. On the rocks with a twist."

The bartender was a young guy with an Irish grin and jokes. "Double the liquor, double the fun. You guys got proof of your age?"

Joe said, "Jim, show him your liver."

The bartender said, "Hey, you want the joint closed?"

Joe said, "Doubles doesn't mean double the rocks."

"How do you think we make our money?"

He left us with our drinks and went up the bar to tell jokes to somebody else. A thin man with a jacket but no shirt walked up to us and said, "Have you been saved?"

Joe said, "Have we been what?"

"Saved from the damnation of sin."

Joe said, "Son of a bitch."

I said, "You picked the place."

"Lust, my friends, lust, greed and hate corrupt the body and so also the soul."

Joe finished his drink. "Let's go."

"The soul never dies. The soul lives forever."

Joe and I crossed Seventh Avenue and Broadway and walked toward Eighth. A guy stopped us and said he just needed seventeen cents more to get to Hoboken and Joe said, "You, too?" and another guy stopped us and wanted to sell us a gold watch so he could get carfare home to his mother's funeral. We passed a guy lying on some concrete steps who looked dead and a kid carrying a cat and a black couple, the woman of which had bright red hair. A thin, black-haired, intense-looking woman came out of a dingy doorway and said something to Joe and Joe said, "Next week, honey. Next week's my birthday and you can give me a present." The woman did not even swear at him. She went back inside the doorway and lurked, like something under a bridge. We passed a couple of sailors who looked as if they were twelve years old and went into another bar and had some more martinis.

Joe said, "You ever get the feeling, Jim, that the world has a worm in it?"

I said, "Often."

"Punks, whores and queers. And then you go up a couple of steps and you get to the unemployed, and then you go up a few more and there's Barlow Matthews."

I said, "There are probably a few steps in between, but that's about the general idea, yes."

"Something wrong with this world, Jim. All the crummy people we've seen tonight—how can people get so crummy?"

I said, "Joe, I guess that's what you do when you don't have anything else to do."

Joe Slattery's words were just a little slurred. Not an awful lot. He did not seem to be leaning or wobbling at all. Big body. God knows how many martinis. "I was one good marine, Jim. Guadalcanal. Tarawa. Iwo."

"I had an idea you were," I said.

"You're good at something, you kind of wonder when they can you. Nobody cans you when you're good, right?"

It was not just being fired. It was that for the first time in his life, Joe had not measured up. He did not even know how or why.

I said, "They changed the rules on you, Joe. It's like outlawing the forward pass when that's what you spent your life getting the hang of."

"Nora. Nora isn't going to understand this at all. Jim, if we have to move out of Westport, it's going to kick Nora in the head. What do I tell her? Dumb broad thinks she belongs for the first time in her life. George? You. Two more of those things."

"Mister, I think maybe you've had enough."

Joe said, "George, if I had enough, what would I want any more for? Now that's logic, George. Just plain and simple logic."

The bartender said, "Logic is not losing my license, mister. How about some coffee?"

Joe said, "Jim, have we been saved from the damnation of sin?"

I said, "I think we left in the middle."

Joe said, "Christ, that was a rude thing to do."

I said to the bartender, "Two more."

"Not for him," the bartender said.

I said, "Joe, this place discriminates against drunkards. Let's go."

Joe took out some bills and said, "That all right? I put down enough?"

The bartender said, "You put down enough if you want to tip me four bucks. One of these is a five, mister."

Joe said, "Mister, you're an honest man. Jim, I've found an honest man. How the hell about that?"

I said, "Let us go elsewhere. Elsewhere we will be appreciated."

The bartender said, "You better keep an eye on your friend. I seen guys like that get like that."

I said, "Guys like what get like what?"

The bartender said, "Mister, I never said a word."

We did get a drink at another place, and then stopped at one of those little hamburger places where the hamburger is the size of a nickel and covered with onions and then we got to a Spanish bar and had two martinis in a booth and Joe decided he wanted chili.

I said to the waiter, "Two bowls of chili."

Joe said, "Beer. What kind of beer they got here?"

The waiter said, "Mexican beer?"

"Why the hell not? We're in Mexico, aren't we?"

The waiter brought us the beers and after a while a fat Latin woman came over and sat down with us and had a beer, too. She said, "How are you going to get your friend home?"

I said, "I'm going to mail him."

"How far do you have to go?"

"Connecticut. About fifty miles."

"I have never been to Connecticut."

"It's just like Manhattan, before they put up the buildings. This is a nice place, you know that?"

The fat woman said, "Do you go home by train?"

I said, "Tonight I have a car."

"You are going to drive?"

"I'm going to try to."

"Please do not do it. Please find a place to stay."

Joe Slattery said, "Bring on the girls. Where are the goddamned girls?"

The fat woman said, "Mister, if you're going to drive, leave your friend here. You can take his wallet—I'd rather you took his wallet."

I said, "Can't do that."

"Then have some coffee. Will you stay here and have some more chili on the house and have some coffee?"

I said, "Coffee, sí, chili, no. Bring him some coffee, too."

The fat woman said, "I will get it myself."

Joe Slattery, by now, was slumped in the corner of the booth, bottle of beer in his big hand, looking a little dopey. "Jim, where are we? I want to go to the Tavern on the Green."

I said, "After we have some coffee, old buddy. The chili made me a little drunk."

"Drunk on chili. That's the goddamnedest—Jim, you're one of the funniest guys I ever met. No kidding. You're one hell of a funny guy."

I do not know whether the next bar was near Ninth or Tenth. I looked at my watch. I could not quite make out what time it was. It was nine-thirty or ten-thirty. This bar was also Spanish. It was pretty crowded.

A pretty black-haired girl came over and asked us what we wanted. Joe said, "If I wanted you, would I order you from you or from the waiter or what?"

The girl laughed and said, "I am not on the menu."

Joe said, "Martinis. We want martinis. That right, Jim? Feel one hell of a lot better if we'd stuck to martinis to start with. Never should have had that goddamned beer."

I said, "Two martinis. Maybe some crackers or something, peanuts, you know?"

The girl said, "Martinis with olives?"

I said, "Lemon twist."

The girl said, "Martinis with lemon twist."

Somehow, in serving us these, some words were exchanged that did not particularly mean anything except that Joe was loaded and that Joe thought she was pretty, but there we were, with a number of Latin guys standing around our booth. One of them said, "We would like to talk to you and your friend outside."

I said, "We didn't come in here to go out there. Friend, we just came in here for a drink. You guys want a drink?"

"We do not like your friend's mouth."

Joe Slattery was leaning against the wall. His eyes were closed. He said, "Jim, are the drinks here?"

I said, "All Mexico is here."

"That pretty little girl?"

"No, but I think we're meeting the family."

"Sometimes, Jim, I don't have any idea what you mean by what you say." Joe rubbed his face and looked at our new audience. He closed his eyes again and said, "Jim, you take care of them. I'm sleepy."

I looked around and took a deep breath and said, "Well now, how do we do this?"

One of the Latin youths said, "Your friend has insulted one of our women. I think it would be better if you waited for your friend outside and we will handle matters in here."

I blinked my eyes a few times because I seemed to see two faces for every one. I said, "Well, we can't do that because—well, because we can't do that. So I guess if we're going to do anything at all, we'd better get it started just as we are. Do I get to get on my feet for this?"

One of the young Latins laughed and said, "It would not be fair. Just tell your friend when he feels better that he had better watch the things that he says."

Even if I had been cold sober I would not have understood

the next thing that took place. Joe Slattery stood the table in our booth on end and pushed it into the lot of them and followed it himself, yelling something that I could not make out. It seemed to me that I heard the thud and swat of a lot of blows, and I got up to lend a hand. I took a swing at somebody and got punched in the jaw and I found myself sitting on the floor. I got up again but had to grip the edge of a booth to steady myself, and I looked around to see who I ought to beat up next, and somebody—or possibly two people—got hold of me and, speaking rapidly in Spanish, hustled me across the floor, around several people who just seemed to be lying about from an automobile accident.

The next thing that I knew I was standing outside on a dark, wide sidewalk, and there was Joe, leaning against an old Buick, and I said, "Some marine you are."

Joe Slattery said, "Jim old buddy, on to the Tavern on the Green."

I said, "How about on to my car?"

"Your car? Jim, it isn't even morning yet."

I now said the first intelligent thing that had occurred to me all night. I said, "Joe, I think I'm going to get sick."

thursday

In the morning, what woke me up was a headache that seemed to grow out of the base of my neck and spread up to the back of my eyes. This was somewhat apart from a separate ache in the left side of my jaw.

I got out of bed and went into the bathroom and turned on the light. My chin was swollen and bruised on the left side. Orange juice. What I needed was orange juice.

I went back out into the bedroom and sat down on the side of the bed and rubbed the back of my neck. Then I looked around. Melinda was not in her side of the bed.

"How do you feel?" It was Melinda with coffee.

I said, "I think I left my head in town."

"Did you have a good time?"

"I don't know. Joe called me at the office. They canned him and he wanted to have a drink."

"Did you fall or were you pushed?"

"Mmmm?"

"You look as if you beat somebody up with your chin."

"Oh. Yeah, something or other happened. Some bar on the West Side."

"How's Joe?"

"I don't know."

"Didn't he come home with you?"

"My car in the garage?"

"Of course. Don't you even remember driving home?"

"I guess I must have. They won't let you take a car on the train."

"Jim?"

"Mmmm?"

"I think we had better have a talk."

"What are we going to talk about, Barlow?"

"You can put it that way, if you want to."

"All right." I drank some of my coffee. "Any cigarettes around?"

Melinda got my cigarettes and lighter from the dresser and gave them to me and held my cup while I lit one. She said, "It isn't just Barlow, Jim. It's us."

I said, "No fun and games, eh?"

"It can't be any fun for you, Jim, knowing how I feel and having to come home to it every night."

"I don't know how you feel. You mean feel about me or feel about Barlow?"

"Both. I suppose. I didn't want it to happen. Jim, it wouldn't have happened if there was anything left between us."

I sat there and smoked for a moment without saying anything. Then I said, "All right. So you're in love with this guy. You don't have any kids, so that makes it nice and neat on your side, but he does have kids, and a wife to boot. That's kind of messy."

"It happens every day, Jim. I think that I heard fifty per cent of the marriages today end up in divorce. It's awkward. Some people get hurt. But it's a case of weighing one kind of hurt against another."

"What makes you think Kate would give him a divorce?"

"I think I know Kate. I don't think she'd stand in the way."

"You know Kate the wife. You don't know Kate the mother."

"Would the children be any happier in a home like that?"

The ache behind my eyes had taken over from the ache in my jaw. What a time to have a little talk. I said, "Of course they would. If Kate says no, do you really think this hot flash of yours or whatever it is will just keep right on burning? The guy will get tired, Melinda. You'll go on meeting wherever you've been meeting for a while, but if Barlow has to go home to his wife and kids every night, you're going to wind up all by yourself."

Melinda said, "Jim, does any part of this conversation seem a little odd to you?"

"What do you mean?"

"You don't even sound like a husband. You're just trying to talk me out of getting another job."

"For Christ's sake, Melinda, I have a hangover and I got slugged last night. What am I supposed to do, go over and tell Barlow to stay the hell away from my wife?"

"That is not what I want you to do. But that's just what you would have done if our marriage had any meaning to it. Jim, I don't even know why you're arguing. God knows this isn't any more of a home for you than it is for me."

"It's a home for me," I said.

"Well, Jim, I suppose if it isn't clear to you yet, I'll just have to put it to you as a direct question. I'd like a divorce."

"That isn't a question. That's a simple declarative sentence."

"But you will agree?"

"Why not? It can't cost any more than the sprinkler system."

"Would you like me to make you some bacon and eggs?"

"You can bring up some more coffee, if you want."

"All right, Jim."

I went into the bathroom. Brushing my teeth with the Broxident machine was more than my jaw could take. I got the front ones and the ones on the far side and called it quits. Shaving was something that I managed by being very careful, but the shower helped some. I put on fresh underwear and combed my hair and put on a pair of socks and my pants and shoes. What do you know, a divorce.

Melinda brought fresh coffee. "Are you sure you ought to go in to the office?"

"I'll just tell them I ran into Forty-eighth Street or something. This happy time with Jack Thompson still on at Barlow's?"

Melinda said, "I think until everything is out in the open for all concerned, it would be discreet to carry on as usual."

"You mean until Barlow talks to Kate."

"You're really the lucky one in this, Jim. You're probably the only one of the four of us who won't come out of it with any scars."

I said, "Maybe that's what they mean by lucky in love. What are the mechanics of a divorce, anyway? Who gets what and how do we do all this?"

"I'll ask Ina Cross for the lawyer who handled her case."

"What case? Don't tell me Ina Cross was married twice?"

"Most people are, these days."

"Do you get a lawyer and I get a lawyer or what?"

"I think we both have to get lawyers. I don't think one lawyer can represent both parties."

"That's a great business they have there. Twice as many lawyers as divorces."

"Jim, the lawyer may say one of us should move out of the house."

"What happens if you get a divorce and Barlow doesn't?"

"Then I get a divorce and Barlow doesn't."

"Kind of burning your bridges behind you, isn't it?"

"Jim, would you want a wife who stayed because she couldn't have somebody else?"

"I guess this is being civilized and adult about it all, right?"

"If it means anything, Jim, I think you're the most civilized, most adult person I know."

"Wait'll you meet your lawyer."

I finished my coffee and put on a shirt, tie and jacket. I looked in my wallet. Forty-five dollars. I had only spent twenty-five bucks last night.

Melinda went downstairs with me to the door to the garage. "Anything special you'd like for dinner tonight?"

I said, "Oh, something civilized and adult."

The office. I think the day that you know you are going to die you still think that the office is a place you have to go to.

Edna said, "What happened to your chin?"

"I beat a guy up with it. You ought to see his fist."

"You should have seen his fist. Brook Parker was looking for you."

"Brook's in?" Brook did not get in when other people got in. Brook did not do anything other people did.

"He was in before I was," Edna said.

"What do you know? Any coffee around here?"

"That Tim Malloy was looking for you, too."

"Well, important things first. You get the coffee. We'll save the world later."

I went into my office. Odd questions began to turn up in my mind. If we got a divorce, was I supposed to move out? And if I did, where was I supposed to live? It seemed silly to go all the way to Westport every night if there was not going to be anybody there.

I wondered if I was supposed to do something about the chinch bugs.

On my desk was a type proof for a Mountainaire trade ad. Trade ads were ads addressed to dealers.

It's a machine. Sooner or later, machines go Zonk. The following speech may keep a customer from chasing you with a stick.

This was a Percy Holland job. The body copy went on to describe Mountainaire's system of roving field engineers for any service that the dealer could not provide the customer himself.

I looked at this copy and rubbed the back of my neck. It had not been set the way Percy wrote copy. Percy used short sentences and short paragraphs. This had all been run together in one paragraph almost five inches wide. One big black blob of print.

I looked for the art director's initials in the little approval stamp. RdF. Rudy d'Franco.

So that was what it was doing on my desk. Rudy had screwed it up and Percy wanted me to see it.

It seemed as if the ache in my jaw was coming back, and the liquor that I had had the night before was doing things in my stomach. A hangover and a divorce were not fit training to go in to see Rudy d'Franco. Still, I was taking the money. There did not seem to be any choice. I got up, waited until my stomach had got up with me, and then took the type proof around to Rudy's office.

When Rudy d'Franco saw me in his doorway, his mouth arranged itself in a little sneer.

I put the type proof on his drawing table. "Look, how would you feel about having this reset?"

"What's the matter with it?"

"You can't read it. It looks like a parade of ants."

Rudy said, "Yeah, well, maybe you didn't see the way he wrote it. It was all stringy. It fell apart."

I said, "What are you talking about? Widows? Rudy, widows are good for you." Widows are short lines at the end of paragraphs.

Rudy pursed his lips. "Look, I don't know if you know design. . . ."

Design. God save us from young art directors. I said, "What good is design if you can't read the ad? What is this, twelve point?"

"Twelve point leaded."

"Well, it looks like a skid mark. Rudy, what makes copy easy to read is short paragraphs and lots of white space." A nice little wave of nausea started to come over me.

Rudy cocked his head. "Look, if you want to talk about copy, all right, but how about not talking to me about art?"

"How about talking about the business we're in?"

Rudy shrugged, "Do you want to be the art director? Be the art director."

"We aren't communicating. Okay. I want this reset with the paragraphs where Percy broke them and I want it set in two columns."

"Anything you say."

"Thank you."

I started back to my office and was stopped by a traffic boy named Earl. I did not know what it was about Earl that was insufferable. I think that it might have been all the suggestions he had for improving my ads. Earl had a Federal Airlines proof.

>   Los Angeles to Toronto
>   does not mean
>   Los Angeles to Chicago to Toronto.

My assistant supervisor had written it. He was on vacation. I said, "I thought this ran."

"That was the full page. This is just fifteen hundred lines. If you want people to see it, you ought to put a black border around it."

I initialed it and said, "You don't put a black border around airline ads." I went back to my office to meditate.

Mel King, our TV producer on Den-Test, came in. Thinning hair, a little belly, earnest-looking eyes. "Jim? Did you and Brook put a Den-Test spot on tape in the Sony room?"

"Brook did. I couldn't make it."

"Would somebody mind telling me why I didn't know about it?"

I said, "I don't think Brook knew you were the producer, Mel. It wasn't a slight, if that's what you mean."

Mel King sat down and lit a cigarette. "Came in this morning and found a note on my desk. Miles Turner wants an estimate on that spot and I haven't even seen it."

Miles Turner was the Den-Test account executive under Bob Coleman. Bob Coleman was in charge of the account and Miles Turner was in charge of leaving notes on people's desks.

I said, "Just a straight stand-up. We can put it on tape. They still want us to futz around with the copy a little. It isn't signed and sealed."

"Will it take a set or a limbo background?"

I said, "Probably limbo, but you'd better talk to Brook."

Limbo meant that there was no background. You shot whatever you shot against white no-seam paper.

"Sixty or a thirty?"

"Thirty. You know Brook. First he told Coleman we wouldn't do a thirty, then we did one."

Percy Holland came in. "Got a moment to look at a Federal ad for Buffalo?"

I said, "Why not?"

Shaggy, potbellied Perce, pipe and all. "Jeff Sermon's been calling me every hour on the hour." He opened a sheet of layout paper and put it on my desk.

Ladies and gentlemen, we are now passing Syracuse. Arrival time in Buffalo will be 20 minutes early.

I said, "What the hell do you know about that."

Percy sat down on my sofa. "Jim, what's this guy Malloy doing here?"

I said, "Just at the moment, Perce, I guess he's doing a commercial."

"Word's going around that he's going to be somebody in this place."

"Perce, all I know is that he seems to be a nice guy."

"Packaged goods, eh?"

"Every time you hear a word from the sponsor, he wrote it."

Percy Holland said, "Well, I guess nothing stays nice forever. I guess the thing to do is just be glad I was around when it was."

I said, "Keep your head down and they won't lay a glove on you."

Lydia came in. Fat legs and goggles and bedspring hair. "This a private game or can anybody play?"

"Come on in. Sit down," I said.

Lydia said, "I have this feeling we're an occupied city. Did you see that decree from Caesar Augustus yesterday?" That had to be Marion Simons' memo on office hours.

I said, "Well, Lydia, it's their advertising agency, right?"

Lydia said, "That is not so."

Percy Holland said, "Atta girl, Lydia. Give them hell."

Lydia said, "Well, it isn't. They didn't make this agency. We did."

I said, "We just dig the coal, honey. They own the mine."

Lydia said, "I'm the mine. They don't own me. Without us all they have are the desks and the typewriters."

Edna came in with my coffee and I said, "The house is buying the drinks. You guys want coffee?"

Percy said, "Not me."

Lydia said, "Black." She looked at me and said, "Why can't we go to the clients and say, 'Hey, we've been doing your ads and we're opening our own shop.'"

I said, "You'd be in court until you were on social security. Also, the clients do not even know us. The clients know the management."

Percy Holland said, "Also, it isn't done and clients don't do things that aren't done. You don't know the client mind, Lyd."

Lydia said, "I couldn't open up my own agency with 19th Century vodka?"

I said, "George would have your head shaved."

Lydia said, "Well, there's something wrong when they make more money on our talent than we do."

I said, "Lydia, get mad at something you can do something about, like chinch bugs."

Percy said, "They're the managers, Lyd. World's always had to put up with managers. They're like boils."

Lydia said, "I commend for your reading anything you can find on the French Revolution."

My phone rang. It was Mel King. "Jim? I got the script. I think you have a problem here."

"What problem?"

"Well, two problems. This script clearly implies that this woman brought her children up on Den-Test. That means the talent you get has to have children who used Den-Test—in fact, we'll need an affidavit. Not only that, she's got to belong to SAG."

"SAG? The Screen Actors Guild?"

"You have to try SAG first."

I said, "And just how in hell do you find who belongs to SAG who has children who used Den-Test?"

Mel King said, "That's casting's job. The only thing is, you may wind up with somebody who never spoke a line on camera before."

I said, "Sensational. Mel, I can't thank you enough for all the help you've been in this life and the next."

When I hung up, I said to Lydia and Percy, "Mel King. Whoever said the impossible takes a little longer must have been a gag writer."

Lydia said, "Jim?"

"Mmmm?"

"Do you have any idea what kind of talk is going around the halls in this place?"

"I don't hang around in the hall, Lyd. What kind?"

"The talk, darling, is that George Brice has a real purge coming. They're saying that memo's just the first sign."

I lit a cigarette. "George isn't that dumb, Lyd. A purge isn't something you advertise. A purge is something you pretend isn't happening at all, and you smile a lot until it's over."

Lydia got up to leave. "Friends, Romans and countrymen, this place is beginning to stink."

Percy Holland said, "Well, I'd better get up to Jeff Sermon before his skin shakes off. Jim, look, I kind of go through life not knowing what's going on, but if there's anything I can do . . ."

I said, "Relax." I did not know what I meant by this. It just seemed to be the thing to say.

Before I could leave for Brook Parker's office, my phone rang. "Jim? Joel Babcock, in accounting."

"Yes, Joel?"

"Jim, Marion Simons just called."

"Now what?"

"Your time sheets."

"Oh, boy."

"Jim, Marion wants your time sheets from January on."

"January?" Eight months of time sheets?

"He was pretty serious about it, Jim."

"Joel, I don't know what to tell you. I couldn't even guess what I spent my time on since January."

"Well, that's what he wants, Jim."

"I hope he likes fiction."

"By tomorrow, he said."

"Joel, what can I say? I'll quit writing ads and spend my days writing time sheets."

"Sorry, Jim."

I walked down to Brook Parker's office. "Hi."

Brook was sitting in one of his director's chairs reading *Vogue*. He said, "You don't give a girl a ring any more, right?"

I said, "What did I do, walk in in the middle of a conversation you were having with yourself?"

"Engagement rings. Giving a girl a ring is kind of medieval, isn't it?"

"It's still done, to the best of my knowledge." You give a girl a ring. You marry her. And twenty years later you wake up one morning with a hangover and she tells you all about the swell divorce you're going to have.

Brook said, "I don't know if that's the right thing to do. An engagement ring. It sounds like something they do in tribes."

I said, "It is. At least, it's what they do in this tribe."

"You don't have any kids, do you?"

"No."

"What do you do with kids?"

"Well, you burp them and change them and buy them a car."

"I'd be a bad father."

"Not if you're worried about it, you won't."

Brook said, "That was a bad meeting yersterday, Jim. They're bad people."

"Who? Den-Test?"

"That guy with the glasses. He doesn't listen."

I said, "I'll meet you halfway. He listens. He just doesn't understand."

"Claudette Colbert. He didn't even know what he was looking at."

I said, "Nope."

"Do you know what Max would have said?"

"Well, I like to think Max would have told him you don't put a lot of other ideas on the idea."

"George didn't say anything."

I did not say anything to this. I had lowered myself into one of his other chairs and lit a cigarette.

Brook said, "I don't know. Maybe this would be a good time to split."

"What do you mean—quit?"

"I could open my own shop, couldn't I? There must be a lot of accounts that would like me doing their work."

I said, "You have it made right here. Christ, they're paying you to be a legend. Find another job like that."

At this point, our leader walked in. George Brice. Gray suit. White shirt. Striped tie. And that fatty pink face and all those teeth.

"Good morning, Brook. Jim."

We both said hello.

George Brice sat down. "I thought I'd bring you up to date on what's happening with Landum."

Brook Parker said, "They don't want to change anything but the idea."

George said, "I was just on the phone with Tom Sloan. They're going to cancel the budget and just keep the brand in production until there's no more sell-in."

Brook said, "If they thought of that two weeks ago, we could have spent our time on something useful."

George said, "Brook, you don't know how useful you've been. Tom Sloan thinks that commercial of yours is one of the world's great advertising ideas. If you want to know, that commercial was more valuable not running than if it had got on the air."

Brook said, "Yeah, well, that's that tricky kind of thinking I'm not so good at."

"Brook, it showed Tom the two sides of the coin. First we said we could do it, and then we did it, and then I was in a position to tell them not to run it."

Brook said, "You mean I served a purpose."

"If there was a Landum product loose this morning, we'd have it in the shop. You've helped put us in a very strong position, Brook."

Brook said, "I don't know. It's a little like building a boat and sinking it."

"I know how you feel, but no commercial on earth could have moved Den-Test, Brook. Isn't it better to do a great commercial and not have it flop?"

Brook said, "George, do you know what? I don't think anybody should be right all the time. I think people ought to be wrong once in a while. Wrong means you tried, you know?"

"Brook, agency presidents are wrong more than anybody else in the business. Jim, would you mind very much giving me a few minutes with Brook?"

This was the first time since George had come in that he had said anything to me at all but hello. I said, "Right."

I closed the door on my way out. I noticed that George did not even begin to speak until I had.

I went back to my office and the phone was ringing. I picked it up and a woman's voice said, "Mr. Simons is calling, Mr. Bower."

I said, "Okay."

Presently Marion Simons said, "Jim? Are you aware that Alec Mayberry isn't in yet?"

I said, "No."

"Kindly see that I have an explanation before lunch."

I said, "How about if I come up and see you? I wanted to talk to you about that memo, anyway."

"I think, Jim, that we've had all the discussions about that that are necessary."

I said, "All right, Marion."

I hung up and thought, What explanation? I didn't know why Alec wasn't in. Melinda, when we divvy up the property, you get the house, the boat and Marion Simons.

I went out to tell Edna about the time sheets. "How good are you at arithmetic?"

Edna said, "I know what a day off costs."

I said, "The management would like to see my time sheets from now back to the Flood. Dig up enough forms to cover January on. I'll give you some kind of guess about the breakdown after lunch."

"January to August? The Bible isn't that long."

I went back into my office and in came George Brice's packaged-goods writer, Malloy. "Talk to you a sec?"

"Why not?"

Malloy lit an unfiltered Lucky Strike. "I'd like to bounce a commercial off you."

I said, "I have an idea George doesn't want you checking with me."

"Yeah, but you know Federal. Jim, would you believe Estelle the Computer?"

"Estelle the Computer."

"Kind of a fortuneteller. She knows all about you."

I thought about this. "What's the visual?"

"Start off with all the wheels and dials in their computer operation, and then, through the magic of ectoplasm and television, there's this gypsy."

I said, "They'll buy it."

"But you wouldn't."

I shrugged. "Well, it's a little gimmicky for me."

"I had an idea it would be." Malloy gave me his Irish grin. "I don't know why the hell gimmicks test so well, but they do. Hell, that's all the little cowboys were, the gimmick."

I said, "How did Rudy take it?"

"I think his pimples are coming back. Well, win, lose or draw, Estelle is it."

"Good luck. George going to keep you on, do you know?"

"A thousand dollars for this one job. That's as far as we got."

I said, "How did you ever get around Rudy?"

"How do you think? I told him George would like it." Malloy gave me a wink as he left.

Brook Parker came in. "What are you doing for lunch?"

"After last night, I don't know."

"What happened last night?"

"Guy I know had troubles so I went out with him. I've done brighter things."

"Want to go over to the Algonquin?"

"It's a little late to reserve a table," I said.

"I already did that."

I looked at him. "All right." I could not remember a time when Brook had thought to do a thing like that.

Brook said, "Can you leave now?"

I said, "Let me check Alec Mayberry's office. We seem to be one Alec short this morning and Marion wants an explanation."

"I got the table for one o'clock. See Marion later."

"Why not? My stomach isn't ready for Marion, anyway."

We walked through Grand Central Station and across Forty-third Street to Fifth Avenue. Brook said, "The thing about getting married is, you don't belong to yourself any more. You have to go home for dinner, you know?"

I said, "You get used to it."

"Yeah. That's another thing I don't like."

"Well, there are times when you want to talk to somebody and if there isn't anybody there, what do you do?"

"What about the times when you don't want to talk to anybody and there is somebody there?"

"Brook, you have more problems that nobody else has than anybody I know."

We turned down Forty-fourth Street and walked by little shops with eyeglasses and typewriters and organs in the windows. I wondered if I was supposed to go home that night. I had to. I did not even have a toothbrush.

Brook said, "I wonder if hell's humid."

We went into the Algonquin and into the Rose Room. Helen, who kind of ran things, took us to a little table for two. I said that we would like to have a couple of martinis while we figured out what we wanted to drink, and Brook said, "There's Bob Gage."

I said, "Who's Bob Gage?"

Brook said, "What do you do, come out once a year and look for your shadow? Gage is Gage."

"All right. We'll try categories. Is he a fireman?"

Brook took his napkin out of the way while Helen put our martinis down. Then he picked up his glass and drank a little and said, "You ever check what you've got coming in your profit sharing and pension fund?"

I said, "Not lately. I read the booklet but I couldn't figure out what it was trying to tell me."

Brook said, "Maybe you better try again."

I had my glass just about to my lips. I put it down again and said, "Oh?"

"The idea is, I'm supposed to tell you what's in the wind so you can quit before you get pushed. It's got something to do with embarrassment."

I drank some of my martini now. "Well. What do you know?"

"George is paying for the drinks. Maybe I ought to pay for them myself."

I said, "Well, I guess I knew it was coming."

Brook said, "I think the way George wants to do it is, you go on getting paid while you look around. I think if you get more money by being fired, you'll still get it. He talked a lot about being nice, you know?"

"Yeah, being nice is a big thing with George. How did he ever stick you with this?"

Brook gave a little laugh. There was no sound, just a sort of twitching of his lips. "It's supposed to make me a part of management. While George was being nice, he made me an executive vice-president. I think that's supposed to make everything come out even." He waved his glass at Helen. "Helen, what are you running here, a desert?"

I said, "Well, if there's any little old thing I can do to make this easier for you."

"He said he wants to talk to you after lunch. You know, if you want to call him names or anything."

"You want to know something? I just lost my wife and my job the same day."

Brook looked at me. "What happened to your wife?"

"Oh, there was something missing in her life and it turned out to be a divorce. This is some day. I have this feeling I was just caught stealing in the officers' club."

"I didn't know you were having trouble at home."

"Everybody's got something."

"You were married a long time, weren't you?"

"Twenty years last week."

"What do you do when you get a divorce? One of you moves out, right?"

"I guess so. I never got divorced before. She's getting this lawyer. He'll probably have a training manual."

Brook did not say anything. He just sat there looking into his drink.

I said, "Melinda—you ever hear of a dopier name for a girl? It sounds like a ten-cent whistle."

"Do you want anything to eat?"

"No."

"You just going to drink?"

"Yes."

"I'm going to eat."

"Order me another drink. I'll be right back."

I got up from the table and walked out to the lobby and went downstairs to the men's room and threw up.

When I got back, Brook said, "You all right?"

"Yep. You order another drink for me?"

"I wasn't sure you'd want one."

"George is paying for it, isn't he?"

Brook said, "Helen? One martini. How's the roast beef?"

Helen said that the roast beef was very good but that we had better order it now. They were doing a land office business in the roast beef.

Brook said, "Sure you don't want any?"

"I do not."

Helen brought my martini and I drank a little of it and then a little more. My stomach seemed to have something jumping around in it. I lit a cigarette and inhaled a great deal of smoke and looked around at the complicated ivory woodwork. What the hell. Everybody gets fired. Everybody gets divorced. What's the matter with you?

Brook said, "George wants to make Percy a vice-president."

I said, "Good. He's a good man, Percy."

"He hasn't done much TV."

I said, "What difference does that make? Percy's worth twice his salary just for what he can do in print."

"Maybe that's what George has in mind. Percy for print and Malloy for TV." Brook bit into a breadstick.

I said, "There are dumber things."

"I don't think I want to work with Malloy. Malloy knows what George wants. That's a bad thing."

I said, "Lydia's good."

"I worked with her once. If you don't like something, she cries."

I began to nibble on a round cracker. "Al isn't bad, either." Al was my assistant supervisor; he was on vacation.

"That isn't the same as being good. What's Malloy doing on Federal?"

I said, "Estelle the Computer."

"What does that mean?"

I said, "I think she's a fortuneteller. She knows all about you."

Brook grunted. He did not have any comment to make about Estelle the Computer.

Presently he said, "You know what? You ought to have some soup."

"All right."

He waved to a waiter and ordered some soup for me. "I think you ought to go away for a couple of weeks."

"Do you know any place where it isn't August?"

"Go out to San Francisco."

"What do you do as executive vice-president?"

"I don't know. I execute." Brook was cutting his roast

beef now. "I told George he'd be better off with you than me."

"They don't pay admission to see me."

"It isn't going to work out. I told George that, too."

"What did he say?"

"He said we were going to have to meet each other half-way. I don't know what that means. He talked a lot about something called creative climate." Brook added, "He uses words like that a lot, doesn't he? Creative climate."

I said, "Well, Tonto, my work here is done. You stay here and help these good people with the harvest."

"I've seen you when you looked better. What if I get you a cab? I always wanted to put in for fifty dollars in cab fares."

"Nope. Got to go back and call George names."

The waiter brought me a dish of soup. I had the soup and some crackers. It was twenty after two. I said, "Hark, the herald angels sing. Helen, I would like a Scotch on the rocks."

Brook said, "You sure you want another?"

"There are no more ads to do, so why not?"

"It's your party."

"It's George's party. No host. Just the guest. You could hold a party like this in a closet."

Helen brought me some Scotch in a short glass. The room was getting to be pretty empty. I picked up the glass and then put it down again. "Oh, for Christ's sake. Let's get back."

We got as far as Fifth Avenue and the hot, wet sunshine began to dissolve whatever it was that had been holding my legs up. I stopped on the sidewalk and stared at the concrete and shook my head. I tried to focus on a gum wrapper. I could feel people flowing around me as if I were a rock in a little river. Oh, boy.

Brook said, "Do you want to go up to my apartment and lie down?"

"No."

"Look, if you stay here, it's littering."

"Let's don't litter."

We crossed the street. This upset a cab driver's life plan and he honked and honked. On the other side, as we got there, a man in his fifties walked by saying, "Fucking shithead son of a bitch. Bastard asshole prick." He was not talking to us. He was just walking along Fifth Avenue talking. A gray Cadillac limousine went by, whispery and as long as something in a dream, and a tall, white-haired woman with three shiny green Lord & Taylor boxes said to another woman,

"That was Bob Hope. Did you see him? That was Bob Hope."
A kid said, "Eddie, will you blow your nose? I can't stand
looking at you."

We had reached the Brass Rail. Brook said, "Let's get
some coffee."

"Okay."

We went inside. It was dark and the brick-surfaced walls
had a cool look. A waitress with an Irish brogue told us that
the kitchen was closed but that we could get sandwiches.

I said, "Just coffee." I lit a cigarette.

Brook said, "Estelle the Computer. Is that any good?"

I said, "Nope. It's good advertising, but it isn't good."

"That's what we're going to be doing now, eh?"

"It isn't what I'm going to be doing." I wasn't going to be
doing anything.

Brook said, "Maybe we won't do that. I think it's time I
took a look at Federal."

I got up from the table. "I think I'll see George tomorrow.
I think I'll go home."

"Okay. Wait until I pay for the coffee."

"Brook, thank you for lunch."

I walked out by myself. The street was very bright. I
walked down Forty-third Street to Grand Central. I felt very
good. I started to whistle. Then I had to stop and hold my
breath. I had to do this or throw up again.

I finally got things calmed down and walked into the station. I went down the wide pale stairs and looked at the big
sign for the next train. The next train was not going to be for
a long time. I went into the waiting room on the Forty-second
Street side and sat on a wooden bench. I just sat there with
my eyes closed and did not think about anything. After a
while, I got up and went downstairs to the men's room and
put a coin in the slot and went into a toilet and threw up
again. Written on the wall was a phone number and the
words "The Good Fairy." I went back upstairs into the Lig-
gett's drugstore and bought some Tums. I went back to the
waiting room and brought a copy of *Time* and sat there,
smoking and eating Tums and turning the pages.

It was strange to get off the train before the rush hour.
There were all those cars sitting in the sunshine. I had the
feeling everybody else was in school and the principal had
sent me home. I walked down to the Triumph and started
the engine and then I did not know where to go. I did not

know whether to go to the New Englander Motel first, or to go home and get my clothes, or what.

I drove home because it was what I always did. I hoped that Melinda would be out and I hoped that she would be there.

Fired. What do you know?

It was four miles from the Saugatuck station to our house and it took about ten minutes over Compo Road and there was the Lincoln. I pulled into my side of the garage and got out and went into the house.

"Oh. Hello." Melinda was on the phone in the kitchen.

I said, "Hi."

Melinda said, "Betty, I'll call you tomorrow. Jim just got in."

I said, "Don't hang up on my account." I went out to the porch and sat down and looked at the trees.

Melinda came out. "I didn't expect you until later."

I said, "I took an early train."

"Do you want a drink?"

"No. I wouldn't mind a Coke."

"I'll get you one."

Melinda did not just come out with the Coke bottle. She had put the Coke into a glass with some ice. We were going to be civilized about everything and when you are civilized, everybody is nice.

I said, "Thank you."

"Did anybody in the office say anything about your jaw?"

"Just Edna. Everybody else made a point of not noticing it."

"Nora Slattery said Joe has a broken hand."

"He hit a few people."

"He was fired. He told you, of course."

I said, "Look, I figured I'd get a room at the New Englander. I don't know what the ground rules are in this game. . . ."

"I think it might be better if I just moved into the other bedroom. I see no need to start a lot of talk, unless, of course, you really want to move into the New Englander."

Anything that I wanted to do was going to be all right with her.

I said, "I don't know. What's this lawyer say?"

"I haven't seen him yet. He's in Hartford today."

I said, "I always wondered who was in Hartford."

"I wish there were some way of calling off this stupid

thing with Jack Thompson. Being Kate and Barlow's guests is going to border on the weird."

"We can always not go," I said.

"What about the Thompsons?"

I said, "Oh, Jack Thompson will go. If Barlow broke every bone in his body and had to call it off, Jack Thompson would just go out and get a box of candy and turn up anyway."

"I detest that man."

I finished the Coke and said, "You can always let the Thompsons go by themselves."

"That's even weirder. That would be grotesque."

"Well, those seem to be the choices," I said.

"I got lamb chops for tonight. You like lamb chops."

"Oh. Good."

"Do you feel all right? Your jaw looks swollen."

"It's all right." I lit a cigarette and looked at our woods and said, "I guess we'll have to sell this place."

"Do we handle it ourselves or do it through a real estate agent?"

I said, "I don't know. Let's see what your lawyer says."

"You ought to get a lawyer, too, you know."

I said, "I suppose."

"Is there anybody you'd like to ask over tonight?"

I think that I stared at her. "What?"

"I just thought it might be more comfortable if somebody else was here."

I shrugged. "They'd have to go home sooner or later. No. I don't want anybody over tonight. I'm still getting over last night."

"If you want to watch television, I can go upstairs and read."

I said, "We can send each other notes."

Melinda did not say anything.

I said, "Okay. Martini?"

"Is that what you're having?"

"I'm having Scotch."

"I think I'll have a gin and tonic."

I went out to the kitchen and made the drinks. The door of the dishwasher was open and I closed it because it was where I wanted to stand. In all the years we had lived here, I had never learned how to turn on the dishwasher. Cleaning out the basement was going to be something. . . .

"I didn't put any lime in it. I didn't see any."

"I forgot to get them. This is all right."

I said, "This is going to be worse than moving. What do
u do with the furniture?"

"I suppose we sell it."

I said, "Maybe we could sell the house furnished."

"We could put it up either way, I guess. I think most peo-
e already have furniture."

I said, "Maybe not. If they're moving out of a furnished
artment, you know?"

"We'll have to go through all the things in the attic. You
n't even breathe up there in this weather."

I said, "That guy going to fix the pool?"

"He said he was."

"Well, that will make up for the looks of the lawn."

Melinda said, "What will you do, move into the city?"

"I haven't got that far yet." What the hell was she going
do? Barlow had not even asked Kate for a divorce.

Melinda said, "Would you like some cheese and crackers?
have that cheese you like."

"What cheese is that?"

"The one with the pistachio nuts in it."

"Oh. No. Some crackers, maybe. I only had soup for
nch."

"That isn't enough for lunch."

"Well, I usually do better than that."

"How did you happen to come home so early?"

"I just felt like it."

"Jim?"

"Mmmm?"

"They say—well, they say divorces always get messy. They
y you say things, bring things up, things you'd never
y. . . ."

I said, "Yeah, well, let's keep this one nice. We'll be a
odel to all young people getting a divorce everywhere."

Melinda gave me what seemed to be a quizzical look, but
st said, "Are you going to get married again?"

"I don't know. I hadn't even thought about it."

"You should. A girl would be lucky to get you."

I said, "Brook's getting married."

"He is?"

"He's already making a problem out of it. He thinks
ngagement rings are medieval."

"Not to the girl, they aren't."

I said, "I have an idea they aren't to Brook, either. I thir he just thinks they should be."

"Would you like me to get you another drink?"

"I can still get the drinks." I went out to the kitchen agai I watched a squirrel come down the side of a tree, burst speed, dead stop, another run, another stop—you'd thi squirrels would get seasick.

Melinda came out to the kitchen and took down t crackers from the cabinet over the range. "You're sure y don't want the cheese?"

"No, thanks."

"We have some mixed nuts."

"A couple of crackers to munch on, that's all."

She said, "I think Slim's on his way back to Montan Today or tomorrow. Did you know the airlines had a pr vision for things like that?"

"Yeah. We used to do ads on it for Federal for *Casket Sunnyside* or whatever it is."

"That's gruesome."

"If you're a funeral director, it's information."

"I can't understand Jean's going back there."

I said, "I can. It's her and Slim against the world. T world's winning."

Melinda said, "I don't think the world is as bad as s makes it out to be. The world is just people."

"Yeah, well, people are what screwed Slim."

"Just some people, just certain people."

"Yep. Only the ones he trusted."

We went back out to the porch. Melinda said, "If you ju had soup, I can put the lamb chops on now. . . ."

"Later. I don't have much of an appetite."

For a moment, Melinda was silent. Then she said in quiet voice, "I'm sorry."

"Don't worry about it. I can still sign my name and dre myself."

"I didn't want to hurt you, Jim."

I said, "No, all in all, you handled it very nicely. What t hell, I knew it was coming."

"We're still friends."

"Sure. Why not?"

"I really wish you felt better."

"I feel all right."

"Would you like to go in and watch the news?"

"It's nice out here. It doesn't seem as hot as it was." I like

o look at the trees. I was going to miss looking at those
trees.

"I guess I'll have to get all new credit cards," Melinda
said.

There was a practical thought. I said, "Lots of problems,
eh? What do you change your name to, anyway? I mean, it's
going to sound funny: 'Do you, Mrs. Bower, take this
man . . .'"

Melinda said, "I hope we'll find a more discreet minister
than that."

"You will. Understanding is supposed to be a minister's
main stock in trade."

"I think I'll go in and turn on the news."

"I'm just going to sit here for a while," I said.

It was nice, just sitting there. This was home. George
Brice couldn't get at you here.

I rubbed my face and sighed. James Bower. Devoted his
life to advertising. It was a little like being good at racing
salamanders. It didn't exactly do much for the lynchings in
the South.

I got up and went into the den. Melinda had turned on the
air conditioner. She said, "I'll put your dinner on any time
you're ready."

"Not yet."

"In that case, you can refill my glass."

"Okay."

When I got back with the drinks, Melinda said, "You
know, you've been acting funny ever since you got home."

"I have?"

"Funny strange. Are you sure you're all right?"

"Sure," I said. "Look, I don't know how these things work.
What if I wanted to keep the house?"

"Live here by yourself?"

"I guess so."

"Why would you do a thing like that?"

"Oh, it's a nice house. I like to sit out on the porch and
look at the trees."

For a moment, she did not say anything. Then she said, "I
don't think that would be healthy."

"Well, that wasn't exactly the question. The question was
what if that was what I wanted to do?"

"Jim, I think that that's something I'd have to ask the
lawyer about."

"Well, ask him, then."

"All right."

I said, "If it will help any, you can stay here after the divorce and I'll get a room somewhere until you—well—make any arrangements you're going to make, you know?"

"It all sounds a little peculiar, but if that's what you want, I'll ask him about it."

Melinda got up from her chair.

I said, "Where are you going?"

"The john."

I sat there looking at the TV screen. A guy with either a yellow tan or liver trouble or an error in transmission was talking about the teachers in New York.

I felt around in my pocket and came up with the paper that the Tums had been wrapped in. Just the paper. No more Tums.

friday

n the morning, I got to the office a little later. It seemed
itting now not to turn up when the place opened.

Edna, my secretary, said, "Alec Mayberry was looking for
ou yesterday. And Marion Simons called twice, and I got as
ar as March on your time sheets just by guessing."

I said, "Skip the time sheets. The coffee wagon gone?"

"I can send out for some."

"Okay."

I went into my office. Now what do you do? Do you call
Marion or do you call George? The thing to do was call
George. That would probably take care of Marion and Alec

and everything else, except for a little talk with Joel Babcock
in accounting about what I had coming.

I dialed George's phone. It was busy.

I hung up and put my feet up on my desk. How did you
go about calling other agencies to say you were available?
Copywriters ought to have agents. Well, there were agents
available. Jerry Fields. Judy Wald. Mitzi Morris.

Samples. I had not kept samples of my ads for years. I had
heard that the proof files kept things for two years. I could
probably get some of my ads from them.

I took a piece of paper and put it into my typewriter.

> *James Bower*
> *Age: 48*
> *Copy Chief*
> *1960–1970*
> *GIBBS & WILSON*
> *Paragon Motors*
> *Federal Airlines*
> *Mountainaire Air Conditioning*
> *19th Century Vodka*
> *Miniflex Cameras*
> *Den-Test Toothpaste*
> *Manhattan National Bank*
> *1950–1960*
> *MERCER AGENCY*

I stopped and looked at this. It seemed silly to list all the
accounts that I had worked on at Mercer. If Gibbs & Wilson
didn't say it all, the names of the shingle and nylon and steel
and lighting companies were not going to help.

I wondered how the employment agencies worked it these
days. When they got you a job twenty years ago, they got 5
percent of your first year's salary or something. I had heard
that the advertising agencies were paying the fee for you these
days.

Barry Gorner from research came in. Pale green suit, dark
green shirt, gray tie. He looked like a gentleman crook. "Don't
get up. I'm not in uniform."

I said, "Doesn't that make you a spy?"

"Final focus session report. Would you like me to autograph it for you?"

I said, "Why, no. That isn't what I'd like you to do with it."

"Do not be crude. The sciences have always had to suffer the barbs of the common people."

I said, "Federal's pretty high on this, eh?"

"Federal is approaching it with an open mind. Which is more than I can say for some people I know."

I said, "Well, Barry, I'll have to read it sometime. I hear it wasn't the butler that did it, after all. It was the computer."

Brook Parker walked in, saw Barry Gorner and said, "Oh. You're cleaning the room. I'll come back later."

I said, "Don't laugh. This is Barry's first novel."

Barry Gorner said, "I hoped you'd write the screenplay. Now I hear George gave it to somebody else."

I said, "That's right. If you're looking for him, Edna can tell you where his office is."

"I wasn't looking for him. I was wondering why you weren't doing it," Barry Gorner said.

I said, "Well, Barry, the reasons seem to change from day to day. Today's reason is that I don't work here any more."

Barry Gorner's grin went away. "No kidding?"

"I'd cross my heart if I could find it."

Brook sat down on my sofa. He did not say anything.

Barry looked at him and then back at me. He looked embarrassed. "How did that happen?"

I said, "As near as I can tell, I didn't walk my post in a military manner."

Barry said, "Well, what are you going to do?"

I said, "I'm a little too old to reenlist. I guess I'll just have to get another job."

"Do you have anything lined up?"

"I'm just starting on my résumé. It's okay if I don't use you as a reference, isn't it?"

"Hell, you ought to be able to get a job anywhere."

I said, "One job is all I need. There ought to be somebody out there who wants a good used copy chief."

Barry said, "Just like that, eh?"

I said, "Yep."

"There ought to be something I can do."

"You can turn Catholic and light a candle for me."

Barry Gorner gave me one of those helpless little shrugs. I think that he was trying to think of some way to get out of the room without actually breaking into a run. "Look, let's have lunch before you leave, okay? I can't make it today, but any time next week."

I said, "Why not?"

"Good, Jim. It's a date. I guess I'd better look up that guy. . . ."

I said, "His name's Malloy. I think he has an office somewhere down around the corner."

"Well, good luck, you know? You let me know if there's anything I can do."

"Sure. Thanks, Barry."

He stopped as if he had remembered that he ought to say something to Brook. He said, "Real kick in the head, eh?"

Brook said, "Why don't you stop looking for things to say? We know you're sorry."

"Well . . ." Barry gave us another little shrug. "See you later."

When he was gone, Brook said, "You get home all right?"

"Oh, sure."

"Talk to George yet?"

"His line was busy. I guess Marion's been trying to reach me. That's probably about Alec."

"How do you feel?"

"Better than I did yesterday. You got me coming off a bad night. Kind of funny. A friend of mine got canned and I went out to keep him company. Whoever thought a thing like that was contagious?"

Brook Parker said, "You did look like you had a fistfight with a bus."

"Crazy marine. I think he took on a whole barful of Mexicans. He walked out and they threw me after him like his hat."

"Tell your wife you were fired?"

"No."

Brook just nodded. "I was just wondering whether it made any difference, you know?"

"Well, I didn't tell her. I'm trying to keep my messes in neat little piles."

"I talked to Coleman."

I said, "What did that get you?"

"Oh, George is the president. They have to back him up. Coleman has answers for everything."

I said, "What the hell. I guess he's right."

Brook said, "What are you going to say to George?"

"I don't know. Throwing rocks is kind of dumb. I guess I'll go up there and he won't know what to say and I won't know what to say and it'll be like that. What do you say when there isn't anything to say?"

Brook said, "You want to start an agency?"

I said, "Without any business?"

"I will if you will."

I said, "All we'd do is run through all the money you get when you quit. I have to pay for a boat, a swimming pool and a divorce."

Brook said, "Okay."

I said, "Well, I guess the thing to do is just go up to George's office and hang around. I'll look in on you after."

Brook said, "Right."

I went up the fire stairs to the next floor and walked down the hall and Marion Simons jumped out of his office and bit me.

"Jim, would you please come inside?"

I felt a little as if the firing squad had finished shooting and was now kicking the body. "All right."

We went into his office. He said, "We had a conversation yesterday that you seem to have forgotten."

I said, "I didn't forget it. You wanted to know where Alec was and I didn't know."

"Nobody seemed to know where you were, either. I called you twice. You didn't even see fit to call me back this morning."

I said, "Don't you guys up here talk to each other? I was fired yesterday."

Marion's little lined face seemed to twitch under the skin, as if a lot of little muscles got together and tried to change position. "I didn't know that."

I said, "Well, that's why I wasn't around. I went home."

"I'm sorry to hear that, Jim."

"Yeah. Well . . ."

"Jim, I hope it wasn't because of any disagreements we might have had. I'd like to think those were matters we could have ironed out between us."

I said, "Marion, I'm not exactly sure why myself. I'm on my way to see George now. I have an idea it was more than just your being sore, though. I think it's just that George has his way of doing things and I have mine."

Marion Simons said, "I wasn't told about it. . . ."

I said, "Look, I know this isn't the time to say it, but I'd still give Alec Mayberry the benefit of the doubt, if you can."

"Why, all right, Jim. I think I'd like to do that as a favor to you; I really didn't know about this at all."

"Just one of those things."

"Jim, when you're through with George, why don't you look in on Mayberry and tell him you talked to me?"

"I will, Marion. Thank you."

I walked down to George Brice's office. "He in?"

His secretary said, "He's on the phone with General Drug, Mr. Bower. I don't know if he has any time this morning."

I said, "Well, I think he wanted to see me. It's up to him."

"I'll go in and ask."

"Thanks."

She went into George's office. Presently she came out again. "As soon as he gets off the phone."

"Thanks." I sat down and lit a cigarette. The trick was going to be finding someplace that paid a lot of money for the kind of ads that I did. I wondered if anybody around town knew my name.

What did you put down on the application, married or single? I wondered what it would do to a computer if you checked both.

"Mr. Bower? You can go in now."

"Thanks."

I went into George Brice's office. The difference between George's office and mine was considerable. Just at the moment, it was like being in a gold police station. Gold carpet, teak desk and George.

"Come in, Jim. Ellen, bring us some coffee, please. Cream and sugar, Jim?"

"Thank you."

"Jim, I don't know whether I did the right thing, asking Brook to talk to you first. I thought that it might make things a little easier."

"It did, I guess."

"I'm sorry this didn't work out, Jim. I had hoped that we could have put something together here."

I said, "George, I don't think it was even supposed to work out."

"Oh? That's an interesting thought, Jim. I'm not sure that I follow it."

I said, "I think it has something to do with perfection. I guess what you're trying to run is a perfect advertising agency, and I think that's against some kind of law, you know?"

"That's a little hard to understand, Jim. I don't really know what you mean."

"Look, do you know where it doesn't work? You can't say

'To be or not to be' is in, but 'That is the question' didn't test well."

George Brice was wearing blue today. He looked very nice in blue. He looked as if he were getting married.

"Jim, isn't that just a little pretentious?"

"Maybe, but what we did here was a kind of art, George. If you don't want to get that fancy, you can call it a knack— it still isn't something you can put through a computer."

"Jim, the only thing I want from a computer is information. I don't want the computer to write the headlines. Or the man running the computer, for that matter."

I said, "Well, what the hell, right?"

"Why, no, Jim. Not what the hell. You seem to be under the impression that all this is happening for a reason that isn't really the reason at all."

"Well, all right, George. What is the reason, then?"

George Brice smiled. "Jim, I'm sure in your heart of hearts you know that as well as I do. Jim, you certainly must realize you haven't met me halfway once. I've tried to talk to you and you wouldn't listen. I told you what I wanted to do with this agency and you couldn't be bothered. Jim, are you really surprised that things turned out this way?"

The door opened and his secretary came in with the coffee. No cardboard containers in George Brice's office. This was china.

I said, "George, I'm not talking about myself. I'm talking about the kind of place you have here. George, you have something special and you're trying to make something ordinary out of it."

George Brice said, "Jim, I'm afraid that all I know is that nothing was going to be done my way at all. Really, Jim, you can't expect me to accept conditions like that."

I said, "What are you talking about? The focus reports? George, all you want to do is give everybody a kit with directions in it. Three easy ways to make an ad. And, George, that's going to kill this place surer than hell."

George Brice leaned forward in his chair and said, "Jim, I cannot and will not have you leaving under the illusion that I'm in some sort of war with the creative department. That isn't true and you know it isn't true."

I said, "The hell it isn't. George, you're in a war with everything around here that's human. Christ, if you hired Van Gogh, you'd have him painting headaches."

It seemed to me as though George Brice's eyes were getting

bigger. It was almost as if he had inflated them. He was staring at me with blue marbles. "Jim, please do not blame me for what I find under the microscope. I happen to have been in testing for over fifteen years. If you have a problem with the public's mentality, take it up with the Deity, but not with me."

I said, "Well, all right, George. That's what it comes down to. You gave the country an aptitude test and the country flunked." I shook my head and added, "Jesus, George, do you know, I'd hate to be you?"

"Fortunately, Jim, that seems to be a fate we've both been spared." Whatever George had got worked up over he had control of again. "Jim, I think the way to look at this is that you put up a fight for what you believed in even when you knew you were going to lose. I respect you for that."

I said, "Yeah, what we have here is a language barrier."

"Well, Jim, in that case, I suppose there's nothing else to say, is there? I do wish you luck. I hope you can believe that." George Brice folded his hands together as if in prayer. "I don't know how much detail Brook went into with you, but in your case I'm asking the board of directors to okay six months' notice. I think we can arrange internally to handle this as though you were let go and still leave you the freedom to resign publicly."

"That's very nice of you, George."

"I believe you can also transfer your insurance—you might like to talk to accounting about that. How's everything up in Westport? Getting out on that Bertram?"

"A little. Had a little engine trouble over the weekend. Well, I guess I can find out anything I have to know from Joel Babcock. You might tell accounting what's up so they'll know what I'm talking about."

"Of course, Jim. Jim, I'd like to hear from you when you get located. Perhaps we could have lunch."

"Why not?"

At this point, George Brice's phone rang and saved us any little problem we might have had with shaking hands. He looked at me with one of those smiles that tell you it is time to go, and I said, "George, I'll see you."

As I was leaving, I could hear him say, "Good morning, John. John, how would you feel about meeting us halfway on that type bill?"

We got to the Matthewses' house at quarter to eight. There

was a Porsche in Barlow's turnaround. The Crosses were there. I said, "If you're interested, this is how top executives handle embarrassing situations. They lose them in a crowd."

Melinda did not say anything. She was wearing a pale blue print dress and carrying a little white purse. Very proper for visiting.

"Keep walking," I said. "The Thompsons are pulling in behind us."

Kate answered the door. "Melinda. Jim." Her voice was quiet. Just the required smile. "Is that the Thompsons?"

I said, "Let us in and you can bar the door."

"Helmut and Ina are here. We asked the Vans and the Reynolds, too."

Melinda said, "Kate," in a very soft voice and went on into the house.

Kate and I simply looked at each other and then I followed Melinda.

In the living room, Helmut Cross said, "Hello, Melinda. Why is it all the pretty girls have fellows with them?"

That's all right, I thought. We'll all change later.

Ina said, "It's my old buddy with the sexy legs."

I said, "My legs are going to the Smithsonian Institution."

Helmut said, "That's only fitting. That's where he got them."

Behind me, Jack Thompson said, "There he is. There's the man of the hour. How's it going, Jim, boy?"

Helmut said, "Good Lord, I thought Kate was kidding."

Ina said, "Hush, Helmut."

I said, "Jack, how are you? Hello, Peg."

Jack Thompson was wearing a copper-colored linen jacket, light slacks and, by God, an ascot. His wife, Peg, was standing beside him like an umbrella stand. She said, "Jim. Melinda."

Kate said, "Jim, would you be a dear and take the drink orders? Barlow's upstairs settling a border dispute over the television."

I collected the drink orders and went into the study and Jack Thompson followed me. "Real nice lunch the other day, Jim. Nice getting together in the city like that."

"Nice of you to think of it, Jack. That should have been on me."

"Come on, buddy. Let's don't start that stuff."

I plucked ice cubes from the bucket and poured as much gin and as little vermouth into the martinis as I could.

Jack Thompson said, "You know what it really is, Jim? It's time. There we go, in and out of the city—you get so busy when you get up there high enough that you lose sight of the things that count. That's what I was talking about the other day. We only get one life, old buddy. You can't get it back with money."

"Can't argue with that, Jack. Excuse me."

I delivered the martinis and went back to make the gins and tonics and the Scotches and sodas. Jack Thompson said, "I've been giving this commuters' club some real thought, Jim. Even worked out an organization chart I'd like you to look at. You know, just to see if you think it's the way Barlow'd like it. Got you way up at the top, old buddy. Jim Bower, director."

He took a folded paper from his pocket and opened it.

I said, "Jack, look, I'm trying to make these drinks."

"Jim, boy, that's the first priority. I just wanted to check with you before I went over this with Barlow."

"Check what with me? You don't have to check anything with me, Jack."

"Jim, what good's a director if nobody checks with him?" With this, he slapped me on the shoulder, and I took the drinks into the other room.

Tom and Betty Reynolds had arrived. Tom said, "My, my, he's still out of prison."

I said, "Hi, Betty. Why can't you ever turn up alone?"

Betty was wearing something that looked like several lightning bolts sewn together. "Jim, if you're bartender, tender me a Gibson."

Tom said, "He's even lifting his hand in gainful employment. Vodka on the rocks, Jim. Do you know how to make it?"

I went back to the study and made these and looked at Barlow's globe, standing there in its mahogany stand. No matter how you looked at it, it was Barlow's world.

I had had three martinis before we got there and it occurred to me that it would not be stupid to change to Scotch. But I did not want Scotch. What I wanted was a martini. I wanted quite a few martinis. I made one and went back to the crowd.

The women seemed to be talking about the price of food. Steak was out of sight. The only thing that was even reasonable these days was eggs. This did not seem interesting. I went over to the men.

Helmut was saying, "You do not buy a Porsche for its resale value. You also do not buy a Porsche for family outings or going to church. You buy a Porsche because of a death wish."

Jack Thompson said, "I was thinking of a Porsche, but the old Jag and I have been through so many wars together I figured I'd see her through another campaign. They don't make them like that one-twenty any more."

Tom Reynolds said, "Personally, I've never understood the Porsche cult. The idea of seeing how fast one can go around a curve without actually turning over eludes me as a source of interest."

Jack Thompson said, "But that's its gestalt. That's the kind of car you buy to wring out, eh, Helmut? The first thing I'd do with a Porsche is take it up to Lime Rock and see what I could do with it."

Helmut turned his back on Jack Thompson and said, "I've always wanted to try a Paragon, Jim. Have you driven one?"

"I had a ride in one," I said. "The importer had a driver take me around the track once. I think he said he had it up to one hundred forty."

Tom Reynolds said, "La Guardia or Kennedy?"

Helmut said, "How did it handle?"

"We got up to ninety in second. As I remember, the only real sensation of speed was the acceleration. It didn't feel as if we were doing much more than seventy when he was going all out."

Jack Thompson said, "Ah, but it doesn't have the soul of a Porsche, Jim, boy. That's what Helmut's talking about. It's what the car expects from you."

Helmut turned to Jack. "You don't own a Porsche?"

"No, I still have the old Jag."

"That was what I thought you said." Helmut walked over to the women.

Jack Thompson said, "Great car, the Porsche. They ought to make you get a special license for it." His voice trailed off. He looked over at Helmut and it seemed to me as if he started to take a step in that direction and then decided not to.

I said, "Tom, are there any vitamins in vermouth?"

"Not in the amounts generally consumed. Are you sure

vitamins are what you're deficient in? I ask only to be sure I get you started on the right program."

"No," I said. "I was just trying to figure out which program to stop."

Ina Cross came over. I had the feeling Helmut sent her to rescue us. "Lover, somebody drank this when I wasn't looking. Would you fix it and make it well?"

"Sure."

I was crossing the room when Barlow walked in. Tall, brown, blond Barlow, white jacket, blue slacks. "Jim, how are you?"

It just popped out. "I'm drinking your gin, Barlow. This is help-yourself day, isn't it?"

Something flickered in his face, but all that he said was, "Be glad to make it for you, Jim."

"Nope."

As I went into the study, I heard Jack Thompson say, "Jack Thompson, Barlow. We met at a dance at Longshore a couple of years ago."

I made Ina's drink and another drink for myself. I did not want to go back to the other room. I wanted to sit in Barlow's big red leather chair and look at Barlow's big globe. I wondered what would happen if I punched Barlow in the mouth. Christ, I'd probably miss.

Jack Thompson was still talking when I got back. "Beautiful place you have here, Kate. We were thinking of a place like this, but Peg said there weren't enough of us to use it."

Kate Matthews said, "It is a lot to keep up, if you don't need all the room."

Tom Reynolds said, "What do you do in winter, Kate? Take the pool to Florida?"

Ina said, "Did you ever get your pool fixed, Melinda?"

Melinda looked startled, as if she had been a million miles away. "No, they're still coming to fix it. Jim says it has so much dirt in it now we'll have to have it dredged."

I sat down in a big blue easy chair and drank some of my new martini and looked out the glass doors at the Matthewses' pool. You could just about see it in the dusk. Dusk was a swell time; nothing ahead of you but night.

Helmut said something to the room in general, but I was not listening, and then Betty said something and everybody laughed. I lit a cigarette and looked out the glass doors. Somewhere over the rainbow, I thought.

Tom Reynolds said, "Jim? Are you with us?"

"What?"

Ina said, "The Vans are here."

"Oh." Neil and Harriet. I got up. It had been nice, just sitting there.

Barlow let them in. I drank a little more of my gin and then put the glass on a table. Then I picked it up and drank a little more as Kate introduced the Vans to the Thompsons. First names would do, I thought. Even numbers would do.

I noticed with a little surprise that my glass was empty again. Well, what the hell. So I was thirsty.

And then there was little Harriet. "Hello there."

"Hi."

"Am I going to see a lot of you this evening?"

"I don't know. How much is a lot?"

"We could have a very interesting discussion about that. Are you going to make me a drink?"

"Sure. I'm agreeing to everything today."

Harriet looked at me as if she were studying my face to remember landmarks. Then she said, "Are you mad about something? I just got here."

"Not me. What can I get you?"

"Gin and tonic."

This seemed to be as good a time as any to make another drink for myself, and I went into the study and there was Helmut.

Helmut said, "I understand we owe the presence of that horse's ass all to you."

"Who, Jack?"

"With mosquitoes, you can at least spray the area."

Back in the living room, Tom Reynolds said, "Barlow, whatever happened to that thing you were writing? 'Thinking for the Beginner.' "

"Oh, another chapter or two and I think I'll have it, Tom."

Helmut said, "Excuse me, what category are we in?"

Barlow said, "Just a little project of mine, Helmut. We have some people on our staff who seem to confuse procedure with thinking."

"You have an instruction manual?"

"A few ideas I've put down, that's all."

Jack Thompson said, "Barlow, if that's what it sounds like, it ought to be compulsory. If we could just get people to think things out—empathize—maybe we could do something about the whole prejudice syndrome."

Jesus Christ, he got *empathy, prejudice* and *syndrome* a
into the same sentence, I thought.

Betty said, "Are you going to have it published?"

"Well, I'm going to have it printed. *Published* may be a b
ambitious a word for it, Betty."

Helmut said, "I have always found that it's the other gu
who doesn't think."

Jack Thompson said, "Well, I think a book like that is ju
what the doctor ordered. If we'd all learn to just stop an
think—it's so damned important and nobody does it."

Even Barlow's eyebrows went up at this. Barlow turned t
me and said, "Jim, how's the advertising business these days
This your slow period?"

Well, Melinda said we were going to be civilized. I sai
"Most of the Christmas stuff is out of the way. We have
few things for next year we're still working on."

Helmut said, "Isn't it bad to go from one idea to anothe
Jim? A mood isn't something you can change like a suit."

"Oh, you get to look at these things as problems some
body brings in, Helmut. It's like working in a clinic."

Tom Reynolds said, "I knew he'd find a way to do i
'Advertising is good for you.' "

Jack Thompson said, "It's all communications. I was talkin
to Jim about that just the other day. Here we are, the com
munications capital of the world, and we don't even kno
how to communicate with each other. If man could onl
learn to talk to man."

He was talking to Jim about it just the other day. I dran
some more of my martini.

Six months' severance, pension plan, profit sharing an
stock. Put it all together, subtract 25 percent for the govern
ment, and things could be worse. I wouldn't even have to pa
alimony. There just wouldn't be anybody to talk to, tha
was all.

Peg Thompson said, "Personally, I think it's time w
crawled back into the sea again. We've done all we can here."

Barlow said, "Oh, I don't know, Peg. I think man is finall
owning up to a few of his responsibilities."

Peg said, "He may be owning up to his responsibilities, bu
it's still the oil he'll fight over."

Helmut said, "Responsibility is a very complicated word
I only feel responsible for things I can do something about
and I do not feel responsible for all of those."

Jack Thompson said, "The thing is, we're all in thi

ogether. You know, Barlow, in a way, that's what Jim and I wanted to talk to you about. Here we are, passing ea h other instead of meeting, and it's all because we don't know how to ake the first step."

Tom Reynolds said, "Jim said that? God in heaven."

I said, "Wait'll you hear the solution he's got."

Helmut had just started for the bar but he stopped and aid to me, "I hope it involves our painting each other's odies."

I said, "You get to paint Tom's."

Ina said, "Lover, what, pray tell, is that all about?"

I said, "Ina, we're ships that pass in the night."

Tom Reynolds said, "Will you give me your word this is not going to be a spiritual experience?"

Kate said, "Time for one more drink before dinner."

Barlow, I noticed, without being the least bit obvious, took Melinda's glass and went into the study. He had not asked Kate whether she wanted a drink or not.

I walked over to Kate and Peg Thompson. "Get anybody a drink?"

Peg said, "You look just the way I'd remember you if I ever saw you before."

I said, "Well, it was a hot night."

Peg said, "I think when you left, I was trying to get back to the sea. I wonder why everybody thinks lemmings are stupid."

I said, "Kate, if I just drink, you won't take it as a comment on the cooking, right?"

Kate gave me a little smile. "It's just a seafood casserole, Jim. Eating it isn't necessary."

"Good."

I went into the study and there was Barlow, turning the globe around with his finger.

When he saw me, he seemed to turn something over in his mind. But then all he said was, "Jim, I'm sorry about this Jack Thompson business. He gave me to believe this was your idea."

I put my glass down and looked at him and I lit a cigarette while I was looking at him, but I did not say anything.

Barlow said, "Well . . ." He gave the globe another turn and went out to the other room.

I made a fresh martini and then stood there and drank some of it and then poured in some more gin. I was standing there, leaning against one of Barlow's bookcases, smoking and drinking and thinking how when I was a kid I wanted to be a cowboy, when Melinda came in.

I said, "He isn't here."

"Can't we still be friends, Jim?"

"Sure. We can go bowling together."

For a moment, I thought that she was going to say something else, but then she left, and I went back out to my big blue easy chair.

Harriet Van came over and sat in the chair next to mine. "How good are you at vibrations?"

"Whose?"

"Everything tonight seems funny."

"Parties get like that sometimes."

"I keep wondering what we're all here for."

"Honey, tonight you're part of the insulation."

"I don't want to be part of the insulation. I wouldn't mind being the wire."

Neil Van came over. "Everybody ready to dunk for apples?"

Neil looked like a cobweb. I said, "Neil, how are you? Where are you?"

"Hovering overhead. I only come out at night." Neil went off toward Helmut and Betty.

I said, "What the hell is the matter with him?"

Harriet said, "He's a people. It's made him bitter."

The room was beginning to look a little watery, as if rain were coming down the window.

Kate said, "First one into the dining room gets something to eat."

Helmut said, "You only have enough for one?"

Jack Thompson came over to me. "When do you think we ought to talk to Barlow, Jim?"

"Jack, I'm not talking to Barlow. If you want to talk to Barlow, go ahead."

"Hey, come on, old buddy, we're in this together."

"Where did you get that idea?" I got up and went into the study. I had to take two sidesteps, one to miss a little table and one to miss the edge of the door. All in all, I did not do badly.

Behind me came Jack. "Jim, boy, what can I get you?"

"Not a thing." I put some ice cubes and some gin in a glass.

"I thought we'd both sort of talk to Barlow, Jim."

"Jack I told you—when was it, Monday? I told you I don't want to get involved, okay?"

Peg Thompson was standing in the doorway, watching us. Jack said, "Jim, I don't know what you mean by involved. There nothing involved in people getting together."

"Excuse me." I took my drink back to my chair.

Peg and Jack Thompson stood in the doorway talking. At least, Peg was talking. Jack just stood there, shaking his head at something.

Helmut and Ina and Tom Reynolds already had their plates and were eating. Tom said, "I have this strange feeling that somebody's going to read the will and nobody got anything."

Betty came over with her drink. "Open warfare has now broken out in the Thompson family."

Ina said, "What about, Betty?"

"As nearly as I can tell, Jack has something in mind and Peg wants him to drop it."

Tom Reynolds said, "Let's all thank Kate for everything and go home."

Melinda, I noticed, was not eating. She was sitting by herself with a drink, smoking. I did not see Barlow. He was either getting a plate of his own or handing them to other people. The room seemed to be tilting.

Helmut said, "Jim, as the only one who seems to know what this is all about, would you mind filling us in?"

"It's an idea Jack Thompson has."

"Is it worth this grand unveiling?"

"What the hell, there's nothing on television tonight."

Peg Thompson and Jack now came out with their plates and sat down. Jack looked around, probably for Barlow, and when he did not see him, began to eat. Peg began to eat, her eyes on her plate.

Now Barlow came in with a plate. Tall, slim, athletic Barlow, controlled, beautiful and quiet.

Jack Thompson said, "Well, as long as we're all together, I guess now's as good a time as ever. How about it, Jim? You want to tell everybody about it?"

"Your idea, Jack. You tell them, if you want to."

"Come on, Jim, boy. You're the writer here. This is an idea Jim and I were kicking around, but I'm going to let him tell you about it because he's the word man."

Peg Thompson just went right on eating. She did not look up at all.

I stared into my drink. A martini looks like a little fish

pond, when you look right into it. I shook my head. "Not my idea, Jack. I told you that."

"Hey, Jim, you aren't going to abandon ship now—the cameras are rolling, Jim, boy."

I drank some of the fish pond. "All right, I think you've all met Jack Thompson. And if you haven't, I'm sure Jack will see that you do before you get out of here."

Melinda lit a fresh cigarette.

Tom Reynolds pressed his fork through the toast and it went clank against the dish.

I said, "Well, Jack wants to start this club. This is very important to Jack because there aren't any other clubs Jack can get into. Jack, am I getting this right?"

Jack Thompson was not eating or, for that matter, even moving. He just sat there.

Ina Cross said, "Lover, I'll have some coffee if you will."

"Can't do that, Ina. Got to tell everybody about my old buddy, Jack. What do you call it, Jack? A commuters' club? Jack's going to start a commuters' club. Now, what this club does is, everybody who won't talk to Jack on the bar car is going to talk to him now because he thought this idea up, see?" I drank some more of my martini. "Now, all Jack needs is a catalyst. That's what Barlow's supposed to be. The catalyst. Very good reason for that, too. If anybody saw Jack's name on this, nobody'd belong to it but Jack."

Jack Thompson got up with his plate in his hand and said, "Well, I don't know what old Jim's making a joke out of it for."

Peg Thompson got up and took the plate out of his hand and put both their plates on a table. She said, "Come on, Jack. We're going home."

Jack Thompson took one or two steps and then stopped and stood there in the middle of the room, looking at me. "Jim?"

Then he said, "You shit, you shit."

"Jack," Peg Thompson said.

She took him by the hand and led him out of the house like a pony.

After a moment, Tom Reynolds said, "Kate, what's for dessert?"

My glass was empty. I got up and walked across the living room to the study. There was a little table that I did not see, and I hit it with my knee and it went bumpety bump on the carpet.

In the study, I started to pick up bottles. The trouble was telling which was the gin and which was the vodka and which was the dry vermouth. Well, the vermouth had the complicated label. That sure wasn't the gin.

"That wasn't really necessary, Jim."

Barlow. "Well, Barlow, I'll tell you. Yes, it was."

"Very well, Jim. If it makes you feel better."

Well, that wasn't gin, and that wasn't gin, and that sure as hell wasn't gin. I put the last bottle down on the little glass-covered bar and thought, What the hell?

I hit him right in the mouth.

There was a sound like some structure turning over and by God, there he was on the floor, lying next to his god-damned world. He was holding his mouth and looking at me. I wondered, inanely, whether that meant that I did not have a right to any more of his gin.

"Jim?" It was Helmut's voice. I looked around and saw somebody fuzzy standing there.

"Helmut, what the hell can I do for you?"

"How about some fresh air?"

"Can't now, Helmut. Got to wait till this bastard gets up."

"Come on, Jim."

I picked up one of the bottles. "Is this gin?"

"That's vodka, Jim."

"It'll do. This is for drinking or for when that prick gets up. It's like the warranty on cars. Twelve months or twelve thousand miles."

Helmut said, "He got up, Jim. He's in the other room."

"No kidding."

"Let's go out and get some air, Jim."

"Think I'll just pour some of this into a glass, Helmut. Doesn't look right, walking around with a bottle."

"I'll pour it for you, Jim."

He took my glass and I heard what sounded like the plink plink of ice cubes. Presently I felt the glass being put into my hand.

"Okay, Jim?"

"Sure."

"Watch the door, there."

"All right."

As we went through the living room, I saw all these pale little balloons. Faces.

"Now we're going around a plant, Jim."

"A plant? Are we outdoors?"

"Not yet."

"Plant's growing indoors?"

"I'm opening the front door now. Easy."

"I've been in and out doors all my life, Helmut."

"Little step here. Easy now."

"Now we're outside, right?"

"That's right, Jim."

"Got the old booze hound out the door, eh? You do good work, Helmut."

"Let's just walk around the lawn for a while, okay, Jim?"

"Helmut, why not?"

"Tree here. Watch it."

"I see it."

"Want to go over this way, Jim?"

"Anyplace you say. Wait a minute. Just want a drink here. Helmut? Goddamned glass is empty."

"You spilled it in the hall, Jim."

"Helmut, I think I'll just sit down here for a while."

"All right, Jim."

I sat down on the grass. I found my cigarettes and lighter and lit a cigarette. "What time is it?"

"A little after ten."

"Helmut?"

"Yes, Jim?"

"I think I broke my hand."

"Does it hurt, Jim?"

"Can't hold this cigarette in it." I took the cigarette with my left hand. Wouldn't that be something? Writer with broken hand wants work.

"Would you like me to get you some coffee, Jim?"

"Yeah."

"Lie down, if you like."

"Helmut, everything's fine."

I sat there on the grass and smoked a little more of the cigarette.

Well, that's life, right? No skyrockets. No parades. You just wind up drunk on somebody's lawn.